THE *Latest* MRS. FURST

SUSAN MARTINS MILLER

RiverOak®
Good News in Fiction

COOK COMMUNICATIONS MINISTRIES
Colorado Springs, Colorado • Paris, Ontario
KINGSWAY COMMUNICATIONS LTD
Eastbourne, England

RiverOak® is an imprint of
Cook Communications Ministries, Colorado Springs, CO 80918
Cook Communications, Paris, Ontario
Kingsway Communications, Eastbourne, England

THE LATEST MRS. FURST
© 2006 by Susan Martins Miller

Cover Design: BMB Design

First Printing, 2006
Printed in the United States of America

1 2 3 4 5 6 7 8 9 10 Printing/Year 10 09 08 07 06

ISBN-13: 978-1-58919-073-3
ISBN-10: 1-58919-073-4

LCCN: 2006928333

With admiration for the friend who knows this road well

~ 1 ~

Dr. Bennett Grey glanced at the brass-framed clock discretely tucked in the corner of his office. His six o'clock appointment was late by at least thirty minutes. But that was no surprise. Mitchell Furst was rarely on time, if he showed up at all.

The streetlight outside his second-story window flickered on. Dusk settled over the street while he had his back to the window, bent over the notes on his desk. The office was a spacious one, with a commodious grayish blue leather sofa and a matching wide chair across from the mahogany desk.

Bennett didn't mind lingering in the early evening. He preferred to let the rush-hour traffic clear, and he generally dined alone anyway. No one was waiting for him at home with a hot meal and a glass of wine. He didn't even have a housekeeper anymore. It seemed silly to pay Anita to keep a house that was so rarely occupied, so he had given her a generous severance and let her go three years earlier. He pushed the vacuum around himself every other Saturday morning. Within four blocks of his home, three restaurants served meals bordering on home cooked. The waitresses knew him just well enough to leave him in peace.

Bennett had been practicing psychiatry for twenty-eight years. His early years at a prison and a local mental-health institution paved the way to a lucrative private practice, most of which took place in this historic building with oak crown molding and plaster walls that grew dingier by the year.

Bennett, a creature of careful habit, rarely noticed. He simply climbed the stairs every morning, hearing the reassuring creak on the fourth step, sent out for lunch at one o'clock, dictated his notes in the midafternoon lull for his secretary/receptionist to transcribe, and prepared for the patients scrambling for after-work appointments.

Bennett reached for Mitchell Furst's file. Mitchell had been his patient on and off for three years. Sometimes months would go by with no contact from him. Other times Mitchell called twice a week to talk; Bennett was never sure why, but he took Mitchell's calls as often as he could. This was an interesting case, perhaps the most interesting Bennett had ever encountered. Every session yielded lengthy notes, replete with objective observation of behaviors, speculation of motive, theories of diagnosis. For some months now, Bennett had tested one particular theory. Mitchell's erratic appearances were just one more indicator of the validity of the theory.

The clock told Bennett that Mitchell was now a full hour late. He had been later than that once or twice before, but more than likely he was not going to show up. The doctor punched the button on his desk lamp, leaving only the ambient light in the corner and the beams from the streetlight outside. He turned to pack his briefcase with reading material to peruse over meat loaf and brown rice. Then he heard the creak of the fourth step.

Jayne Paige-Hamilton shifted her bag of groceries to the other hand. The plastic was already tearing from the weight of the orange-juice carton, and she hadn't even reached her car yet. Periodically she toyed with changing loyalties to a market that dispensed the paper bags she preferred, but this store was on the way home, and she had a strong leaning toward simplicity that played itself out in ordinary decisions.

A thin drizzle that began while she was inside the store now dampened her dishwater blonde hair. She ducked her face into a shoulder to push a stray strand of hair out of her eyes while she fished in her bag for her keys. Once inside the car, Jayne dumped her load of orange juice, frozen spinach soufflé, microwave popcorn, and deli ham on the passenger seat. Because she lived alone, Jayne could eat whatever she wanted whenever she wanted.

Eight years earlier, Jayne had married carefully, she thought, but in the end unsuccessfully. The courtship was romantic enough. Chuck acted attentive, flattering, and thoughtful. While they didn't see each other every day, the dates they had proved companionable and satisfying. After a year and a half of courtship, a five-month engagement culminated in an outdoor summer wedding, complete with a live band and mountains of cake. After the wedding, though, it became clear that Chuck was not prepared for marriage to change his life in any way. He worked long hours and went out for drinks with his coworkers, only occasionally making it home for an overly warmed dinner before tumbling into bed. He seemed content to continue spending time with Jayne only every few days. The thoughtful cards dissipated. Sweet phone messages became matter-of-fact reminders of household details. They talked less and less. Chuck never stopped reaching for her in the dark, but Jayne stopped responding, more often wondering who this stranger was in her bed.

After the baby came, it got worse. Chuck expressed little interest in his infant daughter and less patience for her needs. Jayne had always suspected that Chuck would have preferred that she exercise her reproductive rights when she discovered she was pregnant. But Jayne couldn't do that. A baby was a baby—her baby—and she had loved Claire.

Then Claire stopped breathing one night.

Jayne was devastated, but Chuck took only half a day off of work for the funeral. Jayne left him a month later and he barely seemed to notice. Before she knew it, she had her premarriage identity back, complete with a hyphenated maiden name foisted on her by forward-thinking parents who had married in the late sixties.

Jayne inserted the key into the ignition. The engine, in need of new spark plugs, sputtered but started. As she tooled across the parking lot toward the plaza exit, Jayne sighed. Why was she thinking of Chuck at a time like this? Her feelings for him had died years ago, and she hadn't really missed being married to him. Her work as a graphic designer and artist in a small design shop satisfied her. The tasks varied enough to remain interesting, and Larry, the owner, was companionable without being nosy about her personal life. Her life was not unhappy, even before Mitchell Furst.

She had met Mitchell seven months ago at a friend's late-summer birthday party. When he entered a room full of people, he attracted attention before he even opened his mouth to speak. At the birthday party Jayne had busied herself in the kitchen, mixing punch and pouring wine coolers. While she mingled among the crowd in the next room, his brown eyes had followed her. Her glances stretched into interested looks, and soon Mitchell approached to try his charms on her more directly. His connection to the birthday girl still was not quite clear to Jayne, but he had called her the next day, and within a month he began treating the high summer weeds in her neglected backyard and showing every intention of taking care of Jayne for a long time. Watching him work outside with his shirt off, sweat glistening on his back, made her heart race. She had forced herself to turn away from the window and mop the kitchen floor. But he returned the next weekend, and soon began calling her cell phone several times a day for no particular reason.

Right from the start she liked having him around. His charm seemed irresistible. Jayne had not tried to resist him. Why should she? She was still young, just past thirty, and he had stirred something in her that she had not felt for a very long time. A great conversationalist, Mitchell identified with her deeply held viewpoints on many issues. And his arms around her felt good, really good.

Pulling into the driveway of her rented bungalow, Jayne scanned the street for Mitchell's black truck. When they talked on the phone earlier, he had been indefinite about whether he would be able to come by tonight, but she couldn't help hoping that he would. His truck was not there.

Mitchell Furst pulled away from Jayne's quiet side street just seconds before she arrived from the other direction. His timing was perfect. In a few moments, she would discover his carefully composed note tucked into the scroll of the screen on her back door, where he knew she would enter the house. Jayne would be pleased that he had stopped by and left an explanation. His note said that he had to drive twenty miles out of town because he had promised to check on the forested home of a friend on vacation in Cancún. He would call her when he got back into town, but it might be late. He could see in his mind the smile that would cross her face as she fingered the note and pondered his careful handwriting before turning her key in the lock.

It was well after six o'clock. Mitchell had skipped lunch in favor of a workout at the gym. Now he was hungry. The Capers Café was just around the corner. He could sit at the counter and have something to eat, maybe a cold beer. A parking space opened up just as he made the right turn. Ten minutes later he chomped into a double cheeseburger and asked for extra salt on his fries. He flashed his smile at the waitress and enjoyed the flush it evoked in her cheeks. Satisfied, Mitchell left an enormous tip and sauntered out of the café.

The clock outside the bank read 6:47 in bright white numerals. Bennett Grey would be waiting for him. Mitchell debated whether to keep his appointment. He hadn't seen Dr. Grey in nearly six weeks, so the good doctor would be reservedly curious about what had transpired in Mitchell's life in that time. Mentioning Jayne to him at their last appointment had been a slipup. Mitchell Furst didn't make slipups. He would have to fix it eventually. Tonight was as good a night as any.

Bennett turned the lights back on and closed his half-packed briefcase. The meat loaf and brown rice would have to wait. He heard the door to his waiting room open. Bennett rose, sighed, and crossed his office to welcome his erratic patient.

Jayne tucked the note in a small basket on the top shelf of the baker's rack in her tidy kitchen. Hidden behind a voluminous ivy, the basket was nearly invisible to anyone who entered her kitchen. But Jayne knew it contained a collection of notes from the last seven months, all written in the same hand. She smiled to herself as she thought that she would soon need a larger basket or another system. She couldn't simply discard the old notes.

Shedding her raincoat at the same time she dumped her small cache of groceries on the counter, Jayne was suddenly ravenously hungry and wished she had not bypassed the chips aisle at the grocery store. She popped the spinach soufflé in the microwave and opened the orange juice. A bag of popcorn would be dessert later. She could see Mitchell shaking his head at her menu and insisting that she come out with him for a good steak instead.

While the spinach turned and the microwave whirred, Jayne looked at her mail: an electric bill, a bank statement, a credit-card offer that she didn't open, and an envelope addressed in Leslie's flowing handwriting, done with a favorite green fountain pen.

Jayne slit the envelope open and found an ad for a department-store sale for that coming Saturday morning. With a bold stroke, Jayne's cousin Leslie had circled "Everything on sale. No exceptions" and written across the ad "Be there." Jayne chuckled. Yes, she would be there. Ever since they both turned seven years old and mastered how many nickels made a dollar, Jayne and Leslie had shopped together—for any occasion or no occasion at all.

The microwave beeped. Jayne opened a drawer, retrieved a fork, and plunged into her dinner.

"Hello, Mitchell," Bennett said with professional evenness.

"Hey, Dr. B.," Mitchell responded as he hung his jacket on a coatrack.

Bennett Grey did not think of himself as a "Dr. B.," but Mitchell had persisted in the nickname for so long it seemed futile to resist it. "Come on back." Bennett gestured toward his inner office.

Mitchell sprawled across the leather sofa, and Bennett lowered himself into the chair.

"It's been awhile," Bennett said.

"Yeah, I keep meaning to come by," Mitchell responded, "but I've been busy."

Bennett smiled slightly. "With what?"

"Oh, you know, I'm doing all right at the construction company, but I think I'm ready for something different. I have a hot lead on a job with a finance company."

"Finance? I didn't know you were interested in that."

"Oh, sure. I majored in business, you know. And the real-estate market is booming. I think I could do well working for a bank that does a lot of mortgage work. I should be hearing any day now."

Bennett picked up the pen and pad he usually held during a session and put the date at the top of the page. "I'll be interested to hear how that works out for you. What else has been going on?"

Mitchell needed no further prodding. He launched into a discourse about the unfair hassle he was getting from his current boss at the construction company; how much he was looking forward to a vacation, perhaps between jobs; and how he wanted to study for the real-estate broker exam. If he could sell property and help to arrange financing, Mitchell explained, he stood to do well for himself. It wouldn't be long before he would be investing in property and turning it around quickly for a tidy profit.

Bennett noticed that Mitchell didn't mention Jayne. He debated about whether to push him and decided not to.

Two hours later after a belated dinner, Bennett Grey pulled into his detached garage, locked the garage door behind him, strode toward the house, and unlocked the back door.

Mitchell Furst weighed on his mind. Six weeks ago all he could talk about was the young woman he had met, Jayne. It was as if a guard had come down; Bennett had believed his puzzling patient as he talked about the wonderful woman he was seeing. Tonight Mitchell had acted as if Jayne didn't exist, had never existed. Had the relationship gone sour in those six weeks, or was Mitchell intentionally discounting Jayne's importance to him?

Bennett flipped on a light in the living room and stood face-to-face with an intruder in his home—a computer. Adam, his nephew, had insisted his uncle needed to get with the times and argued persuasively about the benefits of learning to use the computer. Adam was young enough that he had never lived in a home without a computer. Navigating the keyboard or the screen or the "Net" was no more complicated than putting on shoes—for Adam. Bennett was not so convinced. He spied the handwritten note next to the computer.

> *Dear Uncle Ben,*
>
> *See the button that says on/off? Push it. When you've mastered that, I'll come by to show you the next step. I'm finding some great sites that shrink types like you like to visit.*
>
> *Later,*
> *Adam*

Uncle Ben. No one but Adam called him that. Somehow it made him feel like a box of rice. Dr. B. Uncle Ben. What was it about him that elicited these nicknames, he wondered.

He set the note aside, as he had every day since its arrival seven days ago. He had not yet mastered the on/off button. Bennett had reluctantly admitted that the use of a computer at the office proved efficient and easily paid for itself. And he knew his receptionist would not consent to continue in his employ if she could not use one. He just was not ready for the cyber age to invade his private sanctuary.

~ 2 ~

"Try that one on."

Jayne scrunched up her face at Leslie's suggestion. Considering how often they shopped together, Jayne repeatedly marveled that her cousin never quite understood her taste. The cotton sweater Leslie pointed at had zero appeal.

"That's a putrid color if ever I saw one," Jayne said. "Looks like a bad cold or something."

"You just don't like green in general," Leslie pouted, "even though you know it's my favorite color."

Wearing green close to her face made Jayne look ill. Leslie, on the other hand—with her vibrant black hair and deep brown eyes—could wear green and look spectacular. Jayne smiled and reached for the same sweater in burgundy.

"Falling back on your fallback favorite," Leslie said, rolling her eyes. "You must have half a dozen burgundy sweaters."

"Mitchell likes it." Jayne shrugged. "He says it looks rich."

"Whatever that means. Why do you care so much what he thinks, anyway? Buy a sweater because you like it, not because he likes it."

"I do like it. I wouldn't have picked it up if I didn't."

"In the old days, you would have reached for blue. You only switched to burgundy after that guy entered the picture." Leslie suddenly lost interest in the cotton sweaters and began to move down the aisle toward a rack of dresses.

Jayne put down the burgundy sweater and followed her cousin. "'That guy' happens to be important to me right now."

"I don't get why. You could do so much better." Leslie pushed dresses around a circular rack without really looking at them, a fact that did not escape Jayne's attention. Her cousin was working up to saying what was really on her mind.

"Sure, like Chuck," Jayne scoffed.

"Chuck was a mistake. That doesn't mean you have to make another one. You have a clean slate. Don't mess it up with the likes of Mitchell Furst."

Jayne stuffed her hands in the pockets of her light jacket, biting her tongue.

"Really, Jayne, you have to admit he doesn't treat you all that well."

"What in the world do you mean by that?"

"You don't see him for days at a time. You moan to me about that constantly."

"I do not."

"Yes, you do." Leslie shoved four dresses around the rack at one time.

"Well, it's not as if we're married. He has a job and a life; I have a job and a life. I don't expect him to be at my beck and call."

"He stands you up."

"He does not."

"Yes, he does."

"He never breaks a date without a good reason, and he always calls or leaves a note—I have them all if you want to see them. That's not the same as standing me up." *Why does she insist on going around this loop again?* Jayne thought indignantly.

"You have a good life, Jayne. Why mess it up with a man like Mitchell Furst?"

"You're just sour on men because Ray broke up with you."

"I broke up with Ray. Let's get that straight."

"Whatever. This is not the seventh grade. It didn't work out for you with Ray, or with Scott before him. Now you're down on men in general."

"I was down on Mitchell Furst before I broke up with Ray. One thing has nothing to do with the other."

"You barely know Mitchell. You've only met him a few times."

"I don't trust him."

"You can't trust or not trust someone you don't even know."

"I don't trust him," Leslie repeated, "and neither should you."

"Can we just shop, please? Do we have to analyze my life every time we get together?" Jayne turned to a table of handbags on sale.

"You don't need another handbag," Leslie said. "The one you have isn't very old, and it's good quality. It'll last you for years."

"Now you sound like your mother," Jayne laughed. Aunt Beth, her own mother's sister, believed in buying quality and for the long term. You shopped long and hard for something that met your specifications, and then you didn't replace the item for a long time. Aunt Beth made sure everyone knew her shopping policy.

"Sometimes my mother is very wise." Leslie took Jayne's elbow and guided her toward the cosmetics counter.

"When did you decide that?"

"Since she told me it wouldn't work out with Ray and she turned out to be right."

"Mmmm." Jayne opted not to comment further.

"Speaking of mothers, what do you hear from my favorite Aunt Amanda?"

Jayne perked up. "Mom's doing fabulously. She loves her new job. Doesn't regret for a moment moving out of town to start over."

Leslie shook her head. "I still can't believe she really did that. After your dad died last year ... well, I didn't know how your mom could go on."

"She's been a real trouper." Jayne spoke softly, thinking of her father. He had gotten sick with a flu that he couldn't seem to shake. Four months later he died from pancreatic cancer. Frank Hamilton had sold insurance in the same small city for thirty-five years and was well into a second generation of customers—children of his original customers who would never consider going anywhere else. His genuine concern for everyone he met drew people to him; he rarely had to advertise beyond the yellow pages and did a consistently brisk business. After he died and her grief was contained, his widow felt ready to move on to a new city as Amanda Paige, rather than be known as Frank Hamilton's widow. When she received a job offer as a school administrator six hundred miles away, she took it.

"I admire her." Leslie's comment interrupted Jayne's reverie. "She's got a lot of energy, and she thinks about the future, not the past. She's going to be okay."

"It's you and me, baby," Jayne responded. "Since your parents moved 'out to the country,' as they like to call it, we're the only ones from the family left in town."

"We haven't spent nearly enough money yet," Leslie quipped. "Let's get down to business." She reached for a bottle of perfume.

Monday morning, ten thirty. Jayne glanced at the clock on her desk in the small graphics shop. She had hardly moved in three hours. But the focused effort had been worth it. Now she leaned back in her chair, stretching her arms above her head, and considered her half-morning's work. The book cover filled the computer screen. Her client was a small publishing house that produced perhaps a dozen books a year. It was a steady customer, and Jayne always enjoyed the assignments Larry routinely routed her way. This one made her want to read the book, a thriller outside her usual tastes. Maybe she needed a little excitement in her life, if only vicariously.

"Are we going to make the deadline on that cover?" Larry peered over the spectacles that generally sat halfway down his nose. He refused to try bifocals; that would be an admission of his age. With his worn jeans and polo shirts with sport labels, he persisted in making a statement of youth, despite turning fifty last month. Jayne never understood why he resisted his true age. The gray at his temples was attractive in her opinion, and he carried the bit of extra weight around his waist well.

Jayne nodded. "I promised it for tomorrow, end of day. But I'm almost finished. I'm pretty sure they're going to like it. They loved the roughs, and I've stuck pretty close to that."

As Larry nodded his satisfaction, Jayne's phone rang.

"This is Jayne."

"And I'm so glad it is." Mitchell.

"Hello," she responded warmly, spinning her chair away from Larry and dropping her voice.

"What are you doing?"

"Working, of course. A book cover."

"You need a break, I'm sure. If I know you, you haven't been out of that chair all morning."

Jayne chuckled and rubbed the back of her neck. "You know me, I guess."

"Look out the window."

"What?"

"The window. Look out."

Jayne glanced over her shoulder at Larry, who was absorbed at his own computer. Nonchalantly she rose and stepped to the third-story window.

Mitchell stood on the sidewalk below, his cell phone to his ear, grinning as he looked up at her.

"I just ordered coffee and blueberry scones," he said. "Come on down."

"I'll be there in two and stay for ten."

"Twenty."

"Fifteen."

"I'll be waiting."

She hung up and said to Larry, "I'm gonna take a break." He didn't even look up as he grunted.

The ground floor beneath her office housed a coffee shop and bakery that did a steady business all year round. The Victorian decor, well suited to the historic building, put the blueberry scones Jayne loved in a credible setting. This wasn't the first time Mitchell had popped into the shop in the middle of the day. Jayne sometimes met him for a soup-and-sandwich lunch. The two flights of stairs took her to the sidewalk, and she ducked inside. Mitchell sat at a window table that faced the door.

"How did you get away?" she asked him brightly. "I thought you had appointments all morning."

"Finished a little early. Couldn't think of anything I'd rather do than have coffee with you." Mitchell nudged a cup toward Jayne as she sat down. "Mocha latte, double shot, whipped cream, cinnamon sprinkles."

Jayne picked it up. "Perfect." The steam still rose from the scones in the colorful basket.

That night, Jayne cinched her soft lavender fleece robe around her waist and picked up her pen. She had stayed twenty minutes with Mitchell after all and was glad she had. The brief time together fueled her for the rest of the day as sufficiently as a hearty meal. Feeling no hunger, she had skipped lunch in anticipation of seeing him again in the evening. Their dinner date, postponed a couple of hours because Mitchell had an unexpected evening appointment, had just ended. He had left only moments earlier, and his kiss, tender and eager, still lingered on her lips.

Jayne smoothed the paper on her kitchen table and began to write.

Dear Mitchell,

    Once again you've left me befuddled. You stir something in me that I don't understand, awaken feelings I didn't know I had, and make them seem as if nothing else matters. When I'm with you, I don't want to be anywhere else. And when I'm not with you, I can't wait until I will be. I ask myself over and over again if you feel the same. I'm not sure why you would. I wonder every day why you chose me, why you want to be with me, and I'm afraid you'll decide you don't want to be anymore. Maybe you won't call tomorrow or the next day. Maybe one day we'll say good-bye after coffee and I won't know it's over, but it will be. But I hope not. I think I'm falling in love with you, Mitchell Furst, and I hope you're falling in love with me.

Jayne

Jayne laid the pen down and read the letter again. It wasn't so different from what she had written other nights—two dozen letters total, all to Mitchell. Carefully she picked up the paper, folded it across the center, and creased it. From the second shelf of the baker's rack, below the basket of notes from Mitchell, Jayne took a handcrafted wooden box. Her father had given it to her when she was fourteen with the instruction that it was for keeping her private thoughts safe. A few weeks ago she had removed its adolescent contents to a shoebox and begun afresh. Now it contained her letters to Mitchell, all written on the same pale blue stationery but not sent. On paper she freely poured out her insecurities and urgent emotions, telling Mitchell things she would never tell him aloud.

She was falling in love with Mitchell. And she hoped he was falling in love with her. She hadn't been this happy in years. Jayne snapped the box shut, then turned off the light in the kitchen. She wanted to go to bed feeling just the way she felt right then.

~ 3 ~

Bennett Grey stared at the screen, hardly able to believe what he had just accomplished. Adam had persisted, refusing to see his investment in a computer for his uncle go to waste. He had written out specific instructions for Bennett—and then called three times to make sure that he followed them. The boy had always been stubborn, ever since he was two years old and tugging at his uncle's hand, leading him places Bennett would not otherwise have gone.

The computer age was another such adventure Adam was determined to share with his uncle. With a red marker and a bold hand, Adam had numbered the steps Bennett should follow to boot up his computer and then log on to the Internet. Nervously adjusting his glasses more often than actually necessary, Bennett followed Adam's leading if for no other reason than to be able to tell Adam honestly that he had. Bennett had spent most of the evening learning to point and click.

Behind the instructions was a list of sites and "chat rooms" Adam thought his psychiatrist uncle would enjoy. Bennett now found himself in a chat room (whatever that was) full of people who claimed to be psychiatrists. He had his doubts about some of them. But the discussion mesmerized him.

WILMA: It's a fine line. Is it truly antisocial personality disorder, or merely antisocial characteristics?

BJL062: Is it really a line to be crossed or a spectrum, a matter of degrees?

SHRINKO: Definitely degrees. Can't ever be sure.

SIMON: No, it's a line. Recent psychiatric research supports this.

JADA478:Explain, Simon.

SIMON: It's a question of conscience. I have a patient who truly never is sorry for the messes this person makes.

SHRINKO: Maybe he just makes bad choices. Lots of reasons for patterns of bad choices.

SIMON: More than that. Doesn't care who gets hurt. Can't imagine how someone else might feel.

BJL062: That could still be a spectrum.

WILMA: Does it matter? If it's a disorder or a pattern of characteristics, the results are the same.

SIMON: It matters because it changes whether there is hope for improvement.

BJL062: Disagree. Either way, there is no hope. No one is ever cured of antisocial personality disorder.

Because he was not much of a typist, Bennett knew he couldn't keep up with the electronic discussion. And he wasn't sure what he would say. But as he followed the discussion and put together the oblique references to behaviors and attitudes, one patient came to mind: Mitchell Furst. Bennett had speculated for a long time whether Mitchell had antisocial personality disorder—was he a sociopath, to use the language Bennett had learned during his psychiatric residency decades ago? Despite his strong suspicions, Bennett had never been able to bring himself to put the word in Mitchell's file—perhaps because of the very reason that BJL062 expressed: There is no hope.

"Here, let me get your chair for you." Mitchell pulled out the chair next to the fireplace and smiled at Jayne.

Jayne smiled in return. The glow from the fireplace warmed her against the chilled February air. She loved this restaurant, though she had only been here once before for a friend's wedding rehearsal dinner party. It wasn't an ordinary Friday night dinner-date place. It was a place of special occasions.

"How did you get this perfect table?" Jayne made no effort to contain her pleasure at the cozy table next to the fireplace.

"I have my connections," Mitchell assured her. "I went to college with the manager. Paul and I go way back."

"That was downstate, at the university?"

"Right."

"It's great that you both ended up here in town. Do you see each other much?"

"I don't want to talk about him," Mitchell said, reaching across the table for her hand. "I want to talk about you."

"Oh?"

"Actually, us."

"Oh?" Jayne's heart began to beat rapidly.

The waiter came just then with water and a wine list. He ceremonially informed them of the evening's lobster special. Jayne glanced at Mitchell, who then ordered the special for both of them. After the waiter left, Jayne smiled at Mitchell, wondering if he would pick up the conversation where it left off.

"Should we have ordered wine?" Mitchell asked.

Jayne shook her head.

"I used to drink more before I met you," Mitchell observed. "But you know, I don't miss it. You're smart not to drink."

Jayne smiled self-consciously. She could count on one hand the number of times she had tasted alcohol. But she never objected if Mitchell wanted a drink.

"You have such a good influence on me. I used to do a lot of things before I met you," Mitchell continued, once again reaching for Jayne's hand. "I don't miss any of them. Since I've been with you, I can really see the person I've always wanted to be."

"Oh?" Inwardly Jayne chided herself for her lack of verbal skills, but she suddenly felt nervous. What was Mitchell getting at?

"I care about you, Jayne Paige-Hamilton. I can see myself with you for a long time, a very long time. You deserve the best there is, and that's what I want to be. I don't know what you see in me, but I hope you keep seeing it until I have enough time to prove myself to you."

"Mitchell, you don't have to prove anything."

"Yes, I do. I have to prove I'm worthy of a woman like you. I want to be sure we have a long future together."

Jayne thought of the box full of letters on the baker's rack in her kitchen. What would Mitchell say if he had any idea of the feelings recorded on the pages of blue stationery?

The salad came, with bread, followed soon by the lobsters.

Jayne had never felt this way before, not even with Chuck in the early days, the good days. To hear that Mitchell felt the same made it that much sweeter.

Bennett's stomach grumbled loudly. He'd had a full day of patients and had not paused to order the turkey sandwich he had wished for all morning. He dared not leave the building before getting all his notes in order while his memory of eight back-to-back sessions remained reasonably fresh. It was now nearly seven. Mitchell Furst should have arrived an hour earlier. Intuitively Bennett expected his elusive patient not to show. Mitchell's file sat on his desk, ready in case Bennett's intuition proved wrong. He opened it now and flipped through pages of notes from the last few sessions.

Eight months ago Mitchell had nonchalantly reported being in serious financial trouble. But it had not been his fault. He had tried to help out a friend by taking out a loan; his friend promised to make the payments. Then the friend lost his job and skipped town. Now the creditors were pursuing Mitchell. Bennett wasn't convinced Mitchell was telling him the whole story.

When Mitchell lost his job, he attributed it to a temperamental boss who had never liked him. He had even considered initiating legal action because of wrongful termination. An old college buddy who was an attorney said he had a good case. Bennett never heard any more about it.

Then came the session when Mitchell was so excited about having met a woman named Jayne. He never mentioned her again. Now Mitchell was going to become a real-estate broker and make a small fortune.

Bennett's stomach growled again. It was time to give up on Mitchell Furst for tonight and get something to eat. He filed the manila folder in the cabinet along with the others, making sure to lock the drawer.

At the restaurant, he ordered the fried fish. His cardiologist brother-in-law would scowl at the fried batter. What was the point of eating fish, he would say, if you're going to load it down with cholesterol? Bennett smiled as he spooned on the tartar sauce and thought about the computer waiting for him at home. Logging on was now a smooth process that no longer frightened him. Adam laughed at his uncle's growing enthusiasm for the Internet. Several times Bennett had followed the discussion on antisocial personality disorder, although he hadn't yet joined in. He could now decipher the different voices even without the screen names.

BJL062 believed no cure existed and psychiatrists had almost no reason to treat anyone who showed characteristics of antisocial personality disorder. SIMON, on the other hand, believed treatment could be effective for people with characteristics but not the full-fledged disorder. SHRINKO did not want to rush a judgment of anyone and therefore cut off the possibility of hope. WILMA was more concerned about the people who lived with sociopaths, no matter what label you put on them.

The therapists online carefully kept their identities concealed—if in fact all the participants were therapists, which Bennett doubted more and more. Likewise they never revealed anything about their patients that could be traced to them. But Bennett didn't need names and faces of all those other patients. He had Mitchell Furst.

Did Mitchell Furst have antisocial personality disorder? Was there any hope that Bennett could do Mitchell any good in a therapeutic relationship—especially one that seemed to be at the whim of the patient?

The fried fish finished, Bennett decided to do penance by not ordering the strawberry ice cream he craved.

"This is Jayne." Hoping it was Mitchell. Hoping he was standing below the window.

"There's an art show Saturday morning," Leslie said. "We should go."

"Saturday morning?"

"Opens at ten. It's an exhibit of lesser-known artists from the East Coast."

Jayne chuckled. "Is that really how they billed it?"

"No, that's my analysis. The exhibitors are all from the East somewhere, and I've never heard of any of them."

"Ah."

"Well, are you going or not?"

"I'm going to have to let you know."

Leslie was silent.

"What's the matter?" Jayne asked.

"You tell me."

"What does that mean?"

"Why can't you let me know now?"

"I need to check what I'm doing this weekend. That's all," Jayne said impatiently.

"You mean you have to check with Mitchell."

"He and I have talked about a couple of options for the weekend, so yes, I'd like to talk with him."

"Why can't you just say you'll go to the art show with me and plan around that?"

Jayne was glad Larry had stepped out of the office to go see a client. Her voice was rising.

"Leslie, what's going on?"

"Never mind. You don't have to go."

"But I'd like to."

"Is that a yes?"

"I'll still have to let you know."

"Right. Call me." Leslie hung up.

Jayne set her phone in its cradle, shaking her head. Leslie was so unhappy that she just couldn't let anyone else be happy. "That's her problem," Jayne said aloud. "I love her, but I'm not going to let her ruin this for me."

~ 4 ~

JADA478: What about pharmaceuticals? Useful?

BJL062: Nope.

SIMON: Some on lower end of spectrum may benefit.

BJL062: Really doubtful in my experience.

WILMA: What is your experience?

BJL062: Almost twenty years of working with convicted felons. I evaluate readiness for parole.

JADA478: That's hardly a representative sampling of the general population.

BJL062: It's a perfect sampling of the population of sociopaths.

WILMA: That's an outdated term.

BJL062: It's shorthand. We all know what we're talking about.

JADA478: Are you saying that all people with antisocial personality disorder will end up being convicted felons?

BJL062: Some of them are too smart to get caught. Doesn't mean they don't engage in the behaviors.

SHRINKO: Beg to differ. Have seen some patients respond to medications.

JADA478: How so?

BJL062: Must have had someone policing them to make sure they took the pills.

SIMON: They had family support. That's crucial.

WILMA: But don't family members often end up getting hurt?

SHRINKO: It's important for family to be in therapy.

WILMA: Because they get hurt?

SHRINKO: To keep them from getting hurt. To help them take care of themselves.

BJL062: Noncompliance is a major issue in trying to treat this condition with medications. No one can force a grown man to take his pills. No long-term evidence that this approach works.

HOPEFORALL: Sounds like most of you are ready to give up on these people.

BJL062: Just being realistic.

HOPEFORALL: But if you give up hope, it's all over.

WILMA: How does that help family members? They need hope that their loved ones can change.

SHRINKO: That's why it's important for them to be in therapy.

BJL062: We do them no service by setting up their expectations for something that is not going to happen.

SIMON: Change may be unlikely, but not impossible.

Bennett sighed and leaned back in his chair. HOPEFORALL was a new voice who would like what SHRINKO had to say. BJL062 would think HOPEFORALL and SHRINKO were deluding themselves and not helping anyone.

Mitchell Furst rarely spoke of his family. Bennett knew his parents lived in town. And he knew that when Mitchell was very young, his father had been away for months at a time working on an oil rig. Mitchell was eight months old before he even met his father. *What does his family think of him now?* Bennett wondered.

He swiveled away from the computer and reached for a thick, dusty textbook on the shelf behind him. Bennett hadn't looked at this volume of abnormal psychology in years. WILMA, among others, would take issue with the terminology it contained. Words like *sociopathic* and *psychopathic* were out of vogue. *Antisocial Personality Disorder* was the accepted term. It sounded less clinical, Bennett supposed, but he was not persuaded that the newer term changed the substance of the disorder.

As he flipped the pages, he recalled the lectures from more than thirty years ago. He had to admit that most of the case studies related to sociopathy or psychopathy were rooted in the criminal population. While he could believe that Mitchell Furst would engage in criminal activity, Bennett had no evidence that his patient had done so. Was it fair to compare him to a serial murderer who showed no remorse?

Remorse. Now there was an interesting topic. Bennett had long ago stopped taking Mitchell at his word. Too many of his explanations didn't quite add up. Bennett suspected Mitchell was not the victim of circumstances or others' ill will nearly as much as he claimed. Rather, he orchestrated circumstances that had potential for serious harm in the lives of others. But "sorry" was not in Mitchell Furst's vocabulary, Bennett was sure of that.

Bennett wanted to help Mitchell. But did Mitchell want to help himself? That was the question. What was his real motive in coming to see a psychiatrist, even erratically? Was it a cry for help? Or was it all a con? And whom was he trying to con with these visits?

Bennett glanced at the clock above the fireplace. Midnight. He shut down the computer. His arthritic right knee was stiff and didn't want to bear his weight as he stood up. Limping slightly, he made his way to the bedroom.

Jayne flipped through a stack of photos she had picked up at the drugstore earlier that evening. Pictures of Mitchell, mostly, taken around her house, at the park where they had spent a frosty but glorious afternoon two weekends ago, the scenic river bank where they had eaten cold fried chicken and wished it was hot. Pictures of ordinary places with the two of them doing ordinary things.

She took the box down from the baker's rack and looked over what she had just written:

Dear Mitchell,

Today I picked up some photos I just had developed. I must have looked at them a dozen times tonight. The park, the river, my backyard—wherever we are, we seem to have a great time. Every picture makes me laugh again at the jokes we made or remember the conversations where we shared our dreams with each other. So here I am writing to you again, because I feel wonderful just thinking about being with you. I doubt I'll ever mail one of these letters, so I guess I can think aloud as freely as I like.

I wonder why I have never seen the place where you live. I know that it's in a new part of town. I know that you're house-sitting for someone who is working in India for a year, and that he's very particular about what happens in his house. You've told me that looking after people's houses while they're gone has been a great way for you to save money. But you never know how long you'll be living in one place, so you use your parents' address for mail.

I've shared my home with you, and I love having you here. At the same time, it feels a little strange not to be able to picture where you live. I'd like to meet your family. I'd like to get to know the other people in your life who love you. I want us to be totally transparent with each other. I know we've only known each other a few months, coming up on a year pretty soon. But we both want to spend the future with each other. I want you to feel safe in my love so that you can let go and let me know everything about you. Maybe someday I'll be brave enough to say that to you out loud! Until then,

    Jayne

Jayne creased the blue paper and added it to the collection. Mitchell had told her that he wanted to be with her for a long, long time. And after her experience with Chuck, she certainly didn't want to rush into anything. If Mitchell needed time, she would give it to him. And she would take some for herself.

Spring burst upon them abruptly. In the blink of an eye, April filled the trees with green life, and lawns promised summer lushness. Gray winter skies turned a brilliant blue, and windows went up all over town. Jayne relished the warmth of the sun beaming through the window next to her desk at the graphics shop.

"I'm going downstairs for coffee. Do you want some?"

Jayne broke her concentration on the layout in front of her long enough to look up. Mare, the part-time bookkeeper, stood in front of her, mug in hand.

"Coffee?" Mare repeated.

"Oh, yes, please. In fact, make it a latte."

"Right. Double shot, whipped cream, cinnamon sprinkles."

Jayne smiled. "You've done this before. Larry will be back soon. Shall we get him something as well?"

"Plain Colombian blend, no sugar, no milk. The man has no imagination."

"He just knows what he likes."

"Be right back."

Mare scooted out and left Jayne with her layout but returned almost immediately.

"Look who I found on the stairs," Mare said.

Jayne looked up to find Mitchell standing before her. She rose for a kiss of greeting. "Hi! I wasn't expecting to see you today. I thought the new job had you really busy."

"Well, even a busy mortgage broker has to eat, doesn't he?"

"Absolutely. Is it lunchtime already?"

"Close enough. I'm here to steal you away."

"Well, Larry's not here to say no!" Jayne turned to Mare. "Guess I won't be needing that latte after all."

Down on the sidewalk, Mitchell said, "How about the bagel shop a couple of blocks over? I could go for one of their mongo sandwiches." Still holding her hand, he turned up the busy avenue.

"You must be really hungry."

"I am. And I have an important meeting this evening, so I won't get to eat again for a long time."

"Another evening meeting?" Jayne tried not to let her disappointment show.

"I know I've been working a lot of nights lately. It won't always be like this, I promise. But I'm just getting started in this business, and a lot of working people want to arrange their mortgages at night."

"I suppose that only makes sense."

They ate their sandwiches more quickly than Jayne would have liked, and with less conversation. Mitchell left her in front of her building, pleading lateness to an appointment with a prospective customer.

"Hey, are you Connor's dad?" The boy propped his bat on his shoulder and studied the face in the bleachers.

The man laughed. "Yes, I am. How did you guess?"

The thirteen-year-old boy shrugged. "You look just like him. I mean, he looks just like you. I guess you looked like you before he did."

The father beamed. "That's my boy."

"I'm glad Connor came back to the team this year."

"Connor loves baseball. He wouldn't miss this for the world."

"I heard he was moving away."

The man raised an eyebrow. "Where did you hear that?"

"Around school. Is he moving?"

"No, we're not moving."

"But Connor lives with his mom, right? Is she moving?"

For a fleeting moment, the man thought the rumor might be true. Would Rachelle leave town and try to take Connor with her?

"No one's moving," he told the boy firmly. "Connor will be here to pitch for your team just like last year and the year before."

"Well, that's good, 'cause he's the only decent pitcher we've got."

"I think Coach Tom is looking for you." The man gestured toward first base.

The boy turned his head, saw the scowl on the coach's face, and scrambled across the field.

Rachelle would not be taking that boy anywhere. Mitchell Furst would see to that. Pulling a candy bar from his pocket, he settled in to watch his son's first baseball practice of the season. He kept one eye on the parking lot, looking for Rachelle's green Ford Taurus.

The boys were putting away the equipment when she finally arrived.

"Hello, Mitchell." Her greeting was cool.

"Hello, Rachelle." He didn't look at her, but scanned the ball field instead. "I heard an interesting rumor a few minutes ago, but I'm sure it's not true. You're not taking that boy anywhere."

Rachelle's shoulders sagged. "It's just over in Portsfield. Trent's new job is there. It would make things easier."

"Where your husband works is not my concern. I'm the boy's father, and he's not going anywhere."

"Come on, Mitchell. Be reasonable. It's only forty minutes away. It's not as if we wanted to move to Alaska."

"You can move anywhere you want, but you're not taking my son." He turned and looked at her directly. "Is that clear?"

Rachelle didn't respond. She simply raised her eyes to greet her approaching son, the spitting image of his father.

Mitchell was right on time for his six o'clock appointment with Dr. Bennett Grey.

"How has your week been?" Bennett asked. "Are you settling in to the new job?"

"It's a lot of work. It's a good thing I've done this before, or I'd really be struggling to keep up."

"You've been a mortgage broker before?"

"When I was in college, I had to do an internship. I worked with a lending institution for six months during my senior year."

"Well, you must find that helpful now."

"Tremendously. I think it's one of the reasons I got the job. And, of course, my dad taught me a lot too."

"Your dad?"

"He's an entrepreneur with a background in finance. When I was little, he did a lot of investing."

"I was under the impression that he had worked on an oil rig when you were small."

"He did. That was one of his investments, so of course he was working hard to make it work. He ran the on-site office."

"Did it pay off for him?"

"That one didn't. But he's had a lot of other investments that have done very well."

"I'm glad to hear that. Do you mind if we talk about your father for a while tonight?"

"We can talk about whatever you want to talk about. You're the shrink."

"I want to talk about what you find helpful. That way we can get to the bottom of the things that are bothering you."

Mitchell shrugged. "Nothing's really bothering me."

"Most people who come to see a psychiatrist have a reason."

"I just need someone to talk to sometimes. It's not as if I have any deep-seated emotional issues. It's just good to relax and talk."

Bennett nodded. "Yes, it is. Everyone needs to be able to do that once in a while. Do you think you can relax while we talk about your father?"

"Why not? I'm not nervous about anything."

"Good. I don't want you to be nervous when you talk to me. Tell me what your father is like."

An hour later Mitchell Furst was gone, and Bennett Grey wrote case notes in the dim light of his office. He wasn't sure what the objective truth about Mitchell's father was. He might have been an unskilled worker on an oil rig, or he might have managed a small office. If in fact he had invested any money in oil, it was speculative, a small amount, and he almost certainly lost it.

On the other hand, Bennett was sure that Mitchell's relationship with his father was distant and hollow at best. No matter how many stories he might spin about having a nurturing childhood, it was clear to Bennett that Roger Furst had spent little time or energy on the boy who had idolized him.

Jayne sat upright, but she didn't scream. Not this time. It sat on a shelf in the corner next to the closet, a shelf right up under the ceiling. A shelf that did not exist. A shelf made of marble so heavy that it could not possibly be attached to the wall.

The creature was an odd shade of bluish green, clothed but unclothed at the same time, disproportionate limbs hanging out of the wrong places. Its facial features, however, stood out clear and undistorted. She had seen the face enough times to recognize it with certainty.

The first visit had happened right after Claire died. Then it had disappeared for a long time, returning about the time Jayne met Mitchell at that party. Each visit—occurring more and more frequently of late—gave Jayne the feeling that the creature on the shelf had a message for her. But it never spoke. It merely bore into her green eyes with its brown ones, daring her to respond. And then it would disappear, and she could not be sure it had ever been there at all.

She stared back at it, searching to know what it wanted. But it was silent as always. It did not look fierce or unkind—this time. But she hated the clammy silence that came with the being.

"Go away," she said aloud.

And it was gone.

In the morning light the marble shelf was gone as well.

~ 5 ~

"You've been staring at that screen for hours, girl. I've never seen anyone work as hard as you do for so long without moving. Take a break." Mare tossed a paper wad at Jayne to break her concentration.

Jayne rubbed one eye. "You're right. I just can't seem to make these pages fit right in this book. Maybe it would help to take a break." She stretched her arms above her head. "I feel like I'm breaking all kinds of design rules just to get this book to flow right. They want all the chapters starting on a right-hand page, but there's too much copy."

Larry jumped in. "Forget the rules. Follow your instincts. It will be beautiful."

"That's a very touchy-feely thing for a man to say," Jayne commented.

"I'm just speaking the truth. Some of the best work you've done has come when you abandoned the rules."

"Speaking of touchy-feely," Mare said, "I haven't seen that man of yours for several days. What's he up to?"

"He's very busy, but he's doing well," Jayne answered truthfully. If she didn't see Mitchell every night, he called her. His schedule was frenetic, but she never went to sleep without at least speaking to him. In the last month they had grown closer than ever.

"He's got you under his skin, that's for sure. Take one look at that man, and you know he's smitten."

Jayne blushed.

The phone rang. Larry quickly turned his back and lowered his voice, uttering no more than monosyllables. Jayne and Mare looked at each other with raised eyebrows.

"What's the big mystery?" Jayne asked after her boss hung up.

"What do you mean?"

"What was that all about?"

"Just a client."

"I know what you sound like when you talk to a client, and that wasn't it," Jayne said.

Larry looked at his watch. "It's almost closing time. What do you say we all knock off early today?"

Jayne looked quizzical. "I've been working here for six years, and you've never closed the shop even ten minutes early."

"Well, today I am. Save your file and let's go."

"But—"

"Jayne."

Something in his tone made Jayne suddenly compliant. She saved her project file, backed it up on the server, and shut off her computer.

"You ready, Mare?" Larry asked.

"Ready." Mare slung her bag over her shoulder.

They walked out together, conversing about evening plans as they walked down the two flights of stairs.

"Oh, look," Larry said. "Isn't that Mitchell in the coffee shop?"

Jayne peered in, and sure enough Mitchell was flipping through a book while seated comfortably at a table in the middle of the shop.

"He's probably waiting to surprise you," Mare suggested.

"Jayne!" Mitchell sounded pleased as she entered. "I was hoping you would come down soon."

Mitchell took her arm and guided her to his table. Momentarily a platter of a dozen steaming blueberry scones appeared. Her eyes grew wide.

"Did you order these?"

"Are they to your liking?"

"Very much. But so many …"

The shop owner arrived with a huge mug, not a Styrofoam cup. "I hope this is to the lady's liking," he said.

"Oh yes." Carefully she sipped the hot coffee while eyeing Mitchell.

Mitchell took Jayne's hand. "We've had many very nice moments here, haven't we?"

Jayne felt odd. "Yes, I suppose we have," she stammered.

"We've come here when we wanted to talk or when we just wanted to see each other for a few minutes. People are used to seeing us here, you know."

Jayne glanced around the room and realized it was more crowded than usual. All the "regulars" were there. Even Mare and Larry had come in.

Mitchell squeezed her hand. "I couldn't think of a better place to plan all the moments we'll have together in the future."

The owner appeared again with an enormous bouquet of two dozen yellow roses, which Mitchell laid in Jayne's arms.

"Jayne Paige-Hamilton, will you marry me?"

Jayne leaned across the table and whispered a heartfelt "yes" into Mitchell's ear as the crowd around them burst into applause.

Jayne was so overwhelmed at the coffee shop that she hardly noticed when Mitchell slipped a diamond ring on her finger. Now she stared at it, flabbergasted. She had not seen this coming at all. She knew how she felt, but she had not thought that Mitchell was ready for this step, much less that he would go to such lengths to plan the occasion.

From the coffee shop, they had gone to Jayne's house, where Mitchell insisted she change into something stunning. When she opened her closet, she found Mitchell had put his key to her house to good use. A slinky silver dress waited for her with matching shoes on the closet floor. Both fit perfectly. Deftly she piled her hair on top of her head and stepped back to review the total effect. Stunning. She looked stunning. And she felt stunning.

Mitchell took her to an exclusive restaurant she had never dreamed she'd see the inside of. They danced late into the evening—vibrant, energetic dances; intimate, close dances. When he took her home, Mitchell kissed her slowly and deeply at the door, as if he never wanted to stop. She wanted him to come in, to stay the night to celebrate, but he said it was late and he should go. One more long, deep kiss.

And she was left gazing at the extravagant ring on her left hand.

"I expected you hours ago." The young woman was clearly annoyed when she heard the key turn in the lock and saw the door open. "It's Tuesday night. You knew I wanted to go out. You told me you would watch the baby."

He stopped her rampage by quickly gathering her close and kissing her neck in just the right spot.

"I had a late meeting," he murmured in her ear. "I couldn't get away."

"You could have called." She was still protesting, but the gas had gone out of her effort.

"My cell phone was dead." He traced the shape of her face with one finger.

"But it was my night to go out. And you were going to stay over."

"It's only eleven thirty. I can still stay over."

Sadie relaxed. This man had such power over her. She couldn't stay mad at him.

"How's Corrine?" he asked.

"Sleeping."

"I want to see her." He released Sadie and stepped toward the bedroom.

"Don't wake that baby!" she protested but knew it was pointless. He always woke the baby when he wanted to see her.

Without turning on the bedroom light, he scooped up the sleeping infant and kissed the top of her head.

"What did I do to deserve such a beautiful daughter?" he said softly. The baby stirred in his arms. "Wake up, beautiful. Daddy wants to see you."

Corrine cried briefly as she wakened, then grinned in recognition. At eight months, she was at a most agreeable stage—friendly, cooing, smiling.

"Do you know how long it took me to get her down?" Sadie sighed. But she couldn't help smiling at the picture of father and daughter together.

He leaned over the top of Corrine's head and kissed her mother. "I'll put her down again. Don't worry. Then I'll make good on the second part of my promise."

"Mitchell Furst, I don't know why I put up with you."

He reached out with one hand and touched her breast. "Then let me remind you of all the benefits."

~ 6 ~

Jayne and Leslie simultaneously pushed back from the table in their favorite ice-cream shop.

"I feel really wicked," Jayne said with obvious pleasure. "I haven't done that in a long time."

"That's because you only indulge in double-fudge banana splits with me, and you never have time for me anymore," Leslie said. She put some money for a tip down on the table.

"Don't start on me," Jayne warned. "I see as much of you as I ever did. I can't help it if you have no social life."

Leslie put up a hand. "Truce?"

Jayne nodded. "How about a walk? I can only enjoy feeling wicked for so long, then I repent and need to walk off my sin."

Leslie laughed. "You sound like the old Sunday-school days."

"No, they never gave us a chance to enjoy feeling wicked in Sunday school."

"No, I suppose not. Anyway, that was a long time ago. I haven't been to Sunday school since I was nine."

"Me neither. I never even go in a church unless someone I know gets married."

They left the ice-cream shop and squinted into the bright June sun.

"Which way?" Jayne asked.

"You pick."

Jayne opted to walk toward a park about a half a mile away.

"Speaking of getting married, are you really going to do this getting married thing?" Leslie asked.

Jayne wiggled the fingers on her left hand. "I have a ring that says I will."

"You haven't said a word about wedding plans today. Aren't brides supposed to be obsessed with such details?"

Jayne gave her cousin a sidelong glance. "I didn't think you'd want to hear about wedding plans, considering that you don't approve of the groom."

Leslie shrugged. "Hey, it's not the decision I would have made, but it's your life. I can deal with that."

"Really?"

"Really. So what are the plans?"

"We're thinking about the end of October. Mitchell should have some time off by then."

Leslie counted the months off on her fingers. "We have less than five months to make this event happen."

"That should be plenty. It won't be a big wedding. We both want something small and intimate."

"So the question is where. October might be too cold for outdoors."

Jayne nodded. "It'll be inside somewhere. You know, I had a garden wedding when I married Chuck. I really think I'd like to be married in a church this time."

"But you don't go to church."

"I know. But there are plenty of beautiful little chapels around this town."

"You'd better get booked pretty soon." Leslie shaded her eyes and looked ahead to the park. "Let's go watch those boys play baseball for a few minutes."

"Since when are you interested in that?"

"Since I decided I need to let my food digest before I walk any farther."

They climbed into the bleachers. No coaches appeared, and less than a dozen boys between twelve and fourteen years old straggled in for a pickup game. Soon teams organized, one with five players and one with six. The smaller team opted for last bats and took the field.

Jayne watched as a boy warmed up to begin pitching. He looked unusually confident and comfortable on the pitcher's mound. Clearly he found joy in the sport. Jayne knew just enough about baseball to recognize his talent.

When he took off his cap to wipe sweat from his face, Jayne's heart nearly stopped.

The boy on the pitcher's mound was the spitting image of Mitchell.

The angle of the nose, the setting of the dark eyes, the broad forehead, the shape of his mouth, the color of his skin—she felt as if she were seeing Mitchell as a young teenager. She counted the outs until the boy's team came up to bat when he would have to come closer to where she sat.

He was the third at bat. The ball got away from the catcher on the fourth pitch and rolled back toward the bleachers. The batter twisted around and said, "Ma'am, would you toss the ball back over here, please?"

Jayne reached for the ball as he looked at her briefly, without recognition. Of course he wouldn't recognize her. Why should he? They had never met. He was just a boy playing baseball in the park.

"I got it, Connor," the catcher said.

His name was Connor.

"That kid is some pitcher," Jayne said to Leslie casually. "I wonder if he can hit, too."

Connor smacked the ball into center field.

"Guess that answers your question," Leslie said.

Jayne glanced at Leslie, who showed no reaction to the boy now running around first base. But Leslie had only met Mitchell a couple of times. She might not remember his features well enough to be unnerved by the similarity in this boy. Jayne racked her brain trying to think of Mitchell's relatives. He had two sisters with children. Perhaps the family genes were this strong! And he had a cousin, Mason. Could this be Mason's son? Was it genetically possible for a cousin to have a child who looked so much like Mitchell? But if it wasn't Mason's son who swung the bat, then ... Jayne refused to draw the next conclusion.

"Are you ready to walk again?" Jayne asked abruptly, standing up as if to leave Leslie no choice.

"Well, I guess you think I am." Leslie complied and stood up as well. They headed back toward the street where they had left Jayne's car.

Bennett Grey turned on the computer in his living room and impatiently waited for the initial cycle of cyber noises. He was long past being rattled by the rapid clicking noises that meant his computer was preparing for service. He quickly signed on and entered his favorite chat room.

WILMA: What about in-patient programs?

SHRINKO: Some successful ones. Strictly long-term. Families have to be ready for that. Very structured. Patient must earn privileges.

WILMA: Do they seek treatment on their own?

BJL062: In my experience, rarely. Usually through the forensic system. Don't see their own deficits.

SHRINKO: But you work in the criminal justice system, don't you?

BJL062: Yes. But I keep current with research. Also have private practice.

SHRINKO: I think we must look beyond criminal population for accurate conclusions.

HOPEFORALL: Therapy can help. I've seen it in my own practice.

BJL062: Not my experience.

SIMON: I was a prison psychiatrist once. Huge turnover. Kudos to you, BJL062, but few people stay in it long enough to see long-term results.

Bennett sat with his fingers poised over the keyboard. He would need a screen name if he wanted to enter the discussion, and he wanted to. His typing speed—finger pecking, really—was deplorable. He wouldn't keep up for long. Nevertheless, he smiled at the thought of his nephew Adam's pleasure at what he was about to do.

UNCLEB: Challenge of therapy is overcoming fear.

BJL062: Welcome, UNCLEB. A new voice? In practice?

UNCLEB: Yes. Must be intimate with therapist.

HOPEFORALL: Very scary.

UNCLEB: Discomfort is sign of progress.

SIMON: UNCLEB, do you have ASPD patient?

UNCLEB: I believe so.

BJL062: Court ordered?

UNCLEB: No.

BJL062: Comes on his own?

UNCLEB: Yes.

SIMON: Consistent?

UNCLEB: No.

HOPEFORALL: Making progress in therapy?

UNCLEB: Not sure.

HOPEFORALL: Depression may be first sign therapy is working. Shows they're feeling something.

UNCLEB: Not depressed.

The chat rapidly progressed. Bennett couldn't keep up. But he had made an entry. HOPEFORALL insisted that getting a patient to feel something, anything, was key to progress in treatment. Some people had to feel the pain of depression before they could feel love and genuine compassion for another person. Bennett wondered if Mitchell Furst ever felt anything at all. Could he as a therapist lead his patient into the realm of truth and intimacy if the patient didn't want to go there?

Reaching behind him, Bennett picked up a brochure that had come in the mail a few days earlier. A psychiatric conference in September promised to address the question of antisocial personality disorder and effectiveness of treatment options. And it was nearby. He would only have to be gone overnight. Bennett tore off the registration flap and took out his checkbook.

Dear Mitchell,

    I saw something today that I can't make heads or tails of. I can't even bring myself to say what it was, because it would sound so ridiculous. I thought that if I wrote it down, I would know the truth one way or the other. But I don't think so. It's absurd. I'll put it out of my mind.

    I've worn your ring for three weeks now, but I hardly know your family at all. I'm looking forward to your mother's birthday party next week. I hope I'll have a chance to get to know her. We both love you, so we have something in common right from the start.

    You have my whole heart, Mitchell Richard Furst. I wasn't sure I would ever be able to give it to anyone again, but I have given it to you. Sometimes, though, I wonder if I know you at all. It seems like I'm constantly discovering new things about you. Perhaps that's what marriage is—spending years discovering who the person you've given your heart to really is. I admit that scares me sometimes. But I do love you, and I feel sure that you love me.

    Jayne

~ 7 ~

JADA478: I'm concerned about the loved ones.

WILMA: We must take a look at relationship with parents in early childhood.

JADA478: I understand the theory that a distant relationship with the father contributes to the condition.

SHRINKO: Mother is nearly always passive.

JADA478: But what about siblings? And many of these people marry and have children of their own.

SHRINKO: Or don't marry and have children.

WILMA: Are you asking what hope there is for families?

JADA478: Mostly wondering about significant others. What possible attraction would anyone see in an ASPD?

SHRINKO: They're charming. They can be a knight in shining armor if they want to be. They know all the right moves and when to make them.

BJL062: The smart ones can be anything they want to be. They fabricate a complex web of lies that most people can't penetrate and they themselves begin to believe.

JADA478: I've seen some very intelligent women fall for these guys.

BJL062: No surprise. But the women are victims. Important to remember that.

SHRINKO: If they simply have antisocial personality characteristics, they mess up a lot of relationships with irresponsibility and deceit, but everyone moves on or the spouse learns to cope. If they truly have the disorder, they leave serious damage in their wake.

UNCLEB: Skilled at staying in control.

BJL062: Welcome back, UNCLEB. Yes, exceptionally skilled at maintaining control over any situation. They get their way and no one knows they've been conned.

JADA478: So it's all about control?

SHRINKO: Largely. They don't trust anyone, so they have to be in control at all times.

UNCLEB: But in a charming sort of way.

SHRINKO: Exactly.

SIMON: They spin a better lie than anyone, but it's usually credible. And someone with an emotional attachment will not want to believe the incredible, so they will accept things that don't always make sense on the surface.

WILMA: Is there anything professionals can do to help people from becoming victims? Especially women.

BJL062: Doubtful. They don't know what they're involved with until they are victims. Then we can only help them pick up the pieces of their lives.

UNCLEB: Can you help someone who doesn't know she needs help?

SHRINKO: Not really. Sadly, we must wait for them to come to us, and by then the damage is done.

JADA478: Sorry to repeat myself, but what about families? Parents, siblings. Do they disown the patient?

BJL062: That happens in an informal way much of the time.

SIMON: Disagree. Family is family. They tend to think they can help. If they can clean up this one mess, patient will straighten up and not do it again.

SHRINKO: But they always do.

SIMON: Vicious cycle.

Bennett's mind drifted to the young woman Mitchell Furst had once mentioned, Jayne. Mitchell had never talked about her again and repeatedly resisted subtle suggestions from Bennett that might have led the conversation in that direction. Bennett didn't even know if Jayne was still in Mitchell's life.

He hoped not, for the young woman's sake. Mitchell had been keeping his appointments fairly consistently in recent weeks. Perhaps it was time to put him on a shorter leash.

🦋

Mitchell looked at Jayne from the driver's seat of his truck. "You ready for this?"

She nodded confidently. "Absolutely. I've been looking forward to it for a long time."

"My family can be overwhelming. My sisters sometimes don't know when to stop talking, my father is a pompous jerk, and my mother just wants everyone to be happy even if they really aren't."

"It's all right. I can handle it."

"They're going to pounce on you, you know. Ever since I told them I got engaged, they've been nagging me to bring you around."

"And you should have! They're going to be my family, too."

Mitchell held Jayne's hand as he led her up the walk to the small house where he had been raised. Jayne cradled the boxed set of copper candlesticks that she hoped her future mother-in-law would like. Mitchell had been of little help selecting a gift for his mother, but she reasoned that almost everyone appreciated candles.

"You know what, I think the party is actually in the backyard," Mitchell said. "Let's just walk around."

"Oh. Okay."

She followed him through a gate and around the side of the house. About twenty people were gathered in the yard. Jayne noticed that the cake on the picnic table had already been cut, and empty paper plates and cups were strewn around the yard.

"Mitchell, are we late?" she whispered.

"What do you mean?"

"I think they've already had most of the party."

He shrugged. "My sister told me two thirty. Maybe she forgot what she said. The important thing is we're here now, and it's time for you to meet everyone."

A woman about ten years older than Jayne approached and extended her hand.

"You must be Jayne. I'm Brenda Walker, Mitchell's oldest sister."

"It's nice to finally meet you."

"I'm sorry we haven't met before. We kept telling Mitchell to bring you around."

"I'm glad to finally be here."

Just then a small boy tried to tackle Mitchell, who playfully tumbled to the ground.

"My son, Dylan," Brenda said. "Can't get enough of Uncle Mitchell." Brenda gestured for Jayne to follow her. "Come on, I'll introduce you to Mom and Dad."

"I guess that's a logical place to start trying to understand the Furst family tree."

Brenda led Jayne across the yard to a couple in their late fifties seated on wrought-iron patio chairs.

"Mom, Dad, this is Jayne."

"Mitchell's friend?" Roger Furst stood up to shake Jayne's hand.

"His fiancée, actually. Remember, Dad? Mitchell told you he was getting married."

"I'm so glad to finally meet you," Jayne said with perhaps too much enthusiasm. "Happy birthday, Mrs. Furst."

"Thank you. Please call me Leona."

"I hope you'll enjoy this." Jayne handed Leona the wrapped box.

"How thoughtful of you. We were just about to begin the gift-opening ceremonies."

"You have a big job ahead of you, Jayne," Roger said.

Jayne smiled politely. "How do you mean?"

"Getting Mitchell to settle down won't be an easy job, you know."

"I love Mitchell just the way he is," Jayne answered.

"Well, then you've got a bigger heart than most."

"Roger!" Leona's voice was low, but the reprimand was plain.

Jayne glanced awkwardly over at Mitchell, who was now wrestling with no fewer than four nieces and nephews. His grunted protests only egged them on. She'd had no idea he would frolic with children so easily. The thought made her smile.

"Let me introduce you to the others," Brenda offered. "That's my sister Debra over there."

They began walking in Debra's direction. In another few minutes Jayne had the husbands, Ned and Wally, matched up with Brenda and Debra. Their cousin Mason was also there with his son, Ryan.

Jayne couldn't help but stare at Mason and Ryan. The family resemblance was clear. Mason could have been Mitchell's brother as easily as his cousin. The boy could have belonged to either of them.

"Mason and Mandy have split up again," Brenda whispered. "But I imagine you'll meet her soon enough anyway. They always seem to get back together."

Although Ryan was about the right age, and the resemblance was strong, he wasn't the boy from the park. None of the boys scrambling around the yard was the boy she'd seen at the park. Was this really everybody in the Furst family?

I must have been imagining things, Jayne thought. *The similarity can't have been as strong as I thought, or the boy would be here, part of the family.*

Leona soon began opening gifts. Jayne leaned back into Mitchell's chest as they watched his mother open Jayne's candlesticks.

"Those are gorgeous," Brenda said.

"It's about time Mitchell hooked up with someone who has good taste," her husband, Ned, said. "Lizzie certainly never had any."

Mitchell had talked to Jayne in great detail about his relationship with Lizzie, the only other really serious relationship he'd ever had. He had cared deeply for Lizzie but had stopped short of asking her to marry him. Something hadn't felt right, he'd said. Jayne remembered that Mitchell had said his family never really cared for Lizzie. She hoped she was making a more favorable impression.

"Mom, there's no more Kool-Aid," a tired voice whined. Jayne turned to see a child banging on Brenda's hip with a paper cup.

"I'll go make some more." Brenda grabbed an empty pitcher and moved toward the house.

"Please, let me help," Jayne said, separating herself from Mitchell to follow Brenda through the back door.

"These kids go through more Kool-Aid," Brenda lamented. "I'm thinking of buying stock in the company. If I can't get a bulk discount, I could at least make a little profit." Brenda emptied a package of powder into the pitcher. "You could get some ice out," she suggested.

Jayne stepped over to the refrigerator and reached for the freezer door. "Wow! Somebody likes to have pictures of kids!" The refrigerator was plastered with snapshots and school photos.

"That's Mom for you. She likes to have a picture of every child and grandchild at every stage, and she wants them all out where she can see them."

Jayne extracted the ice bucket as Brenda filled the pitcher with water.

"You have three children and Debra has two, right?"

"Right. And Mason's kids are like more grandchildren to Mom. She pretty much raised Mason."

"I thought Mason and Mandy had one son."

"Mason has a daughter, too, from before he met Mandy. She's nearly grown actually."

"Oh." Mitchell had never mentioned that.

As Brenda stirred the drink mix with a long wooden spoon, Jayne scanned the photos on the refrigerator. She recognized a few of them; however, more children were pictured than the ones she had met in the yard.

"Who are all these other children?" Jayne asked.

Brenda picked up the pitcher. "Oh, you'll get to know everyone. Don't worry about it." She pushed open the screen door and went back outside. With a last glance around the kitchen, Jayne followed.

Back outside Jayne cheerfully filled paper cups with grape drink and passed them out to thirsty children. She saw Brenda's three children, Debra's two, Mason's son, and two others. But none of them stayed in one place long enough to converse with. Jayne scanned the yard for Mitchell, hoping he would help dispel the mystery. The extra children might be neighbors or best friends of the grandchildren. If she was going to be part of the Furst family, she wanted to understand how everyone was connected. But she didn't see Mitchell anywhere.

"You hungry?" Debra asked. "Wally's taking some chicken off the grill right now."

"Actually I *am* hungry," Jayne said. "I saw the cake was already cut and thought we'd missed the food."

"One of the kids got into it, so Mom told them just to go ahead. The real food is now."

"Great! I'd like to wash up first, though."

Debra nodded toward the house. "Go through the kitchen to the hall, second door on the left."

"Thanks."

Jayne headed back into the house, still wondering where Mitchell was. When she got to the hall, she nearly stopped in her tracks. Hardly a square inch of wall was visible behind the dozens of framed photographs. She couldn't help but pause to look. In some older photos she recognized Mitchell and his sisters as young children and then teenagers. She smiled at the sight. She would have to remember to ask Leona if she could see Mitchell's baby book. More recent photos of the children now playing in the backyard were grouped together along with the nameless children whose pictures she had seen in the kitchen. Jayne was almost to the bathroom when she halted abruptly. On the wall next to the bathroom door was a picture of a little boy who had to be Connor, the boy in the park. So he was a part of this family! Just how was what she didn't know yet. The boy in the picture was perhaps seven years old, but he was clearly Connor.

Jayne stepped into the bathroom, washed her hands, and meandered through the living room on her way back to the kitchen. Mitchell was in a corner on his cell phone.

"There you are!" she exclaimed. "I've been looking for you."

"I'll see you when we meet next week, then," Mitchell said into the phone. He clicked it shut and turned to Jayne. "Sorry. Had a business call I had to take, and it was too noisy outside to hear anything."

"You never told me your mother was such a nut about photos. I can't believe how many she has displayed around the house."

Mitchell shrugged. "To be honest, no one else pays much attention to them. If she sees a kid she likes, she wants pictures. You'd be amazed how flattering the parents think that is. They give her all the pictures she wants."

"So not all these kids are related to the family?" Jayne asked, confused.

"No way. You just met everybody in the backyard. Let's get back to the party." Mitchell grabbed Jayne's hand and pulled her through the house.

She couldn't help noticing that another photo of the boy in the park sat on the piano in the living room. And this one was recent. He was wearing a baseball uniform.

~ 8 ~

The picture on the piano—apparently a photo of the boy from the park, Connor—haunted Jayne.

After another hour of pleasantries in the backyard, Jayne decided to go back into the house. But Mitchell suddenly insisted they had to go. He pleaded a lot of paperwork waiting in his office that had to be done before Monday. He promised her a late dinner if he could just have a few hours to work. She offered to cook and took a chicken out of the freezer as soon as she got home.

He never showed up for dinner. At ten thirty, Jayne put the chicken and potatoes away. She had lost her appetite.

Dreams woke her three times that night. The creature on the shelf in the corner laughed at her. Twice she awoke with a start after seeing the boy's face clearly. She was sure that Connor had worn the same uniform as the boy in the picture on the piano—the same purple stripes, the same pocket emblem.

For three days she did not see Mitchell. He called her two or three times a day, and they made one plan after another. Meet for coffee. Have dinner together. Cruise the mall. Make a guest list. But something always came up. His new job was demanding.

The dreams continued.

Half believing that she had psyched herself into believing the two boys were the same person, Jayne decided to trade in her tidy purse for a larger, more amorphous bag. Along with her wallet and cosmetics, her keys, and a couple of pens, she dropped in a camera with a telephoto lens. She made sure she had plenty of film.

Then she went to the park after work. A team was practicing, but it was the wrong team. The boys were too young.

Her cell phone rang just as she reluctantly admitted she was out of luck, at least for the day.

"This is Jayne."

"And I'm so glad it is." At the sound of his warm, smooth voice, her doubts faded. The boys could not possibly be the same. Mitchell had nothing to do with the boy in the park. She had just had some crazy dreams.

"Hello, Mitchell."

"Baby, I'm sorry my schedule has been so scrambled up. I am definitely going to see you tonight. What would you like to do? Wedding plans? Movie? Dinner?"

"Oh, I want to see you, too. It's been a lonely three days. But I promised my cousin we'd do something tonight. I'm supposed to meet her in half an hour."

"The three of us can go out together. I'll treat you both to dinner."

"I don't think that's what Leslie has in mind. She's thinking girly stuff."

"You're just saying that because she doesn't like me."

"No, I'm not. I'm sure if Leslie spent more time with you, she would not like you much less than she doesn't like you now."

"Huh?"

"I told you. It's just a thing she has with men. She's been really supportive since we got engaged."

"I don't get a vote, do I." It was a statement more than a question.

"Sorry, no. But I should be home about ten o'clock. Why don't you come over then? I can at least see your face before it's time to go to bed."

"At ten, the evening is still young. I'll take you dancing."

Jayne chuckled. Mitchell was such a night owl. But she wasn't, not on a work night. "I'm afraid dancing will have to wait until Saturday night. I have a breakfast meeting with a new client."

"If I pout, will you change your mind?"

"See you tonight."

Jayne felt happy as she pulled into her driveway that night. She'd had a good time with Leslie looking at bridal magazines, but she was anxious to see

Mitchell. As she scanned her street she saw no sign of his truck. But it wasn't ten yet. She let herself into the house and kicked off her shoes.

Fifteen minutes later, the phone rang. "Mitchell?"

"Yeah, baby, it's me."

"Where are you?"

"Since I couldn't see you, I decided to spend the evening following up leads. And I got a hot one on an expensive property. If I can close this deal, I'll make a pretty penny."

"You mean you're working now?" Jayne heard some muffled background noises. She couldn't begin to guess where he was calling from.

"Yeah, I think it's going to be a late night. I'm doing the wining and dining thing, and I really think it's going to pay off."

"Now I want to pout. I really wanted to see you."

"Me, too, baby. But this could bankroll our honeymoon. Think Hawaii!"

Mitchell snapped his cell phone shut and stepped out of the cubbyhole outside the club's men's room.

"Oh, there you are." A tall, striking redhead slinked toward him. Her tight, short sapphire dress showed off her long legs. "I thought maybe you had escaped my lair."

"Now why would I want to do that?" Mitchell slipped one hand around the woman's waist as she leaned into his chest and played with his collar.

"You'd better not. You promised me the next dance and they're playing our song."

"And I always keep a promise."

"Mmm. I hope so. Maybe I should see what else I can get you to promise."

"Or maybe you should make a few promises yourself." Mitchell put his other hand behind her neck, pulled her head close, and put his mouth down hard on hers.

Hawaii. Jayne liked the sound of that. When she had married Chuck, he had insisted on honeymooning at his parent's time-share condo in Florida, even though they had been there twice before. Yes, Hawaii sounded good.

She ran a hot bath and poured in a generous amount of bubble bath. She lit a candle and turned off the light before easing into the steaming water. She hadn't had a moment to relax all day, and tomorrow was not likely to be any better. With a rubber pillow behind her neck, she soon drifted off.

Then it was there. Not laughing this time, but smirking. Watching her in the bath.

The water was cold. The candle had gone out. Stifling a cry she splashed out of the tub and flicked on the light. The creature was gone.

"I'm a crazy person," she said aloud as she wrapped a large towel around her shaking body. "I see things that aren't there in my own house. How would I know what I saw in a public park?"

But she had seen something. And she couldn't forget it.

She went back to the park the next day after work, still carrying her large bag that could hide anything.

The right team was on the field. Her heart pounded as she scanned the team. It was just a practice. Mothers were chitchatting about their other children and eccentric bosses. No one paid any attention when she sat down on the metal bench. Most of the boys wore shorts and T-shirts. Connor wasn't pitching today; a coach took the mound instead, lobbing pitches at batters. She almost hoped she wouldn't see him. But she did see him, feet spread, hands on his knees, crouched and alert for a fly ball to come to right field.

Jayne took out the camera, the long lens already in place. She lifted it to her eye and focused. The boy's face was dipped in the shadow of his black cap; suddenly she wasn't sure it was the same boy.

Not wanting to appear conspicuous, Jayne nonchalantly stood, slung her bag over her shoulder, and began strolling around the outskirts of the field. She watched as the boy fielded a ball that dropped in the pocket behind first base and hurled it back to the infield. As he threw, his cap fell off. Jayne snapped four pictures before he scooped it up off the ground.

The coach waved the boy in from right field. "Come on in. Your turn to bat a few and show 'em how it's done."

The boy grinned as he trotted in toward the plate. Jayne took some more pictures. His smile was remarkably like Mitchell's. Remarkably.

As the boy dug his feet into the batter's box and took a stance that showed his determination to hit solidly, the coach returned to the mound. Jayne had sauntered over to the third-base line.

"Okay, Furst, here we go."

If she hadn't had the strap around her neck, Jayne would have dropped her camera. Furst. The coach had said Furst. This boy was in the family. This boy had to be Mitchell's son. She snapped three more pictures as he swung at the first pitch and smacked it to left field.

She stopped by a one-hour photo booth, then went home to wait for Mitchell. He was supposed to come over at seven, and she had promised to make good on that home-cooked meal he had missed on the weekend. Earlier in the day, however, she had decided not to start cooking until he arrived—too many broken dates in the last few days.

But he didn't break the date. He was a few minutes late, but he arrived looking relaxed and glad to see her, offering the usual kiss of greeting. She forced herself not to turn away. He glanced around.

"Did you decide you'd rather go out?" he asked.

"Actually, I'm not really hungry."

Mitchell furrowed his brow. "Are you all right, babe? Not sick, are you?"

"Please sit down, Mitchell."

He chose the easy chair across the room from her. She perched on the arm of the sofa.

"Mitchell, I want us to have an honest relationship."

"We do, babe. We tell each other everything."

"Sometimes I wonder if we really do."

"What are you talking about, Jayne?"

"I was so glad to finally meet your family last weekend."

"And they were glad to meet you. My mother called me twice to say that."

Jayne forced a smile. "That's nice to hear." She sighed deeply. "But when I met everybody, I couldn't quite connect all the dots. There were some extra kids there …"

"Family friends," Mitchell said quickly.

Jayne nodded. "That's what I figured. But all those pictures your mom has …"

"Babe, I told you, Mom likes pictures of kids, so people give them to her all the time. She doesn't want to insult any of her friends, so she puts them all up."

Jayne nodded again. "On the piano … I saw a picture of a boy. He was wearing a baseball uniform. Do you know the one I mean?"

Mitchell shrugged. "Not really. She just moves the same pictures around from place to place. I don't really pay any attention."

"So that boy isn't anybody you know?"

"Maybe. I might have met him if he came by the house some time when I was there. What are you getting at, Jayne?"

"It's just that I saw that boy at the park the other day when Leslie and I were out walking. Then I saw his picture at your mother's house."

"Jayne, you're imagining things. Kids look alike if you don't know them well."

Jayne stood up and started pacing. "This boy didn't look like all the other kids, Mitchell. He looked like you."

"What?" He sounded genuinely shocked.

"It was like looking at you when you were fourteen."

"But you didn't know me when I was fourteen."

"Please, Mitchell, I'm serious. This boy is the spitting image of you. And your mother has his picture—several of them, as a matter of fact. I went back to the park today and saw him again."

"It probably wasn't the same kid." Mitchell reached out to catch Jayne's hand, but she avoided him and continued to pace.

"Mitchell, I heard the coach call him 'Furst.' What are the odds that some random kid who looks like you would have that name?"

"You think this kid is my kid?"

She stopped and looked him straight in the eye. "Yes, I do." She handed him the packet of photos. "Is there something you haven't told me?"

Mitchell remained calm and cool as he flipped through the stack of pictures. "I have relatives all over this town. You know that. Just look up 'Furst' in the phone book. My dad has second cousins that we never even see."

"Mitchell, whatever the truth is, I can handle it. I promise. You know all about my past, about Chuck and Claire—everything there is to tell. I can't get over the feeling that there's something you haven't told me. If we're going to get married, we have to be honest with each other."

Mitchell leaned forward in the chair and looked down at his feet, letting the handful of photos go limp. "I've been trying to figure out how to tell you," he said softly.

"So he is yours?"

"Yes, I have a thirteen-year-old son. I got his mother pregnant, so we got married, but it was a mistake. We were young. We didn't know what we were doing. We thought we had to pay for a moment of passion with our whole lives. But we made each other miserable. When Connor was about a year old, we split up."

"He lives here in town, obviously. Surely you see him," Jayne said.

"Yes, I see him. After all, he's my son."

"Does he know about me?"

"He knows I've been seeing someone seriously. He knows your first name. I haven't told him we're engaged."

"I want to meet Connor."

"Well, of course, when the time is right."

"Soon, Mitchell. You have to tell him you're getting married. And I want to meet his mother. It's inevitable that we would have contact with each other at some point."

"Rachelle and I don't really get along, Jayne. She's remarried. I just pick up Connor and drop him off."

"I understand. I just want to meet her. I'm not trying to be her best friend."

"Okay. I'll ask her."

Jayne knelt in front of Mitchell and took his hands. "Mitchell, I've trusted you with my whole life. I've told you everything I've done on every day since I met you. Can you understand how I'm feeling when I find out something like this—in this way?"

Mitchell looked Jayne straight in the eyes, his brown eyes wide with sorrow. "I'm so sorry, Jayne. But you married a total mess-up once before. I didn't want you to think you were doing the same thing again."

"You're not a mess-up, Mitchell. Everybody makes mistakes. Chuck was a mistake for me. Rachelle was a mistake for you. The main thing is to be sure we're not a mistake for each other."

"No way, this time it's the real thing. I swear, Jayne. I've never loved any other woman the way I love you. I've never pictured growing old with anyone but you." He took her face in his hands and kissed her slowly, lingering over the sensation.

It was a long time before Jayne caught her breath. "I love you, too, Mitchell. You have to promise me, no more secrets."

"I promise. No more secrets."

~ 9 ~

She liked Rachelle, although she hadn't really expected to.

At Jayne's quiet insistence, Mitchell had finally arranged a time for them to go out to dinner with Rachelle and Connor. Jayne suggested a gourmet hamburger place with enough raucous music to please any teenage boy. And she was right. Connor chowed down on a supersized cheeseburger and a mound of onion rings so high Jayne could hardly see his face, all the while bouncing to the surround-sound bass beat.

Next time, Rachelle promised, she would bring her husband, Trent, who was out of town. Jayne liked the idea that there would be a next time. Rachelle, tall and very blonde, carried herself with poise and had well-thought-out opinions on a range of subjects, from school vouchers to benefits for military veterans to the complexity of quilt patterns. All Jayne's nervousness at encountering Mitchell's past dissipated the moment Rachelle extended a hand of warm greeting. She was witty and quick with the one-liners. Jayne hadn't laughed so much in a long time. She had to remind herself from time to time that this enchanting woman was Mitchell's ex-wife and that Mitchell had tried to hide Rachelle's existence from her.

Connor seemed to take the news of his father's engagement in stride. After offering polite congratulations, he launched into tales from his base-ball team. He seemed to vaguely recognize Jayne as the "lady from the park," but did not linger on the memory. Apparently he accepted that the incident had been purely coincidental—which it had.

Connor essentially had played on the same team for four years. The coach was one of the fathers, and he managed to graduate each year with his son and coach the next age bracket. He also mysteriously arranged for all his favorite players to appear on his roster. He was a serious coach, requiring two extra practices each week beyond the minimum league requirements. Connor spent a great deal of time on the ball field. But the work was paying off. As the boys grew older, competition grew more serious. They had their eyes set on a state championship next year.

Mitchell seemed pleased and proud of his son. Seeing them side by side, Jayne marveled anew at how closely they resembled each other. Connor clearly enjoyed having his parents together at the same table. Jayne guessed that this hadn't happened for a long time—years, probably—and secretly hoped that it would happen often, for Connor's sake.

Once the shock of Mitchell's having a son had worn off, Jayne had thrown herself into the mode of doing everything possible to minimize stress on Connor and promote positive adult relationships. And once she met Rachelle, she knew for certain that she had nothing to worry about on that front. Though Trent was absent from this dinner, Rachelle obviously was happily married and had done a good job providing a secure home for her child.

For a fleeting moment, Jayne imagined what it might have been like if Claire had lived. It was doubtful that her marriage to Chuck would have survived. She could have come to this table with a child of her own. She certainly had no right to cast judgment on Mitchell and Rachelle for their breakup.

Throughout the evening, Jayne watched Mitchell. Beforehand, clearly he would have preferred that this meeting not take place. In the first tenuous moments of conversation, his eyes flashed back and forth between his former and future wife. At first she thought he was afraid of something, and in between Connor's baseball stories she tried to discern what might be so unsettling to Mitchell. In the end she decided it was nothing specific, just nerves. She reached under the table and put a hand on his knee to reassure him. He covered her hand with his and did not let go for a long time.

In the parking lot Jayne told Rachelle how delighted she was to meet her and said she hoped Connor would agree to be in the wedding party. He grimaced at the thought of getting all dressed up but awkwardly accepted.

"You're going to be really good for Mitchell, I can tell," Rachelle said quietly to Jayne. "I see him changing, and I'm sure it's because of you."

Rachelle's words haunted Jayne. She hadn't seen any change in Mitchell, except perhaps a sense of relief that at last Jayne knew the truth about his past. What changes in Mitchell was Rachelle referring to?

Long after Mitchell left her house that night, she sat up in the living room watching a wide vanilla candle burn. She hadn't expected Mitchell would want to leave so early. It wasn't like him to claim to be tired. Jayne pulled her bathrobe around her and scooped her knees up under her chin as she stared at the glow on the coffee table and tried to process what had happened during the evening.

A few weeks earlier Mitchell's father had suggested that she would have a job on her hands getting him to settle down. At the time Jayne had dismissed the comment as awkward conversation. Now Rachelle was suggesting that Mitchell was changing for the better, which meant there had been a worst in the past. Jayne reviewed in her mind the scores of conversations she and Mitchell had had about their lives.

She knew where he had gone to college, how he had changed majors three times, what jobs he had held, what career goals he hoped to achieve. She had known the facts about his immediate family even though she had not met them until recently. He told dozens of stories about the troubles he and his sisters had gotten into when they were little. She knew all about the train set he got for Christmas when he was seven and how it was still boxed up in his parents' basement until he had someplace permanent to live.

She knew the itineraries of his two trips to Europe, one in college and one the summer after graduation. Florence, Italy, was his favorite spot, and he wanted to take her there someday. She knew which apartment complexes he had lived in over the years. He often pointed them out as they drove past. "Second floor on the north end," he would say. Ever since she had met him, he had been house-sitting at several different locations. The owners didn't want him to have guests, and she respected that.

He didn't like dogs and was allergic to cats. When he was stressed, he liked to work out at the gym so that he didn't take his stress home with him. He told dozens of stories about his best friend, Doug, who had moved to the West Coast three years ago. She knew how Mitchell liked his coffee, what his favorite Italian dish was, that he liked hot curry foods and martial-arts movies. He thought miniature golf was for wimps and could lose himself in a video arcade for hours. He liked to dance and was not afraid of hard physical labor.

"I could write his biography," she said aloud.

All except his relationship with Rachelle and the birth of Connor.

How could he have left out something like that? Rachelle appeared to be a wonderful person, and Connor was a son any father could be proud of. So why the secrecy? Had Mitchell really just been afraid she would reject him if she found out he had an ex-wife and a son? How could he think her so shallow, given her own history?

The candle burned to the edge and Jayne blew it out.

"This is Jayne."

"And I'm so glad it is."

"Hi, Mitchell. I hope you're not calling to tell me you can't make it tonight."

"Absolutely not, babe. Quite the opposite. I think we should paint the town."

"Oh, really?"

"Really. It's Friday. We deserve a night out. Planning a wedding is a lot of stress."

Jayne chuckled. "As if you've been any help with that."

"I'm supplying the groom. That's a big job."

"I suppose so."

"I'll pick you up at seven. We'll go anywhere you want to go."

But they didn't.

"Let's go to the Excelsior Room," Jayne suggested when Mitchell arrived. "Leslie says the music is great and the food is scrumptious. We can dance the night away."

"No, I don't think so," Mitchell said abruptly. "You wouldn't like it there."

"But I've never been," Jayne retorted. "How do you know I wouldn't like it?"

"I know you, and I know the Excelsior Room. You wouldn't like it."

"Leslie and I enjoy a lot of the same things, and she had a great time there last week. I'd really like to give it a try."

"I don't think that's a good idea."

"But Mitchell—"

"Why don't you let me surprise you?" Mitchell suggested, pulling her close and kissing her forehead. "I promise not to disappoint you."

For a moment she was ready to give in. But something felt wrong. She pulled back.

"Mitchell, what's going on? Why can't we go to the Excelsior Room?"

"I didn't say we can't. I just said it's not a good idea."

"For me or for you?"

"What's that supposed to mean?"

"You said we could go anywhere I wanted. I want to go to the Excelsior Room, and you won't take me there."

"Babe, you're making too much of this. I love you. I know you inside out. I've been to the Excelsior Room to wine and dine clients, and I know it's not your kind of place. I just want to make sure you have a terrific evening."

In the end Jayne acquiesced. Mitchell chose a restaurant. The food was acceptable but the music mediocre. They did not dance.

Jayne did not have a terrific time.

The creature leered.

~ 10 ~

For two days Jayne tried to call Mitchell.

She wanted to talk more about his reluctance—even refusal—to go to the Excelsior Room. She left messages on his cell phone and at his office, applauding herself for the great restraint she showed in the words she chose. Each time she called his office, however, he had just left or was tied up on the phone with an important client. He returned her calls at times when he ought to have known that she would not be available. That only heightened her sense of irritation. He ended every message with a cheerful "Love you," sounding oblivious to her distress.

She decided to try his office one more time before lunch. The receptionist answered promptly.

"McCann and Trout."

"Mitchell Furst, please."

"One moment." Pause. "I'm sorry, Mr. Furst is not available. Would you like his voice mail?"

"When will he be available?"

"That's hard to say, ma'am."

"Is he in the building or out on a call?"

"That's difficult for me to say."

"Then how do you know he's not available?"

"Would you like me to try his extension again?"

"No, thank you."

She slammed the phone down. Mitchell would have to be blind and deaf not to know she was upset. He was avoiding her with his charade of busyness and voice-mail affection. Maybe he thought a little time would cool her off. Self-doubt flooded in. Was she making too much of it? Was he really sure she wouldn't have enjoyed the Excelsior Room? If she hadn't been in such a funk, she might have appreciated the place they did go a lot more. And she knew his new job had him busy. Overlooking a client at the wrong moment could mean losing the deal. After all, he was returning her calls and not ignoring her completely. He promised they would see each other soon. He missed her. He loved her.

It would be all right.

Jayne fidgeted her way through the days at work mainly with only her thoughts as company. Larry was on vacation, and Mare only came in for three hours each morning. Jayne plunged into her work with renewed fervor, coming in early and staying late. Leslie called, but Jayne claimed to be too busy to have lunch. The truth was that Jayne did not want to undergo the interrogation Leslie would launch into when she perceived that Jayne was muddled about something. And Leslie could always tell.

And so Jayne worked and ate and went for long walks alone.

BJL062: Hello, UNCLEB. Glad to chat alone.

UNCLEB: Me too. Slow typer. Be patient.

BJL062: Your observations always worth the wait.

UNCLEB: Even if I don't agree with you?

BJL062: We have different experiences.

UNCLEB: I have a patient now. Almost certainly ASPD. Exploring therapies.

BJL062: You will have little result.

UNCLEB: Unless he is not truly ASPD.

BJL062: Does he meet the criteria or not?

UNCLEB: In many ways a classic profile. Erratic. Evasive. Everything that happens is someone else's fault.

BJL062: But?

UNCLEB: But I am not convinced he lacks emotion.

BJL062: How so?

UNCLEB: He mentioned a woman. Seems to care.

BJL062: Promiscuous?

UNCLEB: No hard evidence. But maybe.

BJL062: Probably.

UNCLEB: Going on hunches.

BJL062: Not very scientific.

UNCLEB: Sometimes a hunch leads to hope. Not ready to give up hope.

BJL062: Be realistic, my friend.

UNCLEB: Just want to help him.

BJL062: Probably not possible.

UNCLEB: We disagree once again.

"Why are you so late?"

"I'm not late."

"Yes, you are. You said you would be here two hours ago."

"Well, I'm here now. But if you want me to leave, I will."

"What if I told you that the baby is not even here? Would you still want to stay?"

"Our daughter is beautiful, but she's not as fun as you are." He reached for her and wrapped her in his arms, slowly swaying his hips.

She couldn't resist. She never did.

"My mother is bringing the baby back in an hour."

"Plenty of time." He slid a hand under her top.

Jayne punched the button on her home answering machine.

"Hey, babe. Sorry we keep missing each other. My day is just not the same when I don't talk to you. I'm trying to close a deal tonight, so I'll be out late. If you want, I can come by around eleven thirty. Leave a message on my cell. Love you."

STOP. ERASE.

Jayne was dead on her feet. She intended to be fast asleep long before ten. She was long past having the conversation she wanted to have. Why wasn't that obvious to Mitchell? Or perhaps it was.

She kicked off her shoes under the kitchen table and rubbed the back of her neck. A hot bath and then to bed was what she really wanted. She didn't even want to eat. But first she would have to get something out of her system. She reached for the box of blue paper.

Dear Mitchell,

I love you, and we're going to be married. If we're going to spend our lives together, shouldn't we be able to talk? Oh, I don't mean just on the telephone. I suppose there will be days when it's hard to catch each other at a good moment. But I feel like something went up between us the other night. Now I don't know how to get it out of the way. I want to talk. You don't. Are we that different?

Maybe I'm just being skittish because I've been married before. I don't want to fail again. And you've been married, too. You have a son. We have to think about more than just the two of us.

I hope and pray that we'll make it.

Jayne

Jayne folded the letter in half and reached for the box her father had given her all those years ago. She meant just to lay the letter on top of the pile. Instead, she took out the growing stack and fingered the letters. She didn't need to unfold them and read them. The words of each one played in her mind like a tape.

"Love is scary," she said aloud. She put the lid back on the empty box and dropped the stack of letters in a drawer instead.

When she opened her eyes, she saw only darkness. After a hot bath Jayne had plummeted into a hard sleep. Until a moment ago, She had no idea what time it was. A noise that should not have been there had wakened her. Jayne sat up in bed and held her breath. There it was again. Footsteps. Coming toward the bedroom. Her mind scrambled to think of something within reach that she could use to defend herself.

The bedroom door creaked open. "Jayne?"

"Mitchell! What are you doing? You scared the bejeebies out of me." Jayne reached for her robe and got out of bed.

"Sorry. I didn't mean to. I used my key. I was worried because you didn't return my last call."

Jayne sighed and turned on a light. "That's because I didn't want you to come by this late." She glanced at the digital clock. 12:41. "And it's way past eleven thirty."

"It's been a long few days without seeing you."

Despite her irritation, Jayne had to agree. This was not the time to spill her doubts and questions. Mitchell stepped toward her. She let him envelop her in his arms as she buried her head in his chest.

"I'm sorry about the other night," he said softly.

"Really?" Jayne lifted her eyes to his.

"Yes. I took a client to the Excelsior Room one time. I had a chance to really make a tidy sum. But the whole deal went belly-up when he got mad at the waiter for taking too long to bring more rolls. For some reason that meant he couldn't do business with me. I really hated to lose that deal. Bad memories. I just didn't want to go there."

"Why didn't you just tell me?"

"I don't like to mix business with my personal life."

"But sometimes what happens at work touches your personal life. I would have understood."

Mitchell shrugged. "I know I should have told you."

"You can tell me anything, Mitchell. Really. I want you to. We shouldn't hold things back from each other."

"You're right, babe."

"You know everything about me, and you love me anyway. I can do the same for you."

Mitchell held her tighter. "I'm going to try harder to believe that."

They kissed tenderly and sincerely. Then Jayne pushed away. "It's late. I have to be up early. Time for you to go."

"All of a sudden I'm really tired too. Mind if I just crash here?"

Jayne hesitated. Mitchell had often stayed the night before. But she really wanted to sleep. Next to her in bed, he would be persistent and irresistible.

"On the couch, okay?"

"Are you sure?"

"Yes, I'm sure. You know where the extra blankets are."

Jayne sighed as she turned off the light and snuggled back under the covers. She had to find a way to get Mitchell to trust her. *What happened to make him so insecure about trust?* she wondered. *Why can't he believe that I'll love him no matter what?*

~ 11 ~

The weather was distinctly fallish this weekend. Though it was still mid-August, the blazing heat of summer had abated and left a few days that were sunny yet required a sweatshirt. Jayne rummaged in her closet for one that looked presentable for a Furst family barbecue. She pulled on her new jeans and a favorite soft blue cotton shirt, then pulled the gray sweatshirt over her head and adjusted the collar. She gathered her hair into a ponytail and stood back to inspect herself in the mirror. She liked what she saw—a happy young woman.

Jayne's mother had come to town last weekend to meet Mitchell and bless the engagement. Amanda Paige was smitten with Mitchell as soon as she met him. He treated her with charm, courtesy, and deference, and she was duly impressed by his tender attentiveness toward her daughter. It was obvious that Jayne loved him. Jayne hadn't looked this happy even in the early days with Chuck. Amanda left on Sunday afternoon persuaded that Jayne had made a wise choice.

Jayne wished that she had introduced them sooner. Mitchell should know the family he was marrying into, small as it was, just as she wanted to know his family. Mitchell and Jayne had not seen as much of his parents as she had supposed they would, living in such close proximity. They had had dinner out a couple of times. Mitchell had carefully selected the restaurants, and everyone had a nice time. Jayne surmised that Mitchell didn't feel the need to see them more often because he stopped by the house a couple of times a week to pick up his mail. He had ample opportunity to visit and keep up on their news, which he regularly reported to Jayne. But she wanted to get to know his family better. Today's barbecue at his sister Brenda's was the perfect opportunity.

Mitchell picked her up right on time. She carefully balanced a tray of deviled eggs on her knees while she leaned over to kiss him.

"It's a nice day for a barbecue," she commented.

Mitchell scanned the sky. "No sign of rain. Brenda thinks she's cursed. It always seems to rain when she throws an outdoor party. But today looks good."

"I'm really looking forward to it. Even if it does rain, I'm glad to be spending some time with your family."

Mitchell smirked. "They're not nearly as interesting as you seem to think they are."

"That's not the point," Jayne responded. "They're your family, so they're going to be my family. I ought to know them better."

"Well, they think you're fabulous, so you don't have anything to worry about."

They seemed to be the last to arrive at Brenda's house. The kids already zoomed around the yard with balls and whiffle bats.

"Is Connor coming?" Jayne asked as they got out of the truck.

"Yeah. Rachelle said she would drop him off. I'll take him home later."

"Good. I haven't seen him for a while."

As Jayne went in the house to find Brenda, Mitchell was quickly caught up in a game of Frisbee with the kids. Jayne set her tray of eggs on the counter, where Leona was slicing carrots and celery and arranging them on a tray around a bowl of dip.

"Jayne! So glad you could come."

"I wouldn't have missed today for anything."

"I keep telling the girls we should do this sort of thing more often. We haven't all been together since my birthday, and that was almost three months ago."

"I couldn't agree more," Jayne said heartily.

"And this time Connor will be here."

"I'm looking forward to seeing him."

"He seems to like you quite well."

"I'm glad to hear that. I like him, too."

"He's a good boy. Rachelle's done a good job with him, considering the circumstances."

Jayne wasn't quite sure what Leona meant. What circumstances? But she didn't get a chance to ask. Brenda came into the room with a three-pound package of ground beef.

"Hello, Jayne. Nice to see you again."

"Nice to see you, too, Brenda. What can I do to help?"

"Ned says the grill is just about ready. You can make some hamburger patties while I get some brats ready."

"Sure." Jayne stepped to the sink to wash her hands, then plunged into her task.

"How are the wedding plans coming?" Brenda asked. "Still aiming for late October?"

"I'm afraid I haven't been as on top of things as I should have," Jayne admitted. "I have my dress, and I've talked with a couple of caterers. But we haven't decided where yet, so the date is not final."

"October is only a couple of months away," Brenda reminded her. "If you don't get a place booked soon you'll end up getting married in my backyard."

Jayne laughed. "Worse things could happen. I know we have to get on the ball. Mitchell is just always so busy."

"Don't wait for him," Leona advised. "Just choose a place and let him know."

"Mom's right," Brenda said. "Mitchell can be hard to pin down."

"Well, I do know about a lovely little chapel at one of the big churches downtown," Jayne said. "A friend of mine got married there. I want to take Mitchell to go see it."

"I didn't know you were religious."

"I'm not, really," Jayne said as she pressed meat between her hands. "I went to Sunday school when I was little, but that was a long time ago."

"Well, what about the church you went to then?"

Jayne shook her head. "Too big and impersonal. I want a more intimate kind of place."

"Mitchell in a church," Brenda mused. "That should be interesting."

"Speaking of Mitchell, where's your father?" Leona asked.

"On the front porch. Mitchell's out back with the kids," Brenda reassured her.

Jayne was confused. Why the concern about where Mitchell and Roger were?

"Is something wrong?" she asked.

"Not really," Brenda answered. "It's just that sometimes Dad and Mitchell get into it with each other at these family gatherings."

"I haven't noticed anything."

"You will. I do have to say, though, that Mitchell's been a lot better lately. He seems to be making an effort. But Dad is another question."

"Don't speak ill of your father," Leona cautioned her daughter.

Jayne's mind couldn't keep up with her own questions as she listened.

"I'm just saying what's true, Mom."

Leona put down her knife. "Mitchell and your father have had their difficulties, but don't exaggerate. You'll give Jayne the wrong impression."

Brenda glanced over at Jayne. "Okay, Mom." She said nothing more.

Jayne sprinkled salt on one layer of patties and starting pressing another one in her hands.

"The veggies are ready," Leona declared. "The eggs look delicious, Jayne."

"Thank you." So the discussion was over.

Ned came in to fetch the first round of meat. Mitchell's other sister, Debra, popped into the kitchen to help carry the food outside. Jayne picked up her eggs and Leona's vegetables and followed Debra. Connor had arrived and was tossing a ball underhanded to a younger cousin. Jayne scanned the yard and ticked off names in her head. She could account for all the children with no extras this time. She knew who belonged to whom.

She watched as Connor patiently coached Brenda's son, Dylan, in his batting technique. The advice paid off. Dylan whacked the plastic ball across the yard. A shaggy spaniel Jayne had not noticed earlier leaped to his feet to chase the ball. Jayne and Debra couldn't help laughing as the kids tried to take the ball away from the dog, which had no intention of releasing it.

Roger Furst ambled around the side of the house to join the action in the backyard.

"Well, hello, Jayne," he said enthusiastically. "How is the woman who is going to reform my son?"

"I'm fine, Roger," she answered, "but Mitchell doesn't need reforming, or I wouldn't love him."

Roger half snorted. "Wait until you live with him."

"Dad ..." Debra warned.

"I know, on my good behavior."

"How many of those have you had?" Debra asked as she took an empty beer can from her father's hand.

"None of your business. I'm a grown man."

Mitchell threw the Frisbee one last time and crossed the yard to stand next to Jayne.

"Hi, Dad."

"Hello, Mitchell."

"I think I'll go get the lemonade." Debra quickly left.

"How's your job going?" Roger asked.

"I like it a lot," Mitchell answered somewhat stiffly.

Roger nodded. "Good. I hope you can hang on to this one for more than six months."

Mitchell glanced at Jayne and didn't say anything.

"You have to think about Jayne now," Roger continued, smiling at her. "You can't just quit your job over some little thing."

"I'm not going to quit my job, Dad."

Once again Jayne found herself in the middle of a conversation she didn't quite understand.

"You've been known to do it before."

"I've had good reasons for the job changes I've made. I'm trying to build a career."

"I'm just saying, now you have to think of somebody besides yourself."

"I'm well aware of that, Dad."

"Just don't forget your responsibilities."

"Oh, you mean like you didn't forget your responsibilities?" Mitchell's voice rose with anger.

"I always provided for my family."

"Yeah, from half a continent away, chasing oil that you never found. What about your responsibility to be with your wife and kids?"

"You're not such a sterling example yourself." Roger glanced at Connor, who was once again pitching the ball.

"I learned from you," Mitchell muttered.

Jayne could hardly believe what she was hearing. But she couldn't say she hadn't been warned. She put a hand on Mitchell's arm but said nothing.

Mitchell glared at his father. "Come on, Jayne. Let's go talk to Connor."

Jayne didn't see Mitchell and his father together for the rest of the afternoon. She wanted to talk to Mitchell about what had happened, but she never found a private moment. They stuffed themselves on burgers and brats, played ball, and relaxed with homemade ice cream. The deviled eggs, veggies and dip, and assorted chips disappeared over the course of the afternoon. When it was time to take Connor home, Mitchell made noises about leaving. At last Jayne made her way into the house to find her empty platter. Brenda was loading the dishwasher.

"You know, I saw you and Mitchell talking to Dad," she said.

Jayne wasn't sure how to respond. "Well, I can't say you didn't warn me. I've just never seen them like that before."

Brenda shrugged. "You've only seen Dad a few times. This time he'd had one beer too many, I think."

"Why are they so angry at each other?" Jayne asked.

"Dad wasn't around much when Mitchell was little," Brenda explained. "Then around the time Mitchell was in fourth grade, Dad had a job in town and was here most of the time. Somehow he never got over Dad being gone so much before that."

"I had such a close relationship with my dad that I can't imagine being that angry with my own father for this long."

"Maybe your father will be good for Mitchell."

"He passed away a couple of years ago."

"I'm sorry." Brenda poured soap in the dishwasher and latched the door shut. "Don't worry about it too much, Jayne. It usually blows over. You'll get used to it."

Get used to it? Jayne wasn't sure she wanted to get used to it. *Wasn't there another option?* She would have to think carefully about how to broach the subject with Mitchell when they were alone.

~ 12 ~

"Thanks for a great time, Dad. You, too, Jayne." Connor slid out of his father's truck and jaunted toward his mother, who stood on the porch to welcome him.

"There's Rachelle," Jayne said with enthusiasm. "Let's say hi."

"I usually just drop Connor off," Mitchell responded flatly. He had not even turned off the engine.

"Just for a minute. Please?"

Mitchell couldn't resist the pleading look in Jayne's eyes. "Okay, but make it quick."

Jayne waved at Rachelle through the open window. Rachelle returned the greeting and started down the walk. After giving his mother a passing acknowledgment, Connor bounded into the house.

With Mitchell reluctantly following, Jayne got out of the truck and walked eagerly to meet Rachelle.

"Looks like Connor had a good time at the barbecue," Rachelle said.

"He may not want any dinner. He ate two hamburgers and three brats."

"Any chance he ate anything resembling a fruit or vegetable?"

Jayne shook her head. "Sorry. Unless strawberry ice cream counts."

Rachelle turned to Mitchell. "Hello, Mitchell. How are your folks?"

He shrugged. "Same as they usually are."

Connor appeared at the front door. "Hey, Dad. Come in and see my project. I'm making a three-foot model of the Space Needle in Seattle."

Mitchell glanced at Rachelle, who nodded. "Go on in."

Jayne and Rachelle sat on the front steps side by side.

"It seems like things are going really well for you and Mitchell," Rachelle observed.

"For the most part, yes. We've had a few bumps along the way, but we manage to work them out."

"Any relationship has a few bumps. You seem to be really good for Mitchell. He just seems to have a better grip on himself since he met you, especially since you got engaged."

"What do you mean, 'a better grip on himself'?"

"Oh, you know, the temper thing."

"What temper thing?"

Rachelle looked at Jayne guardedly. "Mitchell has quite a temper. Or at least he used to."

"I've never seen it," Jayne said, puzzled. "He can be pretty stubborn sometimes, but he's never really been angry at me."

"He's been pretty cordial to me lately too. We're actually starting to get along. I think it will be good for Connor."

"Absolutely. I know you and Mitchell haven't really been talking in a long time, just dropping off Connor."

"And leaving phone messages because we didn't want to talk to each other. But that's all changed. Now he calls when I'm home and tells me about his plans with Connor. And he sees a lot more of Connor now."

Jayne hesitated. "Rachelle, can I ask you a question?"

"Sure."

"People in Mitchell's family keep saying how much different Mitchell is now. And now you're saying it. To me he's the same Mitchell I've always known. Is there another Mitchell?"

Now it was Rachelle's turn to hesitate. "Yes, there's another Mitchell. Or there used to be."

Jayne inhaled the weighty silence hoping Rachelle would say more.

"When we were together and he got angry ... well, let's just say it wasn't pretty."

"Were you scared of him? That kind of angry?"

"Yes," Rachelle said quietly, "and I had good reason. I hope you never do."

"Did he ... hurt you?"

"Yes." Rachelle declined to elaborate. Images raged through Jayne's mind, images she could not believe.

"I've never felt scared with Mitchell," Jayne said resolutely. "Frustrated, sometimes, but never frightened."

"Like I said, he's changed. I really think he has. He wants to be with you. He's not with you just because he got you pregnant, like he was with me. I think he'll try very hard to get it right this time."

The screen door swung open. "Ready to go, Jayne?"

She nodded and stood up. How long had Mitchell been at the open door?

Bennett picked up his notepad. "How are you doing, Mitchell? Let's see, it's been five weeks since I've seen you."

"Yeah, I've been busy." Mitchell settled into the grayish blue couch and put one ankle on the other knee. *He looks confident and content,* Bennett thought. *As always.*

"The job?"

"Yeah, it never seems to stop."

"Well, I'm glad you made it in today. I'd like to talk some more about your father, if you don't mind."

"Why would I mind?"

Bennett thought that Mitchell almost certainly did mind.

"Good," Bennett said. "You said that when you were little, he wasn't around much because he was working on an oil rig he had invested in."

"That's right."

"How much did you see your father when you were a child, say, until the age of ten?"

Mitchell shrugged. "He would come home for a couple of weeks maybe two or three times a year. Christmas. Stuff like that."

"Did he stay in touch with you while he was gone?"

"He talked to my mom on the phone and sent her letters."

"But not to you?"

"They always said it was long distance and too expensive for him to talk to everybody in the family."

"How did you feel about that?"

"I don't know. It's just the way things were."

"I know it's hard to think back from your adult perspective. But try, please. How did you feel about not having your dad around?"

"It wasn't that big a deal. There were other kids who didn't have dads around because of divorce. At least my dad came home once in a while."

"How did you feel when he was home?"

"Happy, I guess. Of course, I wished he could be around more. But he always kept the bills paid. We got along all right without him there." Mitchell uncrossed his legs and shifted position. "It was a long time ago. Why does all that matter now?"

"Sometimes looking at where we've come from helps us to see where we're going."

"The past is the past. We can't go back and change it, so what's the point of dissecting it?"

"Our past experiences help to form our values and personality."

"People change. My dad came home to stay when I was ten. We were a normal family after that. And don't ask me how I felt when he came home. We were all glad he was there, even though we got along all right without him."

Bennett nodded.

"Look, I don't want to talk about all this stuff in the past," Mitchell said. "It doesn't matter. I'm grown up now, and I make my own decisions about what I think is important."

"Do you want to talk about the present?"

"Sure."

"What is your relationship with your father like now?"

Mitchell shook his head. "That was sneaky. I see him when I pick up my mail, and we go out to dinner once in a while. We get on each other's nerves sometimes, but we're fine."

"So you would describe your relationship with your father as …?"

"I love him, he loves me. What more do you need to know?"

"Sometimes the people we love are the ones who irritate us the most."

"I argue with my father sometimes, but who doesn't?"

Bennett nodded. "Of course."

"Hey, have I told you I'm getting married?"

Bennett looked up, his eyes widening involuntarily. "No, you haven't mentioned that." He wondered if this was the same woman Mitchell had mentioned months ago and never spoken of again.

"Well, I am. Now that's something that matters—something that's happening now."

"Tell me about her."

"She's an artist and doing very well for herself."

"That's good. How did you two meet?"

"At a black-tie charity event my sister organized. We both arrived with other dates, but I asked her out as soon as I could."

"And ever since?"

"She's my one and only."

"When is the wedding?"

"End of October."

"Getting married is a serious commitment."

"I know that. I'm ready to make a serious commitment."

"How do you think your life will change after you're married?"

"It's only going to get better."

Bennett spent the rest of the session probing Mitchell's readiness for marriage. Mitchell had a casual, ready answer for every question he raised. Frankly, Bennett had not expected anything else. It was typical of Mitchell Furst to try to control every conversation they had. He never seemed to want help with anything, just sympathy for the way his boss treated him or to brag about accomplishments that Bennett never quite believed. Bennett wondered if he should even believe that Mitchell was engaged. He made a note to ask about the engagement during their next session to see if Mitchell was still willing to talk freely about it.

Probing into Mitchell's relationship with his father, both past and present, had been purposeful, and Mitchell's reaction was informative. Bennett knew that people with antisocial personality disorder nearly always have a distant emotional relationship with their fathers, whether the father was physically present or not. The mothers were usually passive. Bennett supposed he could ask Mitchell about his mother in the future, but he knew he would get the same resistance he had received in trying to talk about Mitchell's father. The past was the past. It didn't matter.

The only real emotion Bennett had picked up from Mitchell toward his father was squelched anger. He didn't want to talk about the events of his childhood that may have made him so angry. Mitchell spoke of his father matter-of-factly. Even saying that he loved his father, which Bennett doubted, was another unemotional fact.

Bennett also wanted to see what level of resistance he would get if he exerted more authority than usual in the counseling session. The way Mitchell abruptly changed the subject had come just as quickly as Bennett had supposed it would.

Bennett came away from the session with the sense that Mitchell really did care for his fiancée and intended to make a life with her. But Mitchell was such a master of controlling situations and people that he could be whatever the situation called for him to be. Bennett could not help wondering what type of person he became when he was with this woman. If he really did have antisocial personal disorder, she would almost certainly be his next victim.

And Bennett could do nothing to stop it.

He didn't even know her name, and he couldn't violate the confidentiality of his sessions with Mitchell. The only thing he could do was try to help Mitchell. He wasn't about to give up, no matter what BJL062 had to say.

~ 13 ~

S"So you'll come to the church with me tomorrow?" Jayne asked Mitchell. "Even for a small wedding we have to get the place booked and find a minister."

Mitchell nodded. "Yes, I'll come. Of course I'll come."

"Have you ever even been in a church, Mitchell—for something other than a wedding?"

"My grandmother used to take me to Mass. She always complained because it wasn't in Latin anymore, but even in English I didn't know what was going on most of the time."

"This place will be different. It's a Protestant church. The bulletin will tell you what to do."

"Is that how it was when you were a kid?"

"Yes. Usually I just went to Sunday school and then went home. Every once in a while I stayed for the service."

"Do I have to wear a suit?"

"I don't think it will be that formal. Nice slacks and shirt should be fine."

On Sunday morning, they arrived a few minutes early for the midmorning service and were glad they did. The building was large and overwhelming, taking up an entire block, and it turned out they had parked at the rear of the building and had to walk all the way around to find the front door. They took a bulletin from a friendly usher and awkwardly indicated that they preferred to sit in the back.

The bulletin was easy to follow, and they were comforted by knowing what was coming next, when to stand, when to sit, when to sing. Jayne was pleasantly surprised that she remembered two of the hymns from her childhood days. The more contemporary praise songs were new to her but easy to catch on to. Mitchell did not try to sing.

To Jayne's surprise, Mitchell removed a Bible from the rack in front of them and began to thumb through it. By checking the bulletin and the table of contents in the Bible, he found the Scripture passage in time to follow along as it was read. The pastor's preaching style was humorous but direct. Jayne liked him and could see that Mitchell was paying close attention as well.

They stood for the benediction, amazed at how quickly the hour had gone. By the time they made their way to the lobby, three church members had introduced themselves. Mitchell and Jayne responded warmly to the invitation to come again. *I just might,* Jayne thought.

Once in the lobby, they followed the signs directing them to Peace Chapel. They stepped inside, quietly and reverently. The chapel could hold perhaps fifty people. The pews and pulpit, made from warm, dark oak, were just the shade Jayne loved. Plush maroon carpeting muffled their steps as they walked partway up the center aisle.

"It's beautiful, Mitchell. Perfect. Just the way I remember from my friend's wedding years ago."

Mitchell looked around and nodded. "It's very pretty. If this is where you want to get married, then that's what we'll do."

Surprising Jayne once again, Mitchell slid into one of the pews and indicated that she should sit beside him.

"I didn't expect to like the church service so much," he said quietly.

"Really? You liked it?"

"Nobody in my family except my grandmother was religious. So I never knew what I was missing. But coming here today … it's like finding another piece of myself."

Jayne held her breath, not knowing what to say. She had never heard Mitchell say anything like this before.

"So I think we should come back," he concluded. "I'd like to come back sometime."

"Okay, we will."

First thing that Monday morning, Jayne called the church office and inquired about reserving the chapel on a Saturday in late October. She hardly breathed while the church secretary checked the calendar. Yes, the chapel was available that day. To make specific arrangements, Jayne should call the church wedding coordinator, Noelle Richman.

Jayne then phoned Noelle and liked her immediately. Jayne made an appointment to meet her on Tuesday evening at the chapel to go through a planning checklist and take their time looking at the chapel.

A third phone call connected Jayne to Mitchell's cell phone. She was all set to leave a message, but he answered.

"Hello?"

"We got the chapel!"

"Great! Our date worked out okay?"

"Yep. We're getting married at two thirty in the afternoon, the last Saturday of October, at Peace Chapel."

"So what do we do next?"

"The church has a wedding coordinator, Noelle. We need to meet with her. I hope you're not busy tomorrow night, because I made a seven o'clock appointment."

"That should be fine. Do we meet her at the chapel?"

"Yes. Be on time, Mitchell!"

"I will, I promise. I'll probably have to meet you there, though. I have an early dinner appointment."

"That's fine, just be there."

When Jayne pulled into the church's main parking lot the next evening, she looked around for Mitchell's truck. The few other cars in the lot indicated that the building was sparsely occupied, which was what she expected for an evening in the middle of the week. She considered waiting for Mitchell in her car, but she wasn't sure which parking lot he might choose. After a few minutes, she entered the building and walked toward the chapel.

"Jayne?" A friendly voice spoke her name as soon as she stepped into the chapel, almost startling her.

"Yes, I'm Jayne Paige-Hamilton."

"Noelle Richman." The woman extended her hand. "Nice to meet you."

"Nice to meet you." Noelle looked to be in her midforties. She wasn't very tall, shorter even than Jayne, yet her presence filled the room. Flaming red hair, long and thick, hung loose to declare that she enjoyed every strand. Brightly colored clothing—a blouse and long billowy skirt—declared her bold self-confidence. Jayne was drawn to Noelle, admiring her endearing eccentricity.

"Mitchell—my fiancé—should be here any minute," Jayne explained. "He had a business meeting and said he would meet me here."

Noelle waived a hand. "No problem. That will give us a chance to get acquainted before we have to get down to business. Shall we sit?"

Jayne sat in the pew next to Noelle and turned to face her. "Do you do a lot of weddings?"

"In the spring and summer we're busy every weekend, sometimes three weddings in a weekend. But at this time of year it's slower. And not everyone wants to use the chapel, of course."

Jayne looked around. "It's so lovely. So intimate."

"That's why the people who don't want a big wedding like it."

"We just want family and a few friends. This will be the perfect size."

"Do you come to the church often?"

Jayne shook her head. "Actually, last Sunday was our first time. But we'd both like to come back."

"That's good. Some people never darken the door of a church except for a wedding. I should know. I used to be that way."

Jayne smiled sheepishly. "I guess you could say I'm that way. I haven't been to church in twenty years."

"Oh, darling, you must give it a try. It's a whole different experience as a grown-up."

"How long have you been going to church?" Jayne asked. If she had met Noelle on the street, she would never have guessed her to be a churchgoer.

"Twelve years, four months, and three weeks."

Jayne was taken aback. "How can you remember that specifically?"

"Oh, honey, when you meet the Lord, you don't forget."

"Oh. Of course." Jayne remembered a Sunday-school teacher once encouraged her to ask Jesus into her heart. Is that what Noelle meant?

"I'm sorry for all the years I missed out on being with God's people. Life is just too tough to have to figure it out alone."

Jayne sighed. "Wow. You're right. I never thought about it that way. I've had some times when I felt so alone I might as well have been on an island all by myself." Even as she spoke the words, Jayne marveled that she could speak so freely to a stranger.

"See what I mean? People suffering for no good reason, when they could have the Lord and his people all around them. I'll be looking for you in church next Sunday."

Jayne blushed. "I'll try to come. Mitchell wants to. Speaking of Mitchell, he should have been here by now." She looked at her watch. Fifteen minutes late. Where was he?

"He's probably on his way right now," Noelle said reassuringly.

"I'll just give him a call and see where he is." Jayne reached into her bag for her cell phone and poked Mitchell's speed dial number. It rang four times, then his voice mail came on. She didn't leave a message. "Sorry, he's not answering his cell."

"No matter, darling. We can do the paperwork another time. Why don't you just walk down this aisle and see how it feels. Slow and easy, like a bride."

Jayne felt a little silly walking slowing down the aisle in her jeans, but as she got closer to the front, she started to enjoy herself.

"See there, you're smiling!" Noelle said. "Remember to smile on your wedding day."

"I'll try. I'm sure I'll be so nervous."

"Nah. You'll be marrying the man you love. You do love him, don't you?"

Jayne nodded immediately.

"And he loves you?"

She nodded again.

"That's a good start. Now we just gotta get God in the middle of the two of you."

"I'm sorry—I don't understand."

"You need God, dearie. I have a feeling you're going to figure that out pretty soon. Now how many attendants are you planning?"

"Just one. My cousin. And Mitchell will have his son."

"Ah. He's been married before?"

"Actually we both have."

"Isn't it great that God is a God of second chances? If he weren't, I sure would be in deep trouble. Will your father walk you down the aisle?"

"No, he passed away," Jayne answered. She hadn't thought about who would escort her down the aisle. Maybe no one. A moment of grief flitted through her mind.

"We can figure that out later." Noelle pointed to a door to one side, at the front of the church. "The groom and best man will come in through there. Are you going to want to have everyone dress at the church?"

"I suppose that would be best, if there's a good place."

"Yes, we have suitable rooms." Noelle walked across the front to the other side. "Out this door is a lovely garden, enclosed on all four sides. A lot of people like to take pictures out there, but in October you may think it's too bare."

"I guess we'll have to see what the day is like."

"There's a basic fee for using the chapel, and then add-ons for some of the other things, like flower stands and candelabras. They just want to cover the cost of someone to clean up and put things away properly."

"Of course."

Noelle put one hand on a small organ in the front of the church and pointed to some pipes in the chancel. "The organ is small, but it's just been refitted. It really has a marvelous sound."

"I don't know anyone who plays the organ." Jayne was beginning to panic at all the details she had not thought about.

"I can give you some names of people who do a nice job at weddings."

"Thanks, I appreciate that."

Jayne looked at her watch repeatedly as Noelle continued to point out the chapel's features. Finally, an hour past their appointment time, Jayne had to admit he was not coming.

"I really appreciate the time, Noelle. I'm sorry to have inconvenienced you because Mitchell couldn't make it."

"No problem whatsoever. I'll want to sit down with both of you at some point to go through our checklist of arrangements. But the next step is to talk to the pastor, unless you have someone else in mind to do the ceremony."

"No, we don't. We were planning to ask the pastor."

"I'll set up a time that you can meet him, and then after that we'll take care of the rest of our business. Are you ever free in the afternoon?"

"I could get away from work early, I'm sure."

"And Mitchell?"

"With enough warning, he can arrange it."

"Good. Then I'll call you after I check the pastor's schedule."

"I don't have a lot of time tonight, Sadie." He tickled Corrine's tummy and watched her grin.

"But it's Tuesday." Sadie wiped a dish dry and turned to glare at him.

"I know what day it is. I've just got something I have to do. I have to be somewhere at seven."

"But it's already seven thirty. You're late, as usual."

Mitchell raised his eyes to the wall clock. "I didn't know it was so late." He sighed heavily.

"It's too late for whatever you were going to do, isn't it?"

"Unfortunately, yes. It's all the way across town. And it was important."

"Not important enough for you to remember."

"Don't start, Sadie."

"Well, now you might as well stay." She sidled up to him and ran her fingers through his hair.

"I don't think so. I'm going to have to try to fix something."

She leaned down to kiss him. "But you can come back."

He pulled away from her. "Things are going to be a little different from now on, Sadie."

"What do you mean?" she demanded.

"I'm not going to be able to come around as much."

"But we have something going, you and me. And we have her!" She pointed at the baby, now nearly a year old.

"I'm not saying I'm going to abandon you. Just that things will be different."

"Why?"

"It's complicated."

"I'm not a total moron. Try to explain."

"I don't have to explain anything to you, Sadie. I'm just telling you how it is."

Her eyes filled with tears. "So you're not coming back?"

"Not tonight. I'll call you. Don't try to call me."

~ 14 ~

"This is Jayne."

"And I'm so glad it is."

"Mitchell, where have you been? I tried calling you half a dozen times last night!"

"I'm sorry. I had to go to dinner way on the other side of town. I was on my way to the church when I blew a tire. Talk about destroyed. Wouldn't you know, the spare didn't have enough air in it, either. I had to hitch a ride to a gas station to get some air and then go back and change the tire. The whole thing ended up taking a couple of hours. I knew you wouldn't still be at the church."

"You could have called. I had my cell phone with me."

"My battery was drained."

"Don't you keep a charger in your car?"

"I did something with it, I don't remember what."

"What about when you got home?"

"It was late. I didn't want to wake you like I did that other night."

Jayne sighed.

"Come on, babe, I did the best I could. We can reschedule with Noelle."

"She set up a meeting for us to meet the pastor. Tomorrow afternoon, four o'clock."

"I'll be there. How about we go out for a nice dinner tonight? Let's see if we can fix this week before it gets any worse."

Jayne softened. He really was making an effort. "Okay. But after dinner we need to talk seriously about some wedding stuff. I'm starting to feel a little overwhelmed."

"You got it. I'll help any way I can."

"All right. Why don't you pick me up about six?"

The next day, and at the correct time, Jayne and Mitchell sat nervously in the pastor's office, holding hands.

"Hello, I'm Ken Suiter."

Jayne had to let go of Mitchell's hand to shake the pastor's. "Thank you for seeing us."

"It's my pleasure." He sat in a chair across from them. "Noelle tells me you're getting married the last Saturday in October."

"Yes, that's right."

"You're planning to use the chapel, and you'd like me to do the ceremony. Is that correct?"

"Yes, that's right." Mitchell spoke this time.

"Performing wedding ceremonies is one of my deepest pleasures. I do like to get to know the bride and groom first, though, to see if I can be of any help in making sure you're off to a good start. I'd like to schedule a series of four premarital sessions."

"Um ... okay," Jayne managed to say.

"Don't be nervous. I'm not going to psychoanalyze you. I'll just help the two of you look at your relationship and consider some of the strengths and weaknesses that you're taking into your marriage. And we'll spend a little bit of time talking about the place of God in your marriage. How does that sound?"

"That sounds fine," Mitchell said. "Anything that will help us have a good marriage."

"Great," Ken said. He reached behind him and lifted his planner off the desk. "Since we don't have a lot of time, let's schedule all four sessions now. Would Monday evenings work for you?"

Jayne and Mitchell looked at each other and nodded.

"Good. Then let's plan to meet the next four Mondays at seven thirty. That should keep it simple." He penciled them in. "And now I understand that Noelle will be waiting for you in the chapel. I'll look forward to seeing you next Monday."

They stood and shook hands again, then Mitchell and Jayne headed for the chapel, where Noelle was waiting.

"Ah, the missing groom has appeared. I'm Noelle Richman." Her hair was pulled back in a flaming bush behind her head and swooped as she swung around to face Jayne and Mitchell. Her bright yellow-and-green-striped tunic top didn't quite match the aquamarine pleated skirt.

"I apologize for the other night," Mitchell said, offering his hand. "I had car trouble on my way here, and it took longer than I thought to straighten things out."

"Never you mind. Jayne and I had an exquisite chat. You have chosen an utterly charming lass to spend your life with."

Jayne blushed as Mitchell grinned in agreement with Noelle's assessment.

Noelle opened a folder and took out some papers. She handed them each a checklist. "You're here now, so let's get down to business. This is a list of the decisions you'll need to make for your wedding arrangements. You've probably thought of most of these things, but the list will help you be sure you're not overlooking anything. I'll help make your wedding perfect in any way that I can."

They talked for nearly an hour, marking off items on the checklist, visualizing the parts of the ceremony. Noelle had a story for every occasion—the flower girl who refused to rehearse, the ring bearer who got tired and sat on the pillow he carried, the groom in his eighties who lost his dentures when he kissed his bride. The laughter was refreshing, and the more stories Noelle told, the harder Jayne laughed. Jayne was soon enamored of Noelle and beginning to think of her as a friend.

"That about does it," Noelle said as she closed her folder. "Before you leave, I would like to pray for both of you. Would that be all right?"

Jayne hardly knew what to say. No one had ever prayed for her before—that she knew of. "Sure, of course."

Noelle stood while Jayne and Mitchell sat. With a hand on each of their heads, she prayed aloud.

"Great God in heaven, Mitchell and Jayne are about to stand before you and enter into a holy union. I can see that they love each other. I pray that they would also come to love you and know your redeeming love for them. Show yourself to them in unmistakable ways. You created them and love them. Make them your own. In the name of your Son, Jesus, I pray. Amen."

When she released their heads, they sat perfectly still for a few seconds.

"Go with God, you two," Noelle said. "Give me a call if any questions come up."

Out in Mitchell's truck, they sat and looked at each other. "Has anything like that ever happened to you before?" Jayne asked.

Mitchell shook his head. "My grandmother always prayed in Latin with her beads. A rosary, I guess you call it. I don't really know what she prayed about. Not me."

"There's something about Noelle that I really like."

"She's eccentric, don't you think?" Mitchell suggested.

"Maybe that's what I like. She really believes in this church stuff, but she's not very churchy, if you know what I mean."

"I'd say that's a fair assessment."

"Do you still want to go to church again on Sunday?"

Mitchell nodded.

On Sunday morning they took Jayne's car to church. This time they sat a little farther up, and Mitchell even tried to sing. Ken Suiter was in the pulpit again, giving a sermon about repentance. Mitchell followed along in Luke 19 as Ken read the story of Zacchaeus.

"Zacchaeus was a man nobody liked," he said in conclusion. "But Jesus loved him just the same. Jesus' love radically changed Zacchaeus's life. He turned completely around, changed his ways, made restitution for the wrong he had done. That's repentance—turning around and running toward God instead of running away from him. I pray that each one of you will have that experience of turning around to run toward God."

Jayne held Mitchell's hand during the sermon, wondering what he was thinking. But she didn't ask, because she wasn't sure what she thought of the experience herself. Noelle greeted them enthusiastically after the service.

"That sermon could have been about me," she said. "Running away from God is exactly what I used to do. But no more. Now I run right into Jesus' arms. You will, too, someday." And then she was gone, greeting a friend with a bear hug.

Jayne and Mitchell spent a leisurely Sunday afternoon at her house, napping and reading the paper. Jayne felt utterly content, savoring the sensation and imagining what it would be like to have a whole lifetime of Sunday afternoons with Mitchell. After a casual supper of leftovers, Mitchell got ready to go, claiming an early breakfast meeting.

"Don't forget about tomorrow night," Jayne reminded him. "Our session with Pastor Suiter."

"I don't think I'm going to be able to make that," Mitchell said.

"What? You sat in his office three days ago and said Monday nights were fine."

"Monday nights are fine. Or they would be, if I wanted to be under someone's microscope. I don't think we need to subject ourselves to that."

Jayne couldn't read Mitchell's face. "You mean you don't want to do the sessions at all?"

"Yes, I guess that's what I'm saying." Mitchell might as well have been saying he'd rather have tuna fish than egg salad.

Jayne flustered and expected an explanation. "I thought you liked him."

"I do. I just don't think we need someone else to tell us whether we're ready to get married or not."

"That's not what he's trying to do." Jayne could hardly believe what Mitchell was saying. "If we don't do the sessions, he's won't marry us."

Mitchell shrugged. "Then we'll find someone else."

"We've been together all day. Why didn't you say something sooner? Did you ever really plan to go to the sessions?"

"Of course I did. I've just had a change of heart. We were having such a peaceful afternoon, I didn't want to spoil it."

"Then you knew I would be upset."

Mitchell didn't respond. Jayne sighed heavily.

"We'll find somebody else," Mitchell said.

"How many pastors do you know, Mitchell?"

"I'm sure if we ask around we'll find somebody. We can still use the chapel, right?"

"Yes, I think so. It's only four sessions, Mitchell. One hour each. How bad can that be?"

"It's not necessary. We know what we're doing."

"But what can it hurt? Maybe there are some things we need to find out about each other before we get married."

"Are you having doubts, Jayne?"

"That's not what I said." His accusation stabbed.

"If you want someone to crawl around inside your head, you go talk to him. If I wanted to do that, I'd get a shrink."

"Mitchell, you're not making much sense."

He reached for her hand, lifted it, and kissed her fingers. "We'll find someone else, Jayne. The chapel is the important thing, isn't it? Why does it matter who marries us? You only met this guy three days ago. Why does it have to be him?"

She had to admit he was right. "Okay. I'll ask Mare and Larry if they know anyone. But you have to promise to ask around too."

"Absolutely. So you'll call to cancel?"

Jayne bristled. "Can't you do it? You're the one who doesn't want to go."

"Okay. Give me the number."

~ 15 ~

"Did Mitchell ever pick out a tux?" Leslie asked in the middle of September. She spread her Cobb salad around her plate for closer examination. "Six more weeks, right?"

Jayne groaned. "Don't remind me. I don't think he wants to wear a penguin suit, as he calls them. He's so busy. He calls me constantly, but he has so many appointments I don't see him for days at a time. He always seems to have something else to do when I suggest shopping."

Leslie shrugged. "Does he have to wear a tux? How about a nice dark suit?"

"That's what I'm thinking now too. It's a small wedding, after all. My dress is simple, no fluffy or poofy parts. We don't have to act like we're getting married in Westminster Cathedral." Jayne cut a bite of her grilled chicken breast. "Connor doesn't really want to wear a suit either, but I think Rachelle has persuaded him that it's appropriate."

"Do you talk to Rachelle a lot?"

"Every now and then. She's really very nice."

"Isn't it weird? I mean, she's his ex-wife."

"She's also his son's mother."

"Would you want Mitchell comparing notes with Chuck?"

"It's not the same thing. I don't have a child with Chuck." Images of infant Claire floated through her mind. She blinked them away before the pain could set in.

Leslie shrugged. "Whatever."

They both paused for a few bites of lunch.

"We're going suit shopping tonight whether he likes it or not," Jayne said with fresh resolve.

Leslie chuckled. "Don't you think he'll find a way out of it if he doesn't really want to go?"

"Not this time. No business meetings. No car trouble. We are going to get a suit!"

Mitchell picked Jayne up at her office promptly at five. "Where do you want to eat?" he asked.

"The food court at the mall," she answered.

He looked at her suspiciously. "Why?"

"Because it will be convenient to several stores that sell very nice suits that are quite appropriate for a wedding."

Mitchell groaned. "Do I have to?"

"I can't exactly try them on for you, now can I?"

"All right. I'll shop for a suit. But can we eat someplace decent?"

"Your pick, as long as it's on the way to the mall."

Mitchell cooperated and selected a restaurant halfway between Jayne's office downtown and the mall on the outskirts of town.

"Did you get a new tire?" Jayne asked as she got out of the truck. "I can't tell which one you replaced."

"New tire?"

"Yeah, you said you blew a tire that night you didn't make it to the chapel. Didn't that wreck the tire?"

"No, it was just a harmless flat. The tire shop repaired it the next day."

"Oh." Jayne was sure Mitchell had said the tire had been destroyed in the blowout.

They ate a light supper and proceeded to the mall. With two large department stores that both had expansive men's sections and a men's specialty shop, Jayne was sure they'd find the perfect suit. She was buried in the racks when Mitchell's cell phone rang. "Whatever it is, you're not leaving!" she called out playfully.

He smiled at her as he flipped his phone open. "It's my mother's number."

"Good." Jayne turned back to the suits. Mitchell strayed in the opposite direction. Five minutes passed before Jayne realized that Mitchell was still on the phone several aisles away. She circled around to come up behind him as he leaned against a shelf of hats.

"Mom, you'll just have to tell Shelbi that's not a good time for me."

Jayne caught her breath. Who was Shelbi? "No, that won't work either. Can't you take her?" Mitchell ran his fingers through his hair in exasperation.

"Shelbi's old enough to understand. Her mother has explained all this to her a hundred times." Mitchell glanced around. "I'm going to have to go."

Jayne backed up and quickly retreated, busying herself with the dilemma of a dark navy or black suit.

"Find anything you like?" Mitchell asked.

Jayne tried to look nonchalant. "Not really. How's your mom?"

"She's okay. Why?"

"You talked to her for a long time."

"Sometimes she takes a long time to get to the point."

Like mother, like son, Jayne thought. "You know, the service hasn't been very good in this store, and I'm suddenly really tired. Why don't we call it a night?"

"I thought we had to get a suit tonight."

"There's still time."

Jayne asked Mitchell to take her home, claiming she had a headache and wanted to go straight to bed. Mitchell took the hint and didn't linger.

It was no use trying to sleep. She really did have a headache. It had erupted ferociously as they left the mall and was now pounding, throbbing, splitting open her head and heart.

Jayne threw the covers off and shuffled to the bathroom. Pain reliever or sleeping pill? Maybe both. She decided on the maximum dose of pain reliever and went out to the living room to wait for it to kick in. She wrapped herself in a fleece throw from the back of the sofa and sat in the dark. A scented candle would have been soothing, but even the smallest movement was excruciating. Getting up for matches was unthinkable.

The mantle clock her grandmother had given her ticked steadily as Jayne took deep, rhythmic breaths. Breathing was supposed to be an automatic reflex. Why was it taking so much effort? Then the clock chimed twelve times. Midnight. The night was passing in painful slowness.

Who is Shelbi? The question echoed in her mind. Clearly she was not a business connection, or Leona would not have been calling about her. And

Jayne was sure she had met all of Mitchell's nieces and nephews. Whoever Shelbi was, she wanted something from Mitchell and she had a mother with whom Mitchell seemed to communicate.

A child?

A child!

Shelbi was a child.

Mitchell's child.

Jayne's heart rate jumped as the realization dawned. Mitchell had another child he had not told her about. More secrets, despite his tearful promises that he would not hide anything from her. Suddenly it seemed impossible to breathe, and she needed to throw up.

Throbbing head or not, Jayne raced to the bathroom and emptied her stomach. After swishing water around in her mouth, she sank back onto the bed, unable to keep herself upright any longer and took halting, gulping breaths. Her heart threatened to burst out of her chest at any moment.

Was Leslie right? After Mitchell proposed, Leslie promised to be supportive of Jayne's decision to marry him, and she had kept her word. She had not made one more disparaging remark about Mitchell and enthusiastically offered to help with wedding preparations. Jayne had asked her to handle the flowers. But what did she really think? Did she still believe Mitchell was untrustworthy and undeserving of Jayne? That Jayne deserved someone better than Mitchell?

"Really, Jayne, you have to admit he doesn't treat you all that well."

"What in the world do you mean by that?"

"You don't see him for days at a time. You moan to me about that constantly."

"I do not."

"Yes, you do."

"Well, it's not as if we're married. He has a job and a life; I have a job and a life. I don't expect him to be at my beck and call."

"He stands you up."

"He does not."

"Yes, he does."

"He never breaks a date without a good reason, and he always calls or leaves a note—I have them all if you want to see them. That's not the same as standing me up."

Now they were planning to marry. They would share a life, not have separate lives. With a jolt Jayne realized that she expected Mitchell to be more consistent and reliable once they were living together. Surely he would communicate more if they saw each other first thing in the morning and last thing at night.

No, he wouldn't. If he was keeping secrets now, he would keep secrets after the wedding. If he made excuses now—and she had to admit he did—he would make excuses then.

But no one had ever made Jayne feel the way Mitchell made her feel. Not her high school boyfriend, who really had been just a social convenience with minimal emotion. Not Chuck. His thoughtfulness and attention in the early days had delighted her, and she had loved him. But not like this. Not like she loved Mitchell. Not with the abandon and celebration that she experienced with Mitchell. She always felt safe with him. Her heart lifted every time he walked into a room. Their interludes of physical love were extraordinary. She had given herself to him fully, wholly, without hesitation.

"How can I love someone I don't trust?" she asked aloud. "What kind of an idiot does that make me?"

Her letters on blue paper full of unanswered questions.

Keeping Connor and his first marriage a secret.

His reluctance for her to spend much time with his family.

Not letting her ever see where he lived.

The missed dinners.

Rachelle's observation that Mitchell had changed.

The blown tire that became a fixable flat.

Changing his mind about the pastor.

And now Shelbi.

As Jayne's heart wrenched open, she knew without a doubt that Shelbi was Mitchell's daughter. But who was her mother?

A marriage grows out of love. But it thrives in a garden of trust. That's what Jayne's mother had told her before she married Chuck. Right up to the moment of her father's death, her parents had been exuberant in each other's company. They held nothing back. Trust.

I don't trust him. I don't even trust myself right now. Love is not enough.

She had to call off the wedding.

An awful feeling welled up from her stomach to her throat. She barely made it to the bathroom this time. The clock stuck one as Jayne crept back to her bed.

She slept little, wishing all night that whoever was swinging a jackhammer at her head would stop. The creature came and grinned at her. It was not so much the usual daring leer as an expression of pleasure. Its bluish green color was especially animated, flushing and dancing under its skin from top to bottom.

"You're not there. I know you're not there."

It widened its mouth and laughed heartily, silently. Then it went away.

The clock continued to chime at each ensuing hour. When it struck four, Jayne gave up the pretense of sleep and got in the shower. She knew what she had to do.

Leaving her hair wet, she pulled on jeans and a cotton sweater. Then she pulled a large duffel bag from the closet and began to fill it. She would call in sick—or maybe tell Larry she needed a few days off. He could handle the projects she was wrapping up. Not that she cared about them at the moment.

Mitchell didn't know where Leslie lived. She could go there. Jayne paused. She couldn't go to Leslie's and risk an "I told you so." Not yet.

Jayne went into the second bedroom and grabbed her laptop from the desk. Leslie would find out what was happening in an e-mail when Jayne was safely away from her cousin's immediate volcanic reaction. Jayne knew of a mom-and-pop motel about twelve miles out of town with parking in the rear. She would go there.

Her head had cleared, but not her heart. She sobbed as she finished packing. She avoided the kitchen on her way out. Food, or even coffee, was an impossible thought.

~ 16 ~

Once Jayne arrived at the motel she called in sick, then was left with her raging thoughts. She paced and cried and wrenched a plan from her mind. She would have to tell Mitchell the wedding was off. But she did not want to see him. She did not trust herself to remain composed, and the last thing she wanted to do was fall apart in his presence. It would be too easy to accept the comfort he would undoubtedly offer. His nearness would undo her resolve.

Nor did she want to harden her heart to confront him about Shelbi. What was the point? No longer was she looking at an isolated—though significant—secret, such as Connor had been. A pattern was emerging. Jayne was not interested in untangling the web of Mitchell's explanation of last evening's phone call. No, she would not see Mitchell.

She called his office midmorning. The receptionist said he would be out all day. Relieved, Jayne asked for his voice mail. She kept the message brief and to the point, devoid of the affection she still felt for him. The wedding was off, she said, because she had too many unresolved issues within herself and didn't feel their relationship was solid enough to move forward with such a serious commitment. She had too many questions that he didn't answer.

"Please don't call me," she said. "And please return my house key."

The effort that phone message required exhausted Jayne. She bolted the door and sank into the bed and into oblivion. When she awoke, it was dark. Disoriented, she looked around to get her bearings.

Then she saw it. The being. And it was not alone.

Jayne gasped as the room filled with creatures that couldn't possibly be human, couldn't possibly be real, couldn't possibly be there. But they were. They sat on the desk, the dresser, hung in the doorways, peered out from the closet. Never before had the creature followed her when she slept away from home. Soundless as always, they palpably squeezed her among them, as if to draw her in to become one of them.

Jayne screamed.

They left.

She fell back into bed, frightened. Was she losing her mind completely?

Jayne peered at the digital clock at her bedside. It was past eight thirty. Rattled by the visitors, she suddenly wanted to be out of the room. She reached for her shoes beside the bed, put her hair into a ponytail, and left the motel. Outside, the family restaurant next door beckoned. While the last thing Jayne wanted to do was eat, she craved the sense of normalcy that could come from such a place.

She ordered soup and a half sandwich. With enough time, she managed to slide the chicken soup down her throat, one cautious spoonful at a time. But one bite of the sandwich made her stomach revolt. She pushed it aside and asked for a cup of coffee. When it came, she asked the waitress to leave the pot, which was fresh and hot.

Jayne leaned back against the padded bench in the booth and surveyed the restaurant. A few customers lingered, some with children. Although he was three booths away, a little boy loudly chattered animatedly to his parents about his new trucks. Jayne smiled as she listened to his father soothingly and patiently acknowledge everything the little boy said. Her father would have done that, she reminded herself.

Most days, she missed her father fiercely. Tonight the hollow at her core was cavernous.

After awhile the waitress quit asking if she needed anything else. Jayne left an enormous tip for monopolizing the booth for three hours. It was after eleven thirty when she slowly walked back to her room.

As she took off her clothes and hung them over the back of a chair, she spied her cell phone. She hadn't turned it on all day. Her reflex was to check for messages. But she didn't. *Not tonight*, she thought. *There's time for that tomorrow.*

To her amazement, she slept.

Bennett Grey observed his patient with intense curiosity. Mitchell Furst sat in his usual place on the blue sofa, but he hardly kept still. Bennett had hoped to probe some childhood emotions in this session, but clearly Mitchell had something else on his mind. He not only tried to divert the conversation, which was typical, but he was also downright unresponsive to questions and prompts. He fidgeted in another realm. What he was doing with his hands and feet communicated far more than what he said.

After nearly forty minutes of this, Bennett closed the patient folder and set it aside.

"Mitchell, is there something you'd rather talk about?"

"No. This is fine."

"What is fine?"

Mitchell shrugged. "The stuff you're saying."

"I have the feeling you're not hearing what I'm saying."

"Of course I am." Mitchell's posture abruptly came under control. He stretched one arm across the back of the sofa and crossed his legs, setting one ankle on the opposite knee.

"Well, let's just say I'm finished for now, and you're free to bring up any subject you like."

"I don't have any subjects to bring up."

Bennett chose his words carefully. "It seems to me there's something on your mind. You don't seem as settled as usual."

"Oh, it's nothing, really. Just a little glitch in my love life."

"Oh?"

"It's nothing major. Nothing I can't handle."

Despite Mitchell's calm denial, something clearly unnerved the younger man.

"Are you worried about something?"

"No, of course not. I just told you I could handle it. Jayne and I are just not agreeing on everything about the wedding. I'm feeling a little stressed. That's all."

Bennett shifted his weight. Mitchell would never let a disagreement about wedding arrangements get out of his control. He was feeling something far deeper, but it was likely he didn't even recognize the feelings. Devoid of a healthy reference point, Mitchell would have no words for what he felt.

While feeling some sympathy for Mitchell's agitated state, Bennett's mind raced. He had suspected Mitchell genuinely cared for the young woman to whom he was engaged. At what depth, Bennett was not sure, and whether they really had a future together he was even less sure. But the affection and enthusiasm with which Mitchell had spoken of Jayne struck him as real. And now he watched this clear display of turmoil that Mitchell struggled to keep below the surface. For Mitchell Furst this level of agitation was extreme whether he knew it or not.

Bennett sat at his desk musing on these questions long after Mitchell had left. One of the hallmarks of antisocial personality disorder is lack of affect, Bennett remind himself once again. Lack of emotion. Not having empathy for someone else. BJL062 would say that is the root of the disorder. Without a conscience or emotional structure, such a person would never conform to social norms. Mitchell certainly had many of the generally accepted traits of the disorder. But did the man really lack emotion? If he did, then what was at the root of that evening's display? And if he did experience genuine emotions, did hope exist for mitigating the disorder to some degree?

Bennett leaned back in his chair. He was looking forward to the psychiatric conference on antisocial personality disorder coming up in a couple of weeks.

On Saturday morning Jayne showered and dressed. She didn't want breakfast, but she did need some good strong coffee at the neighboring restaurant again. She felt ready to cautiously check in with the real world. And on a Saturday morning, Leslie might be looking for her.

Sitting with a piping hot mug in front of her, Jayne pulled the cell phone out of her pocket and dialed her home number. When it rang she entered the code to hear her messages.

> Message 1. 10:27. Beep. "It's me. It's supposed to be a nice day on Saturday. Wanna get some ice cream or something? Then I could take you to the florist I found and show you the flowers I picked out for you. Call me in the morning." Beep.
>
> Message 2. 2:13. Beep. "Hi, it's Mare. You're probably sleeping. I just wanted to check on you. Larry said you weren't feeling well, and since you never get sick, I wanted to make sure you were all right. If you feel like it, call me when you wake up." Beep.
>
> Message 3. 4:36. Beep. "Baby, where are you? Can't we talk about this? I know you didn't want me to call, but how can I not

call you? I'll keep my cell on all day, I promise. Please, just call me." Beep.

Message 4. 9.18. Beep. "I keep trying your cell, but I'm guessing you don't have it turned on. Jayne, please, I love you. You're just having prewedding jitters. It's normal. Let's talk about this. I love you." Beep.

Jayne hung up and, trembling, pushed the buttons to check her cellphone messages.

You have seven unheard messages.

Mitchell. She listened to them, one by one, and forced herself to erase them one by one. The messages from early Friday afternoon, when he had just checked his voice mail, were laden with befuddlement and reassurances that whatever the problem was, they could work it out. The messages that came around midnight resounded with near panic. Jayne had never heard that in his voice before. On the last three messages, he rambled until he ran out of time. Not everything he said even made sense.

Eventually she would have to face him. He had left some belongings at her house, and he had her house key. But not today. Not this weekend.

She decided to call Leslie. If she put it off any further, her cousin would hound her.

~ 17 ~

"Hi, it's me."

"Hey, Jayne. Did you get my message?" Leslie asked in her perky Saturday-morning tone.

"Yeah, I did. Um ... I don't think I'm up for much today. Could I just come over to talk?"

"What's the matter?"

"Well, a lot. But I don't want to talk about it over the phone."

"Come over here, then. I'll fix some lunch."

"No, please, don't bother. I don't feel like eating."

Once she had arrived at Leslie's house, Jayne immediately shared her breaking heart. Leslie's shoulders sank as she heard about Shelbi. "I had almost persuaded myself that I was wrong about him," she said softly. "You were so happy, and I wanted you to be happy."

Jayne pulled a fresh tissue from the box and blew her nose for about the twelfth time. "Thanks for not saying 'I told you so.'"

"What can I do to help?"

"Can I stay in your spare bedroom for a while? I don't want to be alone in the house right now. He's still got a key."

"You'll have to get that back from him."

"I know. I'm just not ready to talk to him."

"Of course you can stay here."

"Thanks. I'll check out of the motel and get my stuff."

"Jayne, you're my cousin, and I love you. I want to do whatever I can to help you. But maybe you need something more."

Jayne looked up, questioning.

"Someone to talk to, maybe," Leslie continued. "Someone who can help you understand everything you must be feeling."

"I'm not sure I even know what I'm feeling."

"Well, then, somebody who can help with that. A counselor."

Jayne nodded, having no idea where to find such a person.

"Hello, I'm Brant Lorimer." A friendly man in his late thirties, Dr. Lorimer extended his hand to Jayne. She hoped she wasn't trembling as she shook it. She had never talked to a counselor before—not when Claire died, not when she left Chuck, not when her father died.

Brant Lorimer was a clinical psychologist whose services would be covered by her insurance plan and who offered evening hours three nights a week. His office was a little out of her way, but she decided a little inconvenience was worth it. No one she knew would see her going in or out.

Dr. Lorimer gestured toward a wingback chair. "Please, have a seat and tell me what I can help you with."

His voice was warm and soothing, and his eyes sincere. Jayne's impulse to gush every emotion bottled up inside her nearly overcame her. She fought to stay reasonably coherent.

"I recently broke my engagement," she finally said. "Just a few days ago, actually."

"It sounds like that was a hard decision to make."

Jayne nodded. "It was the right one. It's just that now ... I don't know ... I have all these mixed-up feelings. I still love him very much. But the closer the wedding got, the more I felt like I didn't know who he was. I was married before ... and so was he ... I don't know where to start."

Dr. Lorimer reached for a pad of paper and a pen. "Let's start by getting some basic history. Then we'll decide where to go from there."

He walked her through a form that covered her medical history. When she answered the questions about pregnancy and birth, she told him about Claire's death. His deep and genuine sympathy made her feel as if she could tell Dr. Lorimer the rest of it—and she did: Chuck, her father's death, Mitchell, the secret of Connor, the unanswered questions, and finally, Shelbi. The blue creature in the night she left out, lest he think she had completely lost her marbles.

"I used to be so confident in myself," she said. "I was a good student, I had friends I enjoyed, my family was close, I married somebody my parents really liked. But in the last few years, everything has unraveled. I don't think I've been making very good choices. I mean, why am I drawn to Mitchell when he's this way? Why do I still love him even though I know I can't trust him?"

"Those are all legitimate questions. I can understand why you're asking them. Let's plan to meet a few times so I can get to know you better, and we'll see if we can help you discover some answers."

With a relief that surprised her, Jayne set up four more sessions over the next two weeks.

Mitchell continued to leave messages, but Jayne didn't answer her cell phone. Without going into detail, she told Larry and Mare that she had broken her engagement and did not want to talk to Mitchell, and that she would appreciate it if they would answer the phones, including hers. They mumbled reassurances and probed with their eyes for more information. But she was not ready to say more.

She stayed with Leslie for a week. Her cousin gently cared for her physical and emotional needs and pointed her toward certain realities: She would have to be tested for HIV and who knows what else. It would be naive to think that Rachelle and Shelbi's mother were the only women in Mitchell's past. Jayne pulled herself together. After a week Jayne decided she really needed more clothes.

"I'll go to the house with you," Leslie offered.

"First I want to get my key back from Mitchell."

"Is he still calling?"

"All the time."

"Maybe you should talk to him. Maybe he would stop if you talked."

Jayne left a message on Mitchell's voice mail at work. "Hello, Mitchell. I would like to meet tonight at the bookstore on Eighth Street, around eight. Please bring my house key with you."

"Do you want me to go with you?" Leslie offered again.

Jayne shook her head as she slipped on her warm wool coat. "No. It's a public place with a lot of people around. I'll just get my key, ask him to stop calling, and then go by my house."

"If you change your mind, let me know."

When she pulled into the parking lot behind the bookstore, to her surprise Jayne saw Mitchell's black truck. She could hardly believe that he had arrived early. Locking her car, Jayne collected her thoughts. All day long she had mentally rehearsed what she would say. It would be short, and then she would be out of there.

She entered cautiously, glancing around. Mitchell sat on a purple velvet couch to her left and wore the charcoal gray sweatshirt she had given him just a few weeks ago. Mitchell stood the moment he saw her and motioned for her to join him.

"I'm so glad you finally called me," he started. "I've been going crazy without you."

"I'm just here for my house key, Mitchell."

"Aren't we even going to talk? Let's sit down."

"No, thanks. I only have a few things to say. It won't take long."

"Jayne, honey, please—"

"Mitchell, please listen to me. I'm sure you've had a terrible week. So have I. Believe me, this was not a decision that was easy for me to make."

"Baby, we can fix whatever the problem is." He reached for her, and she stepped back.

"I have too many doubts right now, Mitchell. Some about you, but even more about me."

"We can postpone the wedding, then. We can get married at Christmas, or in the spring."

Jayne shook her head. "No, Mitchell. I'm not going to marry you."

"But I love you!"

"And I love you," she responded quietly. "But we can't get married. Give me my key." She thrust her hand out expectantly, defiantly.

Mitchell reached into the pocket of his sweatshirt. But instead of a house key, he extracted a bundle of letters. A bundle of blue letters. Her letters to him.

Jayne's eyes widened. "What are you doing with those?" Her voice rose involuntarily.

"I went to your house—"

"That's why I want my key back. And my letters."

"I went there to look for clues about where you might have gone. You weren't taking my calls, and I had to know what happened."

"So you were going to track me down?"

"Only if I had to. I hoped you would agree to see me—and you have."

"Nothing is changed, Mitchell."

"No, you're wrong. Everything has changed. I read these letters."

Jayne looked away, gazing at the children's section across the store. "I really wish you hadn't." She hated that he knew those personal thoughts.

"I'm glad I did. I understand now. I understand that you feel insecure about some things—some pretty major stuff. I understand that love is confusing. And I know that I haven't always been honest with you, I haven't told you everything I should have."

"Even when you promised that you would."

"I know. I'm not making any excuses." Mitchell had tears in his eyes that Jayne felt had conveniently appeared. "I know we have some work to do," he continued, "and if you want to postpone the wedding while we do it, I understand. But please, don't give up on me. You're the one person in my life who hasn't given up on me when you had good reason to, and I don't want to lose you."

Mitchell dropped to his knees and grabbed her right hand.

"Mitchell, please." Self-conscious did not come close to describing what Jayne felt as she avoided the eyes of onlookers.

"I don't care if anyone sees me. I'm pleading for the woman I love. I'll do anything you want, be anything you want me to be, answer any questions you want to ask," he choked out between sobs.

"Mitchell, I've never seen you like this. I don't understand what's happening," Jayne stammered.

"I've never felt like this before. I can't let you just walk out of my life. You mean too much to me. I promise, I will tell you everything."

Jayne raised an eyebrow. "Is there a lot that I don't know?"

"No, not really. I've tried really hard to be honest and straightforward since I've been with you."

"So why didn't you tell me about Shelbi?" Although she had promised herself she wouldn't confront him about Shelbi, she couldn't help blurting out the child's name.

He looked up, startled. "You know about Shelbi? Oh, of course. You heard me talking to my mother, didn't you? Is that what this is all about?"

"No, it's a lot more than that."

"You didn't give me a chance to explain. You never asked."

"She's your child, Mitchell, don't tell me she's not. Why should I have to ask about that, especially after you kept Connor from me for so long?"

"I'm so sorry, babe." He had both her hands in his now. Jayne glanced around uncomfortably, hoping no one she knew was in the store.

"After I read your letters, I wrote one too," Mitchell said. He reached into his pocket again and pulled out a white envelope. "Please promise me you'll read this. Promise me you'll see me again after you do."

Jayne hesitated only a second as she looked into his deep brown eyes. She mustered the resolve to say, "I can't promise either of those things." She pulled her hands out of his.

"Okay, I understand. But just think about it. And then call me if you change your mind." He folded the letter and pushed it into a side pocket on her purse.

"May I have my key, Mitchell?"

He stood up, pulled his key ring out his pants pocket, and removed her house key. "You're the best thing that's ever happened to me, and I know you love me. It's not over."

"Good-bye, Mitchell." She barely made it to her car before she broke down. She dared not look back to see if he had followed her. Through her tears she started the car and pulled out of the parking lot.

~ 18 ~

The late-September evening was cooler than most. Jayne snuggled into the sofa and wrapped herself with her fleece robe. A bag of popcorn sat next to her and a vanilla candle burned on the coffee table in front of her. Ambient light filtered around the corner from the kitchen, casting a yellow haze in an otherwise dim room. *Classics to Relax,* a favorite evening CD, played softly through the speakers on either end of the sofa.

Although it was late, she hadn't eaten anything since breakfast. Popcorn seemed like the shortest route to a full stomach. Crunching seemed to help her think—and she had plenty to think about since her return four days ago. Jayne felt better than she could have imagined she would ever feel, especially given the events of the last few days.

She was glad to be back in her own house. Once she had her key back from Mitchell, she felt safe enough to return home. She knew that if he really wanted to get in, he could; but she did not believe he would ever hurt her. Changing the locks had entered her mind briefly, but she hadn't acted on it. She hadn't needed to.

Mitchell was back in her life, never having left her heart.

For two days his letter lay unopened under a pile of advertisements on the kitchen table. Several times she had wanted to toss it straight in the trash. But she didn't. Jayne told herself that she owed it to Mitchell to at least read the letter. After all, they had been engaged.

109

Jayne took a breath and scanned the letter, barely reading the words the first time through. Mitchell had written pages and pages of penitential apology. Then a phrase caught her eye: "I want to know what trust means." Jayne sat down at the kitchen table, smoothed the letter in front of her, and began reading more carefully.

> *I've broken your heart by not being trustworthy. And I've broken my own heart by not trusting your love enough to tell you the whole truth and nothing but the truth. I can't tell you how deeply sorry I am. I don't blame you for breaking it off. You deserve better. You deserve someone worthy of your love and trust. I know I fall far short. But I also know that every day that I've known you, I've wanted to be better. I've wanted to be a better person. I've wanted to have a better life. I've wanted to love better than I ever have before. I want to know what trust means. You make me want all that, Jayne.*

The lump in Jayne's throat grew larger. As much as she didn't want to, she believed Mitchell. It was so unlike him to talk this way—he had to mean it. Maybe she was giving up too soon. Maybe they were on the verge of the relationship she wanted after all.

> *I'm not perfect. Actually, I'm a far cry from perfect. But I want the past to be the past. I don't want the mistakes I've made in the past to ruin my future with you. I don't want my past to hurt you. I want to walk away from my past, let it go, start fresh with you, Jayne. Please give me the chance to do that. Help me be the better person I want to be, that I can only be if you're with me. You've given me the reason I've never had before to change, to be a new man. I know you love me and want to be with me, too. Let's let the past be the past together.*

She did love him. She did want to be with him, body and soul. Her brain could not fathom how her heart could still care for him after his untruthfulness. But she did.

Let's let the past be the past together. That's why he didn't tell her about Shelbi. That's why he seemed secretive sometimes. He was ashamed of his past. If he was ashamed, then he really did want to change. He was trying to protect her and their future together. Jayne saw Mitchell in a new light at that moment.

Thirty minutes later they ordered coffee at a café on Main Street. Their hands tentatively crept toward each other across the table as Mitchell poured out his apologies and promises and dreams of their future. Jayne could hardly believe the depth of his emotion, and soon tears spilled from her eyes as well. She knew people stared at them, but she didn't care this time. By the end of the evening, she was in his arms. She was convinced he wanted to change but just didn't know how.

Leslie, of course, was furious. Her carefully controlled opinions about Mitchell—and Jayne's questionable judgment—unfurled and whipped viciously in the wind of her indignation. Shaking, Jayne held her own while she spoke to her cousin on the phone. She loved Mitchell. They had some work to do, and she knew it would not always be easy. But they would stand stronger if they did it together. Yes, she would still have the HIV test, and whatever the results, she and Mitchell would face them together.

The wedding was back on for the last Saturday in October, just over a month away. Since she hadn't canceled the wedding arrangements during their separation, everything was all set to go, except that Mitchell still needed a suit.

He was now more transparent than Jayne had ever known him to be. He made sure to see her every day, sneaking in several quick daytime visits between appointments and spending long evenings with her. She always knew where he was. When he took Shelbi out for ice cream, he told Jayne exactly where he was going and when he would be back. He seemed almost relieved that Jayne knew about Shelbi now, as if now he didn't have to sneak around. His routine of seeing his eight-year-old daughter once a week or so at his parents' house was no secret. Shelbi's mother wanted nothing to do with Mitchell, but she allowed the little girl to see her father and grandparents. Everything was on the table. Nearly every day he apologized for behaving so badly and set out to prove to her that he intended to change.

Their daily routine settled into a pattern that it had never had before, which boosted Jayne's confidence in her decision to stick with Mitchell. Underneath it all, she liked predictability. She tested the waters with choosing to trust Mitchell, and he did not disappoint her. He came for dinner when he said he would. He picked her up from work when he said he would. He went shopping for a suit when he said he would.

Jayne's relationship with Leslie, however, was strained almost to the breaking point. Although Leslie had decided not to take care of the flowers after all, so far she had not withdrawn as Jayne's attendant. Jayne was determined to give Leslie the space she needed. As the days passed, she made an extra effort to e-mail Leslie a joke that she would enjoy or send her sale ads with notes saying they should investigate them on their Saturday-morning outings. Patiently, Jayne endured the lectures Leslie opened with each time they saw each other. Gradually the rants became less scathing. Although Jayne was not sure that Leslie would ever like Mitchell, she could see that her persistence was paying off. Leslie was too fond of Jayne to give up on their friendship, no matter how much she disapproved of Mitchell.

Jayne debated whether she would continue to see Brant Lorimer now that she had resumed her engagement. But what harm could come from keeping the few sessions she had already scheduled?

"You seem quite sure that you've made the right decision," Dr. Lorimer observed when she told him of the reversal.

Jayne nodded. "I'm not sorry that I broke it off with him. We both learned something from that experience. Maybe that's what we both needed to get a true picture of our relationship. It's so much better now."

"In what ways?"

"Mitchell is more dependable, more open, more communicative. I don't feel like I'm listening to excuses, just the truth. We're really together in a way that we weren't before."

"Do you trust Mitchell?"

Jayne hesitated.

"Do you want to be happy, Jayne?"

"Of course!"

"Then it's important that you're very sure that you know what's real and what's not."

"I do know what's real. The change in Mitchell is real."

"From what you told me, you had good reason to leave him."

"Well, I know, but ..."

"I'm not going to tell you what to do, Jayne. It's your life. And I haven't even met Mitchell, so I can't comment too much about him. My concern is you. You have to decide what makes you happy. I would not presume to make those decisions for you. I only want to help you be sure you're making the right ones."

"I understand. But I think I am, I really do."

"Let me ask you again. Do you trust Mitchell?"

Jayne's shoulders sagged. "Not as much as I would like to," she finally admitted quietly. "In the small things, yes. But I do love him. I can't stop loving him."

"Love is a powerful force," Brant acknowledged. "Sometimes it motivates us to do things that don't seem all that reasonable from another perspective. It's certainly not anything to discount."

"I've never felt this way before. I never knew love could be this powerful. Doesn't that mean something?"

"Of course it does."

"If I focus on how much I love Mitchell instead of not trusting him, I'll build up the positive parts of our relationship. Won't I?"

"Let's talk about trust a bit more. When I asked if you trusted Mitchell, you hesitated and finally said not as much as you'd like to. How do you think your relationship would be different if you did trust him as much as you'd like to?"

"Well ... I guess I'd be less anxious. I wouldn't have to feel afraid of loving him."

"Do you? Feel afraid of loving him?"

"Sometimes. I used to be afraid that he would leave me. I didn't know what he saw in me."

"There's plenty in you to draw any man."

Jayne blushed. "Thank you. When I found out about Connor, well, I was shocked, of course, that he would hide something like that from me. But I still didn't think he meant any harm. He had his reasons, even if I don't think they were very good. But when I found out about Shelbi, well, that was a whole different story. He was keeping secrets even after he promised not to."

"And so you felt ..."

Jayne clenched a tissue in her fist. "I felt betrayed. I was afraid to love him because he might hurt me again."

"And now that's changed?"

"I don't think he means to hurt me. I really don't."

Brant nodded. "That could very well be true. But even in the best of relationships, people occasionally hurt each other. What we do with that hurt is what makes the difference."

"I'm not sure I understand."

"You may never trust Mitchell as fully as you would like. Wounds can be opened again so easily. But I want you to think about whether you trust yourself. If Mitchell should break your trust in him again, can you trust yourself to handle the situation in a healthy way, in a way that takes care of Jayne, not Mitchell?"

"I'm … I'm not sure … I guess I'll have to think about that."

"I'd like it if you would. Then we can talk more about it the next time we meet."

~ 19 ~

Bennett jotted down his last thought in the margin of his program and pocketed his pen in his old but comfortable tweed jacket. He had foregone a tie that morning, opting to be as comfortable as possible in the vinyl-molded chairs that were certain to abound in a conference center.

The morning had been thought provoking, the conference having lived up to its claims so far. A panel of psychiatric researchers presented and debated the topic of understanding antisocial personality disorder from the inside out. They led the audience in looking at the world through the filters that someone with the disorder would have—what "normal" would seem like to such a person. Questions from the audience had been stimulating.

As he listened, Bennett recalled a number of clients from over the years—not success stories, to be sure. He had limited professional experience with antisocial personality disorder, and most of the clients he had treated for it had been ordered by the court to seek professional help or go to jail. But of course the patient that Bennett thought about the most during the presentation was Mitchell Furst.

Much of the question-and-answer time centered on some of the same issues Bennett had encountered in the chat room. Was it possible to have some of the characteristics but not have the full disorder? Was there a spectrum of degrees of the disorder or was it a black-and-white diagnosis?

What if an individual had many of the defining traits, but lacked one or two key ones? Was there a line beyond which there really was no hope for change? Was there a difference between a sociopath and a psychopath?

Just as in the chat room, opinions varied widely. Those who believed in degrees of disorder argued that some people may live a largely reckless life but never do any serious harm to themselves or anyone else, while others with a more serious condition would leave wreckage in their wake everywhere they went. Other panelists argued that only the individuals who leave such wreckage truly have the disorder and most likely will end up in the penal system. Bennett tended to think it was a matter of degrees. Some patients were quickly recognizable as disordered, even criminal, while others flailed their way through life with minor skirmishes that posed no serious threat.

The group reached consensus, however, on two points. First, a lack of conscience was at the center of the disorder. Without any sense of right or wrong in relation to society's expectations, the person with ASPD would never experience shame at breaching those expectations. Second, transformation in an individual with antisocial personality disorder was rare and required intensive therapy and support—more than most families and professionals were able to give. The moderator had cut off the discussion at that point. The question of treatment and intervention options was slated for the afternoon session.

Conference participants milled in small groups, some in lighthearted chatter and others in absorbing conversation. So far Bennett hadn't recognized more than a few people at the conference. Although he remained aloof from the professional network in the local area, he did appreciate this opportunity for a refresher on a specific condition. He was particularly looking forward to the afternoon session so that he could evaluate the strategies he had tried with Mitchell Furst and his assessment of Mitchell's condition. The aisles had largely emptied, so Bennett stood up to get his bearings. Nodding and smiling politely to people as he passed, Bennett made his way toward the coffee bar at the back of the large conference room. He was pleased to discover a wide selection of Danishes as well. As he debated between almond and raspberry, another participant paused beside him.

"Quite a spread, isn't it? They must be afraid we'll fall asleep if they don't ply us with sugar and caffeine."

Bennett glanced at the man. He was younger, perhaps not even forty, dressed in khakis, a blue dress shirt open at the collar, and brown penny loafers.

"Yes, it's difficult to make a choice," Bennett said lightly.

"Are you enjoying the conference?"

"Very much."

The younger man extended his hand. "I'm Brant Lorimer."

"Bennett Grey. Nice to meet you."

"Do you work in a care facility?" Brant took a plate and stacked two Danishes on it.

"Many years ago. Back when we called them institutions. I'm in private practice now." Bennett selected the almond and glanced around for a coffee cup. "How about you?"

"Most of my experience with ASPD is in the penal system. Assessing inmates who are up for parole, treating court-ordered patients, that sort of thing. I don't tend to see them in my private practice."

"I would imagine you never get bored."

"No, I don't. The kind of stimulation I encounter at this sort of event is invigorating."

A light went on in Bennett's head as he added cream to his coffee. "Didn't I see your name in the program?"

Brant smiled. "You've found me out. Yes, I'm on the panel that will respond to the discussion of treatment and intervention."

"It certainly sounds like you have plenty of experience."

"If we run into each other later, you'll have to let me know how you think I did."

Jayne awoke from her Saturday-afternoon nap gradually and peacefully. She smiled as she realized Mitchell had covered her with an afghan when she dozed off on the sofa. Opening one eye, she looked at him sitting in the wingback chair across from her. He had his head bent over a book. Jayne opened both eyes and stretched.

"Hello, sleepyhead."

"Hello yourself. What are you reading?"

"Oh, just something someone gave me."

Jayne sat up. "Someone gave you a book?"

"A guy at the park I walked through yesterday. He had a stack of them. It's a Bible, actually."

"It doesn't look like a Bible." Jayne eyed the colorful cover with bold lettering.

"No, but it really is one. Or at least part of it. It's the New Testament. I'm not sure what that is."

"I think it's about Jesus. And the people who believed in him after he died." Jayne was wide awake now, flabbergasted to find Mitchell reading a Bible.

"Well, I started at the beginning, and it's about when Jesus was born. Christmas and all that."

"Are you going to read the whole thing?"

"I don't know. It was just something to do while you slept."

"You could have woken me up."

"No, you looked too peaceful. I like to look at you when you're sleeping."

"Remember that friend who got married in the chapel?"

"Yeah?"

"She had a part of the New Testament read at her wedding. I wonder if I could find it."

"What was it about? Jesus?"

"Not exactly. It was something called the love chapter, I think."

"There's an index in the back." Mitchell thumbed through the pages as Jayne perched on the arm of the chair and looked over his shoulder.

"There," she said, pointing. "Where it says 'Love is patient, love is kind.' That sounds right."

"First Corinthians thirteen four."

"Corinthians. First Corinthians." Jayne was amazed at what was coming back to her from Sunday-school days.

Mitchell flipped to the table of contents at the front, found the right page, and began to read.

"'Love is patient, love is kind. It does not envy, it does not boast, it is not proud. It is not rude, it is not self-seeking, it is not easily angered, it keeps no record of wrongs. Love does not delight in evil but rejoices with the truth. It always protects, always trusts, always hopes, always perseveres. Love never fails.'"

"Wow," Jayne said softly. "That's a mouthful."

"I remember this from a plaque on my grandmother's dining-room wall" Mitchell said. "I haven't thought of that in years, but I'm sure it's the same."

"Well, you said your grandmother was religious."

"It's very appropriate to a wedding. Maybe we should have it at our wedding."

"Really?" Jayne said.

"Really."

The facilitator of the afternoon panel summarized the presentation of inter-vention options before turning to the respondents. He reminded the audience that treatment options included medication to stabilize behavior, intensive inpatient programs, psychoanalysis, and outpatient psychotherapy, which focuses on helping the patient understand how he creates his own problems and how his distorted perceptions make it difficult or impossible for him to see himself as others see him. Treatment options are fraught with difficulty because emotions are a key aspect of treatment, and individuals with antisocial personality disorder have had little or no emotionally rewarding relationships in their lives. The therapeutic relationship could be the first emotionally satis-fying relationship the patient has and depression the first emotion the patient experiences.

Bennett leaned forward thoughtfully as the moderator pointed out that the patient will resist intimacy and authority figures. Key to the success of any treatment would be finding an effective way for dealing with the patient's self-defeating behavior; patients needed to learn new self-defense mecha-nisms so that in the process of avoiding intimacy they did not continue to cause emotional or physical harm to themselves or others. It was recom-mended that the therapist not necessarily try to make the patient feel remorse or shame over past actions. Rather, therapy should help the client develop a better understanding of how behaving in moral ways that conform to soci-ety's expectations could help him achieve personal goals. The patient would have an exceptional ability to manipulate and deceive, so therapists should avoid power struggles or posturing as an authority figure.

Bennett observed Brant Lorimer during the summation. Clearly he was ready with his own opinion. The facilitator introduced the respondents and it was Brant's turn to speak.

"Good afternoon. It's my pleasure to be with you today to dissect a con-dition that is coming more to the forefront of our society. As we reminded ourselves this morning, we are not talking about the Hannibal Lecters of the world. Most of us do not encounter someone with the disorder in that extreme. But we do encounter individuals with lesser degrees of the disorder along the spectrum, and I do believe there is a spectrum. For the last twenty years, I have worked in the penal system. You could not hope to find a bet-ter concentration of individuals with profiles that suggest antisocial personality disorders in varying degrees.

"In this age of a plethora of pharmaceuticals and psychotropic options, medication is the question that comes first to many minds. We have seen medications change behavior and mental functioning in many other conditions. Why not also for antisocial personality disorder? Our panelists are correct that some studies have suggested a degree of success in treating ASPD with medications. The ratio of success is not entirely encouraging, though. It seems to be trial and error whether one patient will respond to medication or not.

"However, I believe we face a more serious pitfall with pharmaceutical intervention. If a patient is prescribed medication, you must have someone policing the patient to make sure he takes the pills. Noncompliance is a major issue. No one can force a grown man to take his pills. There is no long-term evidence that this approach works.

"It is my opinion that no one is ever cured of antisocial personality disorder. We all know that as the patients enter middle age, symptoms tend to diminish, and the second half of their lives may be much quieter, with more socially acceptable behavior, than the first. But we must be realistic. We do no one any service, especially the families and other victims, if by administering medications we set up expectations for something that is not going to happen."

As the discussion was turned over to the other respondents and then opened for questions from the audience, Bennett replayed Brant Lorimer's words in his mind. He had heard them before, in almost the same verbiage. Or more precisely, he had seen them. On his computer screen. Brant J. Lorimer. BJL062, who believed there was no hope for Mitchell Furst if he truly had the disorder.

~ 20 ~

Jayne smiled at the little girl squirming in the pew in front of her. The child, perhaps four years old, had been amazingly still during most of the service. But at an hour and ten minutes, she had reached her limit. The coloring book was no longer of interest, she had removed her shoes and socks, and she was loudly whispering a series of questions in her mother's ear. The response was a consistent shushing. As the pastor finished his sermon, the child hunched backward in the pew, gripping the back of the bench with her hands and propping her chin on them, staring at Jayne. Jayne winked, which set the little girl off on a course of trying to wink back throughout the closing prayer and hymn.

Although the pew was full, Jayne was alone. Mitchell had not returned to church since deciding he didn't want to do the required counseling sessions. Today he was spending the day with Connor. Jayne had not come every week either, but she thought that maybe she would be more regular. The services triggered childhood memories, only now the words and rituals made more sense than they did when she was seven or eight. Something she didn't quite understand drew her to church, and each time she went she was glad she had.

Earlier in the service Jayne had scanned the congregation with less self-consciousness than her earlier visits. Mustering her courage, she let the usher seat her about halfway up, rather than a pew in the back. She was beginning to recognize a few people, even if she had not yet met them, and that made the experience more comfortable.

Today Noelle sat very close to the front. Her unquenchable red hair gave her away. After the benediction Jayne stepped out of the way of others seated in her pew and waited for Noelle to make her way down the aisle. Jayne smiled when she caught Noelle's eye. Perhaps it was Noelle that drew her back to church. Something inside her always seemed to lift when she was in Noelle's shining presence.

"Is that the spectacular Jayne Paige-Hamilton?" Noelle teased as she stretched her arms out to hug Jayne, an embrace Jayne willingly received and returned. "Where's your sidekick today?"

"Mitchell is spending the day with his son. I'm on my own all day."

"Well, that sounds like a lovely opportunity to pamper yourself."

"Actually, I was wondering if you would like to go out to lunch? My treat. Are you free?"

"Darling, what a delicious idea! I need to drop some things off in the church office, then we'll be on our way."

A few minutes later they settled into a booth at a Mexican restaurant a few blocks from the church. With a basket of chips and a bowl of salsa between them, they relaxed and waited for the cheese enchiladas they had both ordered.

"I haven't been here in years," Noelle said, surveying the decor, "or any other Mexican restaurant, for that matter."

"Oh, I'm sorry! I wouldn't have suggested this if I'd known you don't care for Mexican. Why didn't you say something?"

Noelle shook her head. "No, dearie, it's nothing you did. Actually, I love Mexican food! The place just reminds me of a piece of my past."

"Oh." Jayne was unsure what more to say. "I'm sorry."

"You have nothing to be sorry about, Miss Jayne. It all happened in another life, and you couldn't have known anything about it."

"I'm sorry. I didn't mean to dredge anything up."

"Would you stop saying you're sorry!" Noelle scolded. "You're not dredging anything up. I used to go to Mexican restaurants a lot. One in particular. But I was running with a nasty crowd. I thought they cared about me, because my own family sure didn't. I was too afraid to be on my own, so I stayed with them when I shouldn't have. We used to hang out at a place called El Señor's." She began laughing unabashedly.

"What's so funny?"

Noelle grinned at Jayne. "In Mexico, 'El Señor' is how they refer to the Lord. I hung out at that restaurant for years, not knowing that the real El Señor was preparing me to meet him. Looking back, it's a miracle that I did. Sometimes God just puts the right person in your life to get you where you need to go. Right?"

"I suppose so," Jayne said timidly.

"My mind was as beat up as my body in those days," Noelle went on without shame or hesitation. "I did everything I could to convince myself that no one could possibly love me. Somehow I thought it was my fault that my mother resented me for ruining her life and my father didn't even know I existed. I was fourteen when I left home. I didn't see my mother again for sixteen years."

"I can't imagine that!"

"That's because you had parents who wanted you and loved you. I had no one. Oh, a teacher here and there felt sorry for me, and we had a neighbor once who made sure I had decent clothes to wear to school, even if they were hand-me-downs. My mother was too drunk to care most of the time. No one loved me at home. So I went looking for love in all the wrong places and all the wrong people."

"I'm sorry you've had such a hard life," Jayne said sincerely. This luminescent woman across the table, who exuded joy from the inside out, who shimmered with confidence and the brilliance of surety—how could she possibly have grown from that broken, neglected girl?

"I used to wish it had been different. But I don't worry about stuff like that anymore, sweetie girl. When I met the real El Señor, everything changed. Not all at once, mind you. My wounds ran deep, and it took me a long time to really believe that his love ran even deeper. But no matter what I did, he loved me. I tested that over and over until I finally gave in and believed that his love was light years ahead of anything I had ever imagined." Noelle paused and smiled at Jayne. "You're not really sure what I'm talking about, are you?"

"Well, not entirely. You're talking about Jesus?"

"You got that right. I'm talking about *life*, baby. Real life."

Their food arrived and they plunged in. Jayne hoped that Noelle would keep talking.

"I'm wondering what your thoughts are about trust this week." Brant Lorimer prompted Jayne to resume their discussion.

Jayne had thought long and hard about this discussion—and not without some anxiety. Did she trust herself? The question had weighed on her heavily the last few days, especially during the night when her sleep was disturbed by intruders she knew were not there, not real. But she also knew they certainly were there, were real. If she saw things that weren't there and believed they were there despite knowing better, could she trust herself? Could she trust her judgment about Mitchell for now or the future? Could she trust how she might respond to future disappointments?

Not knowing how Dr. Lorimer would respond, she chose her words carefully. "There's something I think I should tell you about."

"Of course. What is it?"

"It's kind of confusing for me." Jayne began having trouble breathing.

"Take your time, Jayne. Deep breaths."

"I'm okay. I mean about the breathing."

They sat in silence while she composed herself once again.

"Sometimes I see things," she finally said, "things that I know in my head can't be there, but they feel so real."

"What kind of things?"

"Well, not things, exactly. More like, I don't know ... beings."

She recounted for Dr. Lorimer the visits of the bluish green creature that leered and scoffed in the silence of darkness.

"Is this my subconscious telling me I'm doing the wrong thing? If I felt surer of myself, if I trusted myself more to make good decisions, would it go away?"

Dr. Lorimer shifted in his chair. "I'm glad you told me about this. I do think we should talk about it."

Jayne didn't like the look on his face. It was too controlled in a man who was normally more expressive. She regretted bringing the subject up. Dr. Lorimer was going to tell her she was crazy, and she didn't want to hear that.

"I only brought it up because sometimes I don't trust myself after one of those visits. But just for a few minutes. Then I'm back on track with what's real. Otherwise it doesn't really bother me. Not during the daytime. It's not a big deal." She hoped she sounded casual. Why couldn't she stop talking? Jayne gulped air.

"Dreams often serve a valuable purpose in our mental health," Dr. Lorimer said calmly. "Sometimes they seem so real that we think we can actually touch something in the dream and feel its hardness or coldness. So it's not necessarily a bad thing that this happens. We can explore what it might mean in your situation, as it relates to your ability to trust yourself as well as other areas of your life."

But it's not a dream, Jayne wanted to say. *I really do see it. It really is there.*

"So you don't think I'm hallucinating?" she asked.

"Not in the popular sense, no. You don't see monkeys hanging from the ceiling during the daytime or anything like that. The experience is very specific in its time and place in your life. The fact that it happens while you sleep is probably significant, so we can talk about some of the things the mind does during sleep, both for restoration and self-defense. Let me give you a couple of things I'd like you to read."

He got up to look through a bookcase.

But I'm not asleep, Jayne thought. *When it's there, I'm wide awake. I know what time it is. I know if I'm cold or warm.*

Jayne glanced at the clock as she dropped the pasta into the boiling water. Mitchell had called ten minutes earlier, so she knew he was on his way. As she stuck her head in the refrigerator looking for the lettuce to make a salad, she heard the back door open.

"Hey, baby, come here," he said with open arms.

Jayne abandoned the lettuce hunt and eagerly stepped into his embrace. She buried her face in his shoulder, hoping to hide the drained look she had seen when she last looked in the mirror. Her session with Dr. Lorimer had taxed her far more than she had bargained for. She banished conscious thought, wanting only to feel Mitchell's arms around her, his mouth on hers, the warmth of his shoulder against her cheek.

After a long kiss Mitchell released her and reached into his khaki pocket. He pulled out a neatly folded stack of money.

"Mitchell!" Jayne's eyes widened as she saw the number fifty on the outside bill and gauged the depth of the pile. "What in the world?"

"My friend in India is back for a while. He gave me a bonus for looking after his house all this time."

"That's some bonus!"

"It's eight hundred dollars, Jayne. I want you to take it and use it for the wedding. I know you've been putting some expenses on your credit card."

"Mitchell, I don't know what to say." She forced herself to reach out and take the money.

"I said I was going to help out with the wedding, and I am. Oh, yeah, I also found someone to do the ceremony."

"You did?" Jayne hadn't wanted to admit that she was getting a little anxious about that detail.

"Yep. I have a client whose husband used to be a Baptist pastor. He agreed to do it."

"Wow. Thanks!"

"You didn't think I'd welsh, did you?"

"Well, no, of course not." She stretched up to kiss him again. The pasta pot boiled over, but she didn't care.

~ 21 ~

"Here you go."

"What's this?" Mitchell put down the sports section and looked dubiously at the stack of envelopes Jayne slid across the table.

"Invitations."

"What are we invited to?"

"Silly. We're inviting people."

"To what?"

"Our wedding, of course. Don't pretend you don't know about this, because we've talked about it half a dozen times."

"Yes, and every time we agreed you were doing the invitations. You know how to do that nice fancy writing."

"It's called calligraphy. And I am doing it. For the addresses I have. You haven't given me your list, so I can't address the invitations. So here."

"I'll get you the list."

Jayne shook her head. "Nope. Too late. It's time for me to move on down the checklist. You're on your own now, buddy."

Mitchell picked up one of the invitations and studied it. "You know, this is very nice. You did a great job designing this."

"There are some perks to being a graphic designer."

"You should try to sell this design."

"You think so?"

"Sure. Why not? Or do others. You could have your own little business on the side."

"You're trying to change the subject."

"What was the subject?"

"Invitations. Address them and mail them by Saturday. The wedding is in three weeks. I already put stamps on a bunch of them, but if you need more stamps, I've got plenty extra."

"Yes, ma'am." Mitchell playfully saluted.

Jayne chuckled and pulled her list closer to her. With a bold stroke, she crossed off "Mail invitations."

Later that week, between phone calls at his desk at work, Mitchell addressed one envelope to his cousin Mason, and wrote the names of his parents and two sisters on three more. He would drop those by his parents' house sometime. The others he set aside. Maybe his mother would have some ideas; he'd have to ask her later. Maybe her brother would want to come. Mitchell had last seen his uncle three years ago at some cousin's wedding.

On the spur of the moment, he decided he would swing by his parents' after work, bum dinner off of his mother, stop by Jayne's for a couple of hours, then go out. Jayne would be tired, anyway. She'd appreciate an early evening. He could plead an early-morning breakfast meeting and she wouldn't ask any questions. Or he could say he wanted to work out at the gym before he went to bed. The action at the Excelsior Room would just be getting started.

Mitchell glanced at his calendar and remembered he had an appointment with Bennett Grey. *Not today,* he thought. *I'm not in the mood for that.* He figured he would make a few more phone calls to follow up on leads, then scoot out the door on the early side. No one would know he wasn't headed for a late-afternoon business meeting.

Mitchell left Jayne's bungalow around nine thirty that evening. She had pouted a little when he said he needed to go, so he had suggested that she pamper herself with a candlelit bubble bath. Her invitation to join her was tempting, but his mind had already wandered to the Excelsior Room. As he pulled away from the curb, she stood at the window, holding the curtain back. She was beautiful in her own way, he acknowledged, but the routine they had fallen into in the last few weeks was beginning to constrict him. He deserved some time on his own.

When he strode into the Excelsior Room, jingling his keys on one finger, she was there as he had hoped. Those long legs were irresistible, and she knew it. Her skirts were always pleasurably short, and her form fitted his so nicely when they slow danced.

"Hey, stranger, where have you been the last few weeks?"

"What does it matter? I'm here now."

She leaned into him and kissed him generously on the mouth. He did not resist.

"Let's dance," she murmured, hanging her arms on his shoulders and beginning to sway her hips.

"The dance floor is over there."

"We'll get there," she said, seductively sliding her spiked heeled feet in the direction of the dance floor.

Mitchell smiled and put his hands on her bottom.

When the music changed and the beat picked up, she spun herself out of his embrace, flung her arms over her head, and began the uninhibited gyrations he so loved to watch. With her eyes closed and her head tilted back, he knew she was his for the taking.

"Mitchell Furst?"

He turned to respond to the male voice behind him but did not answer.

"Sir, three individuals at the bar have identified you as Mitchell Furst. Are you Mitchell Furst?"

"I might be."

"Then this might be for you." The man pulled an envelope out of his inside jacket pocket and handed it to Mitchell, who took it before he realized what he had done. The man was gone as rapidly as he had appeared.

She stopped dancing and looked at him, questioning.

He shrugged and stuffed the papers in a pocket. He might or might not decide to look at them.

Two hours later he and his dance partner made their way to the bar.

"I bet I know what that envelope was," she said.

"It doesn't matter what it is."

"Legal stuff."

"So what if it is?"

"Don't you even want to know what it is?"

"I already know."

"I confess I'm curious."

"Why is it any of your business?"

"Oh, baby, don't get nasty with me. You know you want to keep coming back for more."

Mitchell shrugged and took a sip of his beer. "Child support."

"How much?"

"More than I'm going to give."

"How old is the baby now?"

"Four months, I think. But she's been harassing me since way before he was born."

"Have you seen him?"

"Once."

"Aren't you curious about him?"

"It's not worth putting up with his mother. Besides, how can I be sure he's even mine?"

"A woman knows these things."

"Women have been known to lie."

"You could take a paternity test."

"My guess is that's what these papers are about."

"So?"

"So nothing. She's not going to push me around to solve her problem."

"Don't you think you had anything to do with this?"

"If she didn't want a baby, she should have made sure it didn't happen. There was no question that she wanted the action. She could hardly wait to get her hands on me. I told her to get an abortion."

"Let me guess—she didn't want to do that."

"Not this time. I don't know why it was so different from the time before."

"When are you ever going to settle down?" She picked up her white wine and leaned back in the chair to study him.

"Oh, about the time you do."

"Then I guess we'll be running into each other here for a long, long time."

"I certainly hope so."

"Come on, Mitchell. We've got to get there before the shop closes." Jayne tugged at his shirt as if to pull him out of the chair.

"Yeah, I know. I'm just tired. It's been a long day."

"You shouldn't schedule so many breakfast meetings, or at least not so early."

"I have to do what's most convenient for the customer."

"Then stop working out so late at night."

"I gotta stay buff for you." He grinned at her.

"Well, the mall has more normal hours than you like to keep, and I think you look pretty buff in a dark suit, so we have to get over there. You need one last fitting to be sure the alterations are right."

Jayne glanced at her watch as they entered the mall at the entrance nearest the men's store. She was so focused on arriving punctually that she didn't notice the tall, dark woman pushing a stroller right across their path or the well-dressed man beside her.

"Oh, hello," the woman said, looking at Mitchell.

Mitchell smiled politely. "I heard you got married," he said, "but I didn't know you had a kid."

"Well, I do, as you can see." Reserved. Not exactly chums.

"I remember you wanted children."

She paused awkwardly and glanced at Jayne. "Yes, I always wanted children."

The man beside the woman put his hand out toward Mitchell. "I'm Jeff, the father of this gorgeous little boy."

"Mitchell. Nice to meet you."

Jeff glanced at Jayne, and Mitchell took the hint. "This is Jayne. Dolores and I used to go out—a long time ago."

Jeff nodded. "Yes, she's mentioned you."

Funny, Jayne thought. *Mitchell has never mentioned Dolores.* "How long have you been married?" she asked.

"Three years," Dolores responded.

"And the baby?"

"Almost a year old."

Mitchell stepped away slightly. "Well, it was nice to see you, but we've got to get going before everything closes up."

"Mitchell," Jayne said as they picked up the pace, "why didn't you tell her we were getting married? After all, we're here to pick up your wedding suit."

"Oh, I don't know. I guess it just didn't seem like the thing to say."

"You didn't even introduce me as your fiancée."

"Well, it's not like she's a close friend or anything. We went out a few times a long time ago. It was nothing. I haven't seen her since." He put an arm around Jayne's shoulder and kissed the top of her head. "I'm sorry I didn't introduce you properly. I guess all this wedding stuff is getting to me. I just want to focus on us right now."

Jayne nodded but didn't respond.

~ 22 ~

Adorned in deep red roses, Peace Chapel was utterly beautiful. At least that's what Jayne thought as she stood outside the doors looking through the glass panels. A single rose was fastened to the end of each pew, each blossom in turn pointing the way toward the front where she would see Mitchell in a few minutes. Throwing tradition to the wind, they had breakfasted together. Mitchell ate heartily, Jayne lightly. Her stomach was quivering—not with nerves but with excitement. And now she was moments away from marrying Mitchell Furst.

The iron candelabras on either side of the altar were ringed with roses, a white one for every three reds, on a generous bed of baby's breath. Connor had just ceremonially lit the candles and quietly taken his seat in the front pew, awaiting his father's entrance. Restful organ music wafted toward the hall, classical selections that the organist had suggested and Jayne had quickly agreed to when she heard them. Jayne smoothed the skirt of her elegant, slim champagne-colored dress and checked to see that the tasteful veil had not slipped out of place.

"Little miss, what are you doing out here? How did you escape my watchful eye?"

Smiling, Jayne turned to the scolding Noelle, who was swishing her own colorful skirt down the hall.

"I just wanted to see the chapel before everything started. It's so beautiful. So peaceful."

Noelle squeezed Jayne's elbow. "It's your day, so it's your right to have this moment. It does look splendiferous, if I do say so myself."

"You've done a wonderful job, Noelle. How can I ever thank you for helping to pull all the arrangements together?"

"No need, no need. Getting to know you in the process has been ever so delightful."

"I feel the same about you." And she really did. Jayne felt she had made a friend in her wedding coordinator and hoped their relationship would continue after today's ceremony.

"I've been praying for you and Mitchell."

"You have?"

"I pray for all my couples. I ask the Father to use your wedding day, full of love and excitement, as a picture of the love he has for you. I pray that your love for Mitchell and for the Father will grow leaps and bounds every day."

"Thank you, Noelle. I really appreciate that." Jayne no longer felt odd when Noelle said she was praying for her. The prayers in the church services she had attended had given Jayne a glimpse into the meaning of sincere prayer. Since she was unsure how to pray herself, she took comfort in knowing that someone was praying for her.

"I do have one silly little question," Noelle said.

"Oh?"

"Right now you're Jayne Paige-Hamilton. Are you going to be Jayne Paige-Hamilton-Furst?"

Jayne chuckled. "I haven't decided. That's a mouthful, isn't it? Mitchell says he's fine with whatever I decide. Jayne Furst. Sounds kind of Plain Jane. Mrs. Mitchell Furst. That doesn't sound like me, does it? Maybe I'll just be Jayne Paige-Hamilton with a secret married identity!"

"You're only moments away from your new life, dearie. Are you ready?"

Jayne nodded. "I am. Things have been so great with Mitchell lately. And once the stress of the wedding is behind us, we can settle in and start making each other really happy."

"How about one last check in the mirror before we find your uncle and let your cousin know that it's time to start?"

Jayne dutifully followed Noelle back to the dressing room and touched up her lipstick. Leslie was doing the same.

"It's just about showtime," Leslie said.

"I can hardly believe the day has really come."

"Well … you came to it in sort of a circuitous way. If there's anything—"

"Don't ask me if I'm sure, Leslie. I don't know if anyone is ever really sure about things like this, but I'm as sure as I can be. I know what I feel deep inside, and I know that no one else makes me feel that way except Mitchell. He loves me, and I want to marry him."

"Then let's go do this!" Leslie pecked her cousin on the cheek. "My father is looking quite dapper."

"I'm grateful he agreed to walk me down the aisle."

"Of course he agreed. What did you expect?"

"Ready, ladies?" Noelle prodded. Together they walked back to the chapel. With the doors now open, Jayne could get a better view of the guests. Her family was there, of course, along with several of her college friends. She had also invited a few of her favorite clients with whom she had become friendly and was delighted when she saw them seated toward the back. Larry and Mare sat near the front with their spouses.

Mitchell's parents sat in the first row on the groom's side; behind them sat his sisters and their families as well as his cousin Mason and his son. For a fleeting second, it occurred to her that no one Mitchell knew had come except for his family.

"I believe that handsome hunk of a guy is looking for you," Noelle whispered, as Mitchell came in through the side door. He and Connor took their places at the front of the chapel, along with the minister. Father and son were the spitting image of each other, Connor being only slightly smaller than his father. Jayne could not imagine either of them looking more handsome than they did at that moment in their dark navy suits. Mitchell looked up and caught Jayne's eye. She couldn't help but smile.

"That's right," Noelle said. "You keep that smile on your face. Leslie, it's your turn." The organ music changed, signaling the beginning of the bridal procession.

Leslie let out a breath and straightened her shoulders. Her light blue dress draped her tall figure attractively as she took slow steps to the music. At the front she pivoted and turned to face Jayne. Jayne's mom rose to her feet and the guests followed suit. The organ swelled as Jayne, on her uncle's arm, floated down the aisle. It seemed to her that the moment froze in time. The aisle was short, very short, but it seemed to take an eternity to reach the front of the church and take Mitchell's hand. When she did, she saw the tears welled up in his eyes. That was all it took for her own tears to begin flowing.

They sniffled and choked their way through promises to each other. When the pastor read the passage from 1 Corinthians, Jayne felt a warmth surge through her. She and Mitchell turned to face the small assembly as the minister introduced them as husband and wife. Nearly running down the aisle, they threw themselves into each other's arms as soon as they reached the hallway.

Four days, three nights. That's what they would have together, just the two of them, to celebrate their love. Months ago Mitchell had tantalized Jayne with the possibility of a trip to Hawaii, but being a realist Jayne knew something modest was far more likely. They managed a lakeside resort that was in its off-season, about two hundred miles from home. The reasonable rates allowed them to stay in a luxurious room with elegant rosewood furniture. Mitchell was quickly on a first-name basis with the kitchen staff because of his frequent room-service orders and generous tips. Jayne was once again amused by Mitchell's ability to come into any setting and to take friendly control. She let him prevail upon the hotel staff to indulge her every whim.

For a day and a half, they played the role of honeymooners in the extreme and didn't leave the room. Finally they ventured out to explore their surroundings. Jayne's artist eye delighted in the glimmering colors in the water and the shapes and shadows that danced across the nearby hills. She chided herself more than once for not bringing a sketch pad and pencils.

Jayne and Mitchell had never been away together before—away from jobs, families, schedules, commitments, ringing phones. Their biggest decision during their honeymoon was whether to have an early or late supper. The bride could not have been happier with the temporary simplicity of their existence. When they wanted food, it was a phone call or a short walk away. When they wanted privacy yet freedom to enjoy the outdoors, the lounge chairs in the courtyard behind the hotel beckoned. When they returned to their room, it was tidied.

Jayne held Mitchell's hand contentedly as they spent a long afternoon leisurely walking around the six-mile perimeter of the lake before renting a rowboat on a night with a full moon. In the middle of the lake, Mitchell let the oars go idle and kissed Jayne sweetly and often while they drifted. The lights onshore glimmered a lifetime away. Jayne soaked up every sensation of the moment.

The next day Jayne parked herself in a sunny spot with a light blanket and a good book while Mitchell took advantage of the hotel's workout room. He brought her an overflowing fruit plate for lunch and she didn't even have to get up to enjoy it. In the evening he snatched her away for dancing and dinner at one of the elegant establishments on the other side of the lake. The food was rich, the dancing exhilarating. Unwilling to make choices, they shared four desserts, laughing with every delectable bite. As they drove back to their room, Jayne laid her head on Mitchell's shoulder and felt her satiated body relax more than it had in months. It was nearly midnight.

"Tired, sweetie?" he said softly.

"Mmmm. It's amazing how tired being happy can make you."

"Looks like I should tuck you into bed pretty soon."

"Only if you come too." She kissed his cheek.

"It's going to be hard to go back to the rat race."

"Let's not talk about that. We still have one more day."

After their lovemaking, Jayne stretched out on the bed, her head on Mitchell's chest, and fell asleep. She didn't see the blinking light on his cell phone signaling he had a message.

It was no Excelsior Room, but it would do.

He was thirsty, that's all, he told himself, and couldn't sleep. A walk in the night air would be just the thing to settle him down to sleep a few hours. Mitchell sauntered into the bar, only a ten-minute walk from the bed where he left Jayne sound asleep. He stuffed his cell phone in his shirt pocket.

Flagging the bartender's attention, he signaled for a beer and chose a booth. It was the middle of the week in the off-season, and the place would close in another hour or so. Mitchell hadn't expected many people in the bar, and he was right. Sipping the beer slowly, he leaned back and looked contentedly around. At the end of the bar sat a young man who looked like he should be at his high school prom. Fake ID. Near the door two women, perhaps thirty or so, sat talking. He watched their animated conversation, sensing his moment would come soon.

It did. One woman stood and left the bar, leaving her companion looking bored. Mitchell caught her eye and raised his beer glass. She smiled.

When she woke, he was not there.

"Mitchell? Mitchell, are you in the bathroom?" Jayne got up and gently pushed the bathroom door open. Mitchell was not there. *Maybe he got hungry,* she thought as she peered at the clock. It was nearly two in the morning. Jayne returned to the bed and pulled the blankets up around her neck. *Where could he go at this hour around here?* she wondered. *Was he having trouble sleeping?* She was far too drowsy to think about the question for long and was sure that Mitchell would turn up soon. Cuddling a pillow in place of her husband, Jayne drifted off to sleep.

Two hours later she sat bolt upright. "What are you doing here?" she screamed as the blankets fell away from her. "I don't want you here!"

Beside her Mitchell sat up. "Jayne! What's wrong?"

"Why are they here? Why can't they leave me alone?"

"Who? What are you talking about, Jayne?"

"They're right there," she said, pointing above the dresser.

"Who's there?"

"Them. The ones. The ones who come. The ones—"

"Jayne, I think you're talking in your sleep. It's a dream. Lie down and go back to sleep."

She shook her head vigorously. "No, it's no dream. Can't you see them? How can you not see them? There're so many of them."

Mitchell rubbed his forehead and looked around the room. "I don't see anything, Jayne. It's just the two of us. We're on our honeymoon, remember?"

The being grinned, of course, as the growing entourage began to dance on the ever-enlarging shelf.

"Go away!" she insisted. Still it grinned. "Mitchell, turn on the light!"

"Jayne, I think you should just lie down."

"Turn on the light, Mitchell!"

He snapped it on. The shelf disappeared.

Jayne was breathing heavily. Mitchell wrapped her in his arms and held her tightly.

"You'll be all right. It's just a nightmare. Shhh." He smoothed her hair with one hand.

"Mitchell, you don't understand—"

"Shhh. We'll talk about it tomorrow. Just try to relax and get back to sleep."

Gradually her breathing became more even. Mitchell's heartbeat pulsed in her ear, comforting her like a puppy with a ticking clock. She did not want to let go of him. What could she say to him in the morning so that he would understand? She had kept this secret from him all these months, always hoping that it would go away. She reminded herself that she was no longer alone. Maybe if Mitchell knew about them and shared her bed every night, they would stop coming. She did not want them. She wanted only Mitchell.

~ 23 ~

"Married three months and still girlishly giddy," Leslie said, shifting her shopping load in her arms. "I think we've established that marriage is fabulous."

"You think I'm talking too much, don't you?" Jayne said smiling. "I don't care. I'm a happy new bride and it's my right to torture you with it."

"I'm glad to know your husband will still allow you to shop with me."

"Don't be a doofus."

"What's he up to today?"

"He took Connor to the batting cages. Gotta stay in shape during the off-season, you know. It's hard to believe it's the end of January already. Spring training is just around the corner."

Leslie shifted her load once again as they strolled across the mall parking lot. "How come I bought so much more than you this time?"

"I spent a small fortune on stuff for the wedding and honeymoon. And then Christmas came along. I had to draw the line somewhere."

"You're not going on that budget kick again, are you?" Leslie teased.

"Maybe. Here's my car. Where did you park?"

"Farther over."

"Do you want to go into town for some lunch?" Jayne asked as she tossed her purse and small package onto the passenger seat.

"Sorry, can't. I promised my mom I'd do an errand for her. Then I have to be out at her place 'in the country' by three."

"Why did they move way out there, anyway?"

"The leisure life of the gentleman farmer, I suppose."

"Tell your mom hi," Jayne said lightly.

"Call me."

"I will."

Leslie trudged through the melting snow to her car and spilled her load onto the backseat. Twenty minutes later she parked in an obscure strip mall on the other side of town. Several of the shops had stood vacant for more than a year with windows displaying large "Space Available" signs. But a quilt shop, a restaurant, and a few other small businesses continued to hold their own.

Leslie headed to the quilt shop to pick up a family heirloom quilt her mother had left to be mended; however, the smells wafting from the restaurant made her check her watch to see if she had time to grab a quick sandwich after all. She peered into the window to check out the place.

Her shock made her quickly step away from the window. Surely he hadn't seen her. Leslie leaned against the brick wall, trying to look casual as she watched, and debating whether to go in. Did she even want to hear what was going on inside? She watched through the glass, following their movements.

Inside the restaurant a young woman dug in a Spider-Man backpack for a favorite truck while her companion tickled the tummy of her four-year-old son—their four-year-old son.

"He's obviously glad to see you. You should come around more often."

"Yeah, Daddy. Play with me more." The little boy looked up hopefully, his brown eyes matching his father's. "Can you come tomorrow?"

"Sorry, buddy, not tomorrow. But I will as soon as I can."

"Why don't you stay for a few days?" the woman whined. "Lately you always have to rush off. You used to stay over a lot more. We could all use some time together, maybe even a weekend away."

"I know, I know," he answered, "but life is complicated right now. This job has me running every minute of the day and night. Appointments come up. It's hard to make plans."

"I thought you said things were going to settle down." She wiped up the ketchup that dribbled down the boy's chin.

"I'm still hoping they will. I just can't say when." He reached across the table and squeezed her hand, fixing his eyes on her.

"We miss you, you know. We both do."

He looked down at his son as he played with his cheeseburger. The boy smiled with his mouth full, and Mitchell playfully punched his shoulder.

Leslie couldn't hear the conversation, but she couldn't miss the familiarity with which the three spoke and gestured to each other, especially the woman when she looked at Mitchell. Leslie put her hand on the door, ready to push it open and let Mitchell have it. But the little boy—he shouldn't have to suffer through the kind of scene her confrontation would create. However, Leslie could conjure no legitimate explanation for why her cousin's husband should be in an obscure café acting so friendly with another woman and her son. More secrets.

Jayne sat on the sofa with her feet on the coffee table and a sketch pad balanced against her knees. A small photograph of Connor in his baseball uniform was taped to the top of her pad. Her tongue peeked out of the left corner of her mouth as it always did when she was intent on a drawing. The charcoal pencil drawing would be a great thank-you gift to Connor for submitting to wearing a suit for the wedding. Realistically, he would probably outgrow the suit before he had another occasion to wear it. But he would always have a baseball uniform, she was sure of that. So that was how she wanted to capture him.

A rap on her front door startled her. She caught herself just before the stray mark met the paper. Carefully she set the pad on the coffee table as the knocking became more urgent.

"I'm coming, I'm coming." Jayne opened the door and her cousin charged in. "Well, hello to you, too."

"This is no time for pleasantries, Jayne. You'd better sit down."

Jayne's eyes widened. "Is Aunt Beth all right?"

"She's fine. I ran that errand for her. But something happened while I was doing it."

"Are *you* all right, Leslie?"

"Please sit down, Jayne."

"You're making me really nervous."

"I don't feel so great myself."

"Get to the point, please." Jayne sat on the edge of the couch in front of the sketch.

"You remember Grandmother's double-wedding-ring quilt, right?" Leslie sat in the chair directly across from Jayne and looked her squarely in the eye.

"Yes."

"Well, Mom found a quilt shop that was willing to try to repair it. She wanted me to pick it up on my way out to see her."

"So ... did something happen to the quilt?"

"No, Jayne, the quilt is fine. But next to the quilt shop is a restaurant, just a small café really. Hardly more than a hole in the wall. I looked in the window as I passed by, and I saw Mitchell."

"Mitchell? But he's at the batting cages with Connor."

Leslie shook her head. "Maybe he went there this morning, but that's not where he was a little while ago. He was at that restaurant, and he wasn't alone. I wanted to go in and smack him!"

"Leslie!"

"Jayne, your husband was sitting in a booth with a woman and a little boy. Does that not set off any alarms for you?"

"Did you go in?"

"No. For the kid's sake."

"Then you can't be sure it was Mitchell. You were looking through glass with the glare of the sun—"

"It was Mitchell, Jayne."

Jayne sank back into the sofa and sighed. "Maybe she's a client."

Leslie shook her head. "I don't think even Mitchell would be that cozy with a client. I think that little boy is his, Jayne."

"But—"

"I know, you're going to say that after keeping Connor a secret from you, he came clean. And then there was Shelbi, and he promised he had told you everything. He was very convincing at the wedding about how he feels about you with all those tears."

"He loves me!" Jayne lurched forward on the sofa.

"Maybe. But he's not telling you the truth."

"I don't believe it." Jayne's jaw locked in determination.

"How can you say that, Jayne? After all you've been through?"

"That's the point, we've been *through* it. We're in a different place now. We want the same thing from this marriage. The last three months have been wonderful. 'Love keeps no record of wrongs.' That's what we said at our wedding."

"That's a lovely poetic phrase, but this is real life. *Your* life. Considering his track record, you can't put your head in the sand about this."

"I at least owe him a chance to explain."

Leslie scoffed. "I'd like to hear that explanation! This time you should have someone with you when you confront him."

"I'm not so sure about that. You're not exactly handling it calmly."

"I can't believe you're not more upset than you are."

Jayne put her hands over her eyes. "I'm not sure what to believe at the moment."

"When did he say he would be home?"

"He wasn't sure. He was going to call. He said maybe he and Connor and I would go out to dinner together."

"Has he called?"

"No, but it's only four. Mitchell never eats before seven."

"Don't let this sit, Jayne. As soon as Connor is gone, you have to talk to Mitchell."

Jayne nodded mutely.

"Promise me, Jayne."

Unconvinced, Leslie left. Jayne settled in to wait.

The phone finally rang.

"Hi, babe."

"Hi, Mitchell. Where are you?"

"Having dinner with Connor."

"I thought I was supposed to join you."

"I didn't think we had actually decided that."

"I could meet you now."

"Nah, we're way out of town. We've already ordered. We'd be done eating by the time you got here. Why don't you just have your favorite popcorn and spinach soufflé dinner, and I'll bring you dessert?"

"Okay." Jayne worked hard to keep her voice steady. "I'm kind of tired anyway."

"So get comfortable and don't worry about us."

"When will you be home?"

"I'm not sure. That depends on what Connor feels like doing. We may catch a movie or something. And then I might go work out."

"But we haven't seen each other all day."

"I know, sweetie, but we have all day tomorrow."

She let it go. "Say hi to Connor for me."

"Sure will. Love you."

"Love you, too."

Jayne put the phone down and glanced at the drawing in progress. After Leslie's departure, she had forced herself to go back to work on it and was satisfied with how it was shaping up. Connor looked happy, as he usually did in real life. Fleetingly Jayne wondered how much Connor knew about his father's past. On an impulse she picked up the phone and dialed.

"Rachelle?"

"Jayne? Is that you?"

"Yeah. Just wanted to let you know I heard from Mitchell, and he and Connor are going to hang out for a while longer. Maybe go to a movie."

"When did you talk to Mitchell?"

"Just a few minutes ago."

The silence was deafening. Jayne's pulse quickened.

"Rachelle, what's going on?"

"Jayne, Mitchell dropped Connor off before lunch, and now he's at a friend's to spend the night."

Jayne started to shake.

"Are you all right, Jayne?"

"Fine. I must have misunderstood Mitchell."

"Jayne, be careful. And don't doubt yourself."

"I'm sorry I disturbed you. Good night."

He didn't answer his cell phone. She dialed the number three times. When she heard him come in at eleven, she burrowed under the covers and feigned sleep.

~ 24 ~

Larry was gone for the day on Friday and Jayne was grateful for the solitude as the afternoon waned. When she worked alone, she focused on her project and shut out the world—both the outside world and her own inner world. Designing her latest book-cover project occupied and challenged her mind, allowing her to forget for hours at a time the news Leslie had brought on Saturday and the difficult days since.

When she had woken on Sunday and padded into the kitchen, she saw a hefty piece of double-chocolate rum cake in a plastic restaurant container in the middle of the kitchen table. Mitchell had brought her the dessert he had promised, something that should have made her appreciate his thoughtfulness. Instead it reminded her of the confusion and questions of the evening before. Jayne considered the container. It was generic, revealing nothing about what establishment it might have come from.

Though it was Sunday, she opted not to go to church. It was already getting late, and Mitchell was showing no sign of waking up. Over the past three months, she had gone to church erratically; Mitchell had only gone twice.

As she reached in the refrigerator for the orange juice, Jayne steeled herself for the reality that she was going to have to talk to Mitchell about what Leslie had observed. But what was the right approach? Why should she have had any qualms that he was telling the truth in the first place? If she hadn't called Rachelle, her fleeting doubts might have passed, and she would have let the warmth of his love surround her even as she sat sketching alone.

But she had called Rachelle. Mitchell would certainly think she had been checking up on him and demand to know why. Jayne had been in enough scraps with him to know how skilled he was at dominating the argument and making her feel as if she were the offending party. She didn't want to feel that; she would have to pick her time and place carefully.

Their Sunday had passed peacefully with brunch out, several games of racquetball, making a mess of the Sunday paper, and taking a nap before dinner, none of which required a great deal of conversation. They shared the piece of chocolate rum cake late in the evening. Mitchell rambled on about what the week would be like with appointments and business meetings and declared that they both needed an early night. Atypically for Mitchell, he was in bed before eleven.

Monday morning threw them into the usual weekly whirlwind. Mitchell kissed Jayne's forehead and was out of the house before she was even out of bed. Jayne had several deadlines and planned to work through lunch the next few days. On a few days Mitchell met her for a midmorning coffee break in the shop below her office, but neither of them felt like they could stay very long. Too bushed to cook, Jayne stopped off for take-out food several evenings in a row. Mitchell was attentive and home every evening, reaching for her in the dark. Once again, Jayne was troubled by trying to reconcile the Mitchell who held her and slept beside her each night with the man who kept secrets.

Above all, though, she knew she was in love with Mitchell Furst.

On Thursday, she planned to meet Noelle at Peace Chapel after work. Noelle had been impressed with the wedding invitation that Jayne had designed and recommended her to another couple who wanted a custom invitation. Jayne had worked up two options and was ready to present them. Meeting at Peace Chapel seemed convenient because the couple was meeting Noelle at the church anyway. In the solitude of the late afternoon, Jayne placed the two designs between tracing paper and inserted them in a protective envelope.

Jayne was the first to arrive at Peace Chapel. The lights were off and the doors closed. Opening the doors and bypassing the light switches, Jayne slowly walked up the center aisle and sat in a pew about midway up. She had not entered the chapel since her own wedding more than three months ago.

She pictured it as it was that day, candlelit, wrapped in the fragrance of roses, the organ swelling, and Mitchell waiting for her with tears in his eyes.

He did love her. She was sure of that. Maybe he just didn't know how to express it in all the ways she expected—the ways that her own parents had expressed their love and trust for each other.

She heard the words of 1 Corinthians 13 ring in her head. "Love is patient, love is kind. It does not envy, it does not boast, it is not proud. It is not rude, it is not self-seeking, it is not easily angered, it keeps no record of wrongs. Love does not delight in evil but rejoices with the truth. It always protects, always trusts, always hopes, always perseveres."

I've got plenty to learn about love, she thought. *It could take a lifetime to understand what those words mean. Leslie is wrong. They are not just poetic phrases. They are about real life. I just have to figure out how it all fits together.*

The steps on the carpet behind her made so little sound that Jayne did not hear Noelle approach until she touched her shoulder. The older woman sat in the bench behind her and leaned over the back of Jayne's pew.

"You're sitting here in the dark all alone. Praying?"

Jayne shook her head. "Not exactly. Thinking."

"Joe and Tammy just called and said they're running a little late," Noelle said quietly. "We have a few minutes. Anything you want to talk about?"

Jayne shifted so she could look at Noelle. She forced a smile. Noelle wasn't pushing, simply inviting. She waited patiently through the silent moments.

"I guess Mitchell and I are having some trouble adjusting to living together," Jayne finally said.

"Most couples do."

"I know. But I don't mean like who puts the cap on the toothpaste or who should take out the trash. It's more than that. I love Mitchell, and I know he loves me. But ..."

"But love is not enough?"

"I want it to be. I think about those verses from First Corinthians. If we could love like that, wouldn't love be enough?"

"Honey, that's God's kind of love. It goes against our own ways. God wants us to love that way, but it's not as easy as reading the words."

"Things keep getting in the way. If love keeps no record of wrongs and always trusts, why do I have the questions I have about Mitchell?"

"Dearie, I don't know what your questions are, and you don't have to tell me. But I want you to know that nothing is beyond the power of God's love. Whatever your problem is, God's love can take care of it."

Jayne was silent, so Noelle continued softly.

"I once knew a girl who had a baby when she was sixteen. She loved that little baby boy more than anything in the world. But a lot of things got in the way of that love, like you said. She didn't do a very good job taking care of him. This girl was pretty messed up herself, hanging with the wrong crowd, drinking, shooting up. She tried to get it together after the baby was born, but it was too hard. Her hurts were too deep. One day she left that little baby alone all day and all night. The neighbors heard him wailing and called the police. They took the baby away, took him to someone who could take care of him.

"Now that girl woke up fast. She had just lost the only thing that mattered to her. She couldn't make anyone understand how much she loved her son and how much she didn't want to keep making the mistakes she was making. They wouldn't let her have her baby back, but she was determined that some day she would be a fit mother and they would have to give him back. So she got into a program, got her GED, got a steady job. Finally they let her have some visits, as long as someone else was there too. Trouble was, when she saw him, she would just feel sad all over again and go back to making mistakes and have to get cleaned up all over again.

"It took a long time to get her life together. Years, really. By that time, her little boy was seven years old and had been in the same foster home all that time. He was lucky he didn't get bumped around. These were really good people, and they wanted to adopt him. She watched them in the park with the little boy when no one knew she was looking. This girl knew what they were like. They loved that little boy and took really good care of him. And he loved them. She could see it in the way he ran to them, the way he wrapped his arms around his foster mom's neck, the way he called to her when he fell and scraped his knee. When the lawyer said they wanted to adopt him, she faced the hardest decision of her life. Because she loved that little boy too. She wanted him back in her arms. She wanted to be the one he ran to. But she wasn't. He hardly knew her.

"Finally she decided that if she really loved him, she would give him up. It broke her heart. But she did it. She signed the papers giving up her parental rights. Then she went back on the bottle for almost a year. She didn't think the hurting would ever stop, even though she knew she did the right thing. But healing did come. Wholeness came. And she finally understood who she was."

"That was you, wasn't it?" Jayne finally asked.

"Yes, honey, it was. Love is not easy. It's a lot of work. But in the end, love is what brings healing. God's love heals those deep hurts."

"Did you ever see him again?"

"When he grew up, he wanted to find me. He's married and has two children of his own. He sends pictures once in a while."

"He loves you now?"

"He was curious."

"Does he blame you?"

"Happily, no. He loves his parents. He believes me when I say it was hard to give him up, but the way he sees it, my giving him up saved him from a lot of grief. He would be a different man today if I had gotten him back. And he's really proud of the man he is—and so am I. He's a good parent. His kids have a good life, a stable family, because I loved him enough to give him up. Love has long-reaching arms."

"Noelle, you've had so much pain. The problems I deal with are nothing in comparison."

"I don't tell you my story so that you'll feel sorry for me or scold yourself for feeling bad. I tell it so you'll know that God's redeeming love really does bind all wounds. Jesus didn't die in vain."

"Well, at least your life got better after that."

"Not for a very long time, dearie, a very long time. But God was patient with my willfulness; he was kind in my distress. When I was ready to face up to him, he kept no record of wrongs."

"You're so full of hope, probably the most hopeful person I've ever met. Most people with your story would feel like all hope is gone. But you love life, every minute of it. It's amazing."

Noelle smiled. "You're really close."

"Close to what?"

"Believing, my good friend."

Jayne was speechless.

"Do you have a Bible at home?" Noelle asked.

Jayne nodded, remembering the Bible with the colorful cover that Mitchell read from time to time.

"Go home tonight and find the book of First John. It's in the New Testament, toward the back. Read it, and then maybe we can talk again."

"I will," Jayne said softly and meant it.

Footsteps in the hall drew their attention to the doors, which Noelle had propped open.

"Ah, Joe and Tammy have arrived," Noelle said cheerfully, and she moved to greet them. "Another lovely couple who want to bind themselves together. We're going to get God in the middle of you, don't forget. This is Jayne Paige-Hamilton, the artist I told you about. I just know you're going to love what Jayne has to show you."

Jayne laughed. "You haven't even seen it yet yourself."

"I have faith, honey."

~ 25 ~

The weekend came again. Rachelle dropped Connor off on Saturday morning before Jayne even realized that Mitchell was up. As the front door slammed shut, Jayne woke to the aroma of breakfast. Mitchell was already in the middle of fixing waffles, bacon, eggs, and juice. She heard him greet Connor and lay in bed a few minutes listening to the murmur of their voices, Connor's pitch rising in exuberance, probably about a baseball game.

As Jayne stumbled into the kitchen still rubbing the sleep out of her eyes, she observed that Mitchell had fixed enough food for a football team. But she knew the Furst men would make it all disappear and leave only the evidence of the cooling waffle iron. Mitchell greeted her with a kiss and Connor with a grin as he stuffed half a waffle in his mouth.

An hour later they had left. Mitchell had dutifully cleaned up the kitchen and, as Jayne had suspected, no leftovers remained. She had nabbed one waffle and two strips of bacon before Mitchell and Connor inhaled the heap of food on the kitchen table.

Leslie was spending the day with her mother, so Jayne was on her own, a rare event for a Saturday morning. She stayed in her bathrobe, flipping idly through magazines until late morning, and then indulged in a long, soothing shower. As she shampooed and rinsed her hair, she tried to remember what Mitchell had said he and Connor were doing today. Sports, no doubt, then perhaps the video arcade, where Mitchell could spend hours that took about twenty years off his age. He had promised he would be home by midafternoon because Connor was going to a laser-tag birthday party.

Jayne toweled her hair dry and dressed in her oldest, softest jeans and sweatshirt. She glanced out the window, longing for spring. A day to herself would be a perfect time to drowse in a chaise lounge in the sun, but the mid-February air was still too nippy. As she considered her indoor options versus a growing list of errands, she saw the mail truck ease away from her driveway and on to the next bungalow. In her bare feet Jayne scampered outside. Three mail-order catalogs—how did she manage to get on so many mailing lists?—the phone bill, an ad from an appliance store she had never entered, and a pale pink envelope. Once inside Jayne let the rest of the mail drop to the table and fingered the envelope.

"E. Furst" it said in the upper left corner. It was addressed to Mitchell. The postmark was from two states away, two days ago. E. Furst. E. Furst? Jayne racked her brain trying to remember if Mitchell had any relatives out of state with a first name beginning with E. She came up blank over and over again. The handwriting and stationery were distinctly feminine. Jayne glanced again at the rest of the mail. Nothing else had Mitchell's name on it. In fact, she realized, in the months since their wedding, Mitchell had not received any personal mail at her address. She assumed he was still picking up mail at his parents' and had just not gotten around to putting in an address change with the post office.

So why did he get this letter?

How would someone who didn't know Jayne know that Mitchell would receive a letter sent to this address?

Who was E. Furst, and how did she—and it was a "she"—get this address?

Jayne slipped the envelope into her purse and pulled a jacket out of the front closet. Suddenly it was urgent that her day be fully occupied, until midafternoon. She had to get out of the house.

Connor whacked the ball solidly and gleefully watched it clang against the far side of the batting cage.

"That would have cleared center field," his father said. "Betcha can't do that again."

"We'll see about that!" Connor swung at the next automatic pitch, slamming it even harder than the previous one. "A homer to right field."

"You're just trying to show off."

"I can't help it if I'm a better ballplayer than my old man."

"Whoa. Watch your choice of adjectives." Mitchell swatted playfully at his son. "Let's hit for about another ten minutes, then hit the arcade."

"What's the rush?"

"I know you wanted to do both before your party."

"But the party's not till four."

"Right, but I have to check on the house I'm watching."

"Aw, Dad!"

"Sorry, Connor, but I've put it off for too many days already."

"Can't I come with you?"

Mitchell shook his head. "You know the answer to that."

Connor sighed. "Okay. Then I'd rather just stay here and hit."

"Fine by me. That'll give me a chance to prove myself." Mitchell squared off with his bat, ready for the pitch.

When Jayne pulled into the driveway a little after three, she saw Mitchell's truck. As she got out of her car, she reached in her purse and fingered the slim envelope. She forced out a deep breath and reached for the dry cleaning she had picked up and the sack from the drugstore.

Mitchell was sprawled on the couch with a magazine. "Hey, babe!" He sat up and looked at her cheerfully.

"Hi." Jayne paused to hang the dry cleaning in the front closet. "How was everything with Connor?" she called over her shoulder, hoping she sounded nonchalant.

Mitchell followed her into the kitchen. "The little punk thinks he can outhit me." He squeezed her shoulders and kissed the back of her neck.

"Well, he can, can't he?" Jayne began unpacking the bag.

"Don't rub it in."

Jayne shrugged off her jacket, letting it drop to a chair. "Mitchell, I'd like to talk about something."

"Sure, babe. What?"

"Let's sit down."

"You look entirely too serious." Mitchell sat in a chair across from Jayne.

"Well, it is something serious."

"Are you okay? Not sick or anything."

"Nothing like that." Jayne reached into her purse and pulled out the pink envelope and slid it toward him partway across the table. Her fingers remained on the envelope. "This came for you today."

Mitchell wrinkled his forehead as he looked at the envelope. He did not reach for it. He shook his head, puzzled. "What is it?"

"A letter, obviously. From an E. Furst."

"E. Furst?"

"Who is that, Mitchell? I can tell from the writing it's a woman."

"I'm not really sure. I guess it could be my cousin's ex-wife."

"Your cousin Mason?"

Mitchell nodded.

"I thought Mandy was his ex. Haven't they broken up and gotten back together several times?"

"Right."

"Mandy doesn't start with an E, Mitchell."

"Mandy is a nickname, from her middle name. Her name is something like Ellen Amanda or Elise Amanda, something like that. I don't really remember."

It is possible, Jayne silently conceded, *but not even remotely likely.*

"Why would Mandy send you a letter?" Jayne gently moved the letter back toward her side of the table. Mitchell shrugged and stood up. Casually, he stepped to the cupboard for a glass, then went to the freezer for some ice cubes.

"How should I know?"

"Has she ever written to you before?"

"Not that I remember. Why is this a big deal, Jayne?"

"I haven't even met Mandy. She wasn't at the wedding."

"I guess she and Mason were 'off' that week. She's probably just sending best wishes or something." He poured a glass of ice tea and leaned back against the sink looking completely unflustered. Jayne, on the other hand, was barely hanging on.

"Four months after the wedding? And why wouldn't she address it to both of us?"

He shrugged again. "Not everyone is as efficient with etiquette as you are."

Jayne was silent.

"Don't make a big deal out of this, Jayne. I'm sure it's nothing. I won't even read the letter if you don't want me to. Just toss it."

"How would Mandy get this address?"

"She probably filched it off the wedding invitation I gave Mason."

"On one of their 'on' days?"

"I guess so." He took a long sip of his tea.

"Mason doesn't strike me as the type who would keep a wedding invitation. He's not that sentimental, is he?"

"You don't really know him all that well, do you?"

"No, I guess not," Jayne admitted, hearing the steady, accusing tone in Mitchell's voice and looking into his unwavering eyes. She had only met Mason a few times and had never had an extended conversation with him. "Look at the postmark, Mitchell. Why would Mandy go two states away to mail you a letter?"

Mitchell dumped the rest of his tea down the sink. "I don't know what this is all about, Jayne, but I do know I'm not going to stand around and listen to this. You're implying things."

"What am I implying?"

"You have no reason to imply anything. So just lay off."

Jayne pressed her lips together and said nothing.

Mitchell set his glass in the sink a little too hard. "Look, Jayne, I'm going out. Maybe when I get back you'll be a little more reasonable and quit being snoopy about somebody else's junk mail."

"It's not junk mail, Mitchell. It was personally addressed."

"Forget it, Jayne. I'm out of here." Mitchell slammed out the back door, leaving Jayne sitting at the kitchen table with the pink envelope in her lap. She heard the engine of his truck rev up as he peeled away from the curb.

Jayne didn't move for a long time. She had debated all day about reading the letter and had decided she owed Mitchell the courtesy of talking to him first. Now that he had made no effort to take the letter or shown any interest in reading it—well, perhaps she could look at things differently. If he was sure it was harmless, surely he couldn't object if she read it. If it was harmless, she would apologize profusely.

Jayne slit the envelope and extracted a folded sheet of paper that matched in color. After another five minutes, she unfolded the sheet.

You're going to have to face reality one of these days. I have some legal options, and I will not hesitate to use them if you do not comply with the terms of our divorce. The next letter you get will be from my lawyer.

Clearly it was not from Mandy, whose first name Mitchell had probably made up. This letter had no signature.

Jayne trembled, yet could barely move. Short, rapid breaths overwhelmed her as she forced herself to reach for the phone.

"Rachelle, this is Jayne."

"Is something wrong?"

"Did you write Mitchell a letter?"

"A letter? Why would I do that? I mean, once upon a time, maybe, but not now. We talk at least once a week because of Connor. You know that."

"And you're on friendly terms?"

"For the most part. Jayne, you know all this. What's going on?"

"Who is E. Furst?"

Rachelle's silence spoke volumes.

"Rachelle, was Mitchell married another time?"

Rachelle sighed heavily. "I hoped he had told you all this."

"So he was!"

"I'm not sure what's going on, Jayne, but I'm sorry you're being hurt by whatever it is. It wasn't my place to tell you. You and Mitchell seemed so tight, I was sure he had."

You were married to this man, Jayne's head screamed. *You have his child. You could have told me.*

"So who is E. Furst?" she asked calmly.

"Elizabeth."

"Elizabeth? Lizzie? Lizzie! Mitchell's old girlfriend, Lizzie?"

"That's right."

"He told me he broke it off with her because it just didn't feel right."

"Well, I guess you could say that's true. He's the one who walked out."

"But they were legally married?"

"As far as I know, yes. I didn't hear much from Mitchell in those days."

"When was this?" Jayne could hear her own voice rising but was helpless to stop it. "How long ago did all this happen?"

"I'm not sure, a few years ago. Three or four."

"How long were they married?"

"Not long. Maybe a year and a half, and it was always rocky."

"Kids?"

"No, Jayne, no kids. Although ..."

"What? Rachelle, just tell me."

"I have a feeling that Lizzie was pregnant, but Mitchell didn't want her to be. So—"

"An abortion? He made her have an abortion?" Jayne trembled so violently she could barely hold the phone to her ear.

"I've never been sure. But I think so. It wasn't too long after that when Mitchell left."

"Did you know where he went when he left?"

"No one did, for about a year. Then he showed up acting like none of it had ever happened."

"What am I going to do, Rachelle?"

"I can't tell you what to do, Jayne. But I do think Mitchell loves you and he's trying so hard."

"Apparently not enough to be honest with me." Jayne could contain the sobs no longer. She missed the cradle when she tried to hang up the phone.

~ 26 ~

After Mitchell stormed out, Jayne had sobbed for hours before rummaging in the medicine cabinet for some sleeping pills. When she woke briefly at four, Mitchell was beside her, his chest moving up and down evenly. She slid back into a deep sleep almost immediately.

Four hours later, Mitchell awoke her with a kiss and an enormous cranberry muffin.

"What do you want to do today, babe?" Mitchell asked as he set a breakfast tray on the bed.

Jayne's eyes followed him as he opened the closet and rifled through shirts.

"They say it's going to be sunny," he said as he selected a gray pullover that he wore nearly every weekend. "Maybe we can do something outside. Oh, maybe I should ask if you want to go to church."

Jayne still said nothing, trying to make heads or tails out of Mitchell's breezy demeanor. Had the ugly argument been a dream? The letter, had she held it in her hand?

"So? Church?"

Jayne shook her head. "Not today."

"Are you feeling all right?" Mitchell furrowed his brow in concern as he looked into Jayne's eyes.

Jayne could hardly believe Mitchell would ask such a question. Not if last night was real. "Well, I'm still upset."

"Upset? Oh, about last night?"

"Yes."

"Jayne, I think we let that get out of hand. We have to learn not to fight about stuff like that."

"But Mitchell—"

"Come on, Jayne. Let's just have a great day."

"I read the letter, Mitchell."

"That's all right. I'm sure it was nothing."

Jayne pushed herself upright and moved the tray to one side. "Whoever she was, she was upset about the terms of your divorce."

"Divorce? Rachelle?" Mitchell bent over to dig in the closet for his tennis shoes.

"No."

"Well, that's the only divorce I've had." He tossed one shoe toward the bed and resumed the hunt.

"Lizzie is a nickname for Elizabeth. Could the E be for Elizabeth?"

"I never married Lizzie. I told you that."

"She seems to think you did."

"Well, she's wrong. We got really close, and in her mind, I guess we were married. Like common law. But it was nothing legal. I said I would help her out after we split up so she could get back on her feet."

"And did you?" She would match his calm word for word.

"Of course. But she had trouble separating real life from her romantic fantasies. That's why I knew it wouldn't work between us."

"So you think the terms of your divorce means the financial help you were giving her?"

"That's the only thing it could be. I haven't heard from her in years. But if she's still nuts about that stuff, we should just ignore her."

"So you're not mad that I read the letter?" *Slow and easy,* Jayne told herself, *and you'll find out what you need to know.*

"Of course not. I told you it was nothing, and it was. I shouldn't have blasted you the way I did." He jiggled her big toe under the blanket. "Come on, let's get going."

Where are we going? Jayne wondered. *Where are you taking me?*

As she showered and dressed, she had no idea if she could keep up the front that everything was just fine. But that was apparently what Mitchell expected. She just hoped he would stay on his side of the bed that night.

On Monday morning, Mitchell looked for his blue dress shirt with the thin yellow stripes. When he found it in the hamper and expressed disappointment that he couldn't wear it, Jayne promised to get the laundry started that evening. At midafternoon he called to say he would be late getting home. Jayne was grateful. The energy required to maintain a front of happiness and understanding was enormous.

When she got home from work, she dumped her coat and briefcase on a chair, opted not to eat—her stomach was one big knot—and headed for the bedroom hamper. She dragged it to the small laundry room off the hall and dumped its contents on the floor. Mindlessly Jayne sorted the whites, colored, and darks, checking pockets as she went along.

The back pocket of one pair of Mitchell's pants felt a little thick. Jayne reached in expecting to find a wadded-up handkerchief. Instead she found a stack of papers that had been folded several times down to a thick square wrapped in blue paper. She'd seen that color before. It was legal blueback paper. Holding her breath involuntarily, she unfolded the papers and scanned the front page. Mitchell was being sued by a woman named Karen Blackstone to determine paternity of her son.

Jayne collapsed onto the pile of colored shirts, the document falling from her hand.

That was where Mitchell found her two hours later. She heard him calling her name as soon as he came in the house, but she could not bring herself to answer. His steps echoed rhythmically as he moved into the kitchen, then the bedroom, then the study. Finally he opened the door to the laundry room.

"What are you doing, Jayne?"

"Laundry," she muttered, not looking up at him. "I emptied your pockets." Her eyes moved to the legal document.

Mitchell sighed. "It's nothing. I promise. It's an old girlfriend I haven't even seen in years. We only went out a few times. Believe me, we never did anything that would make me that kid's father. A simple blood test will prove it."

"Have you had the test?"

"No, because I don't think I should have to. She can't just go around making those kinds of accusations."

"Have you spoken to a lawyer?"

"Not yet. Why don't you get up, Jayne. It's silly to be sitting here in a pile of dirty laundry."

"I think it's fitting."

"What's that supposed to mean?"

"Look at my life."

"I don't know what you're talking about, but I wish we could talk about it somewhere else. Aren't you hungry? Should we go out to dinner?"

"I thought you had a business dinner."

"We ended up not eating after all."

Jayne stared up at Mitchell silently.

"Jayne, come on. You're being weird. I thought we were over that."

"I don't believe you, Mitchell."

"About what? Dinner? Really, I didn't eat. I'm starving."

"This is not about dinner. I don't believe you about Lizzie, and I don't believe you about Karen Blackstone." As the words came out of her mouth, her heartbeat accelerated rapidly and she could not take a breath no matter how hard she tried.

The next minute Mitchell was beside her on the pile of laundry, sobbing.

"Mitchell?" Jayne's shoulders heaved in shock as she inched away from him.

"I'm so sorry, Jayne."

It was Mitchell's turn to talk, and she would wait as long as it took. She wasn't going to try to make this easy for him.

"I might be that boy's father. I probably am. I shouldn't even bother with the paternity test. My name is on the birth certificate because there really wasn't any doubt at the time." Mitchell reached for Jayne's hand. She snatched it away.

"I want to tell you everything, Jayne. I promise. Everything."

"The truth this time?" *This time? There can't be another this time.*

"Yes, the truth. Nothing but." He swallowed hard. "But you have to listen to me. I haven't told you everything because I didn't think it had anything to do with you, with us. It's all in the past."

"Then why does it feel so much like the present?"

"Please, Jayne, try to understand."

She pressed up against the dryer, her face expressionless, waiting.

"Jared Blackstone is my son. But my relationship with his mother was never serious. It's just one of those things that happened."

"It's a child, Mitchell."

"Yes, yes, I know. I'm sorry."

"So you have Connor and Shelbi and Jared. You've been married to Rachelle and Lizzie. Is that it? Is there anything else you're not telling me?"

Mitchell sighed, propped his hands on his knees, and hung his head. "There's Trevor. He's four."

The child Leslie saw him with.

"And Rusty is six."

The knot in Jayne's stomach surged into her throat. "How many? How many children do you have, Mitchell?"

"That's all. I've told you all of them."

"Five."

"Yes. Five."

"How many could you have had?"

"What do you mean?"

"Have you ever had a girlfriend who was pregnant and you didn't want her to be? So you made sure she wasn't?"

"What?" Mitchell lifted his head.

"You know what I mean." Jayne looked him square in the eye.

Mitchell turned his head away. "I … I … I'm not sure."

"I think you are. Leave honesty out of the picture for the moment. Have you never heard of self-control? Birth control? Having a relationship before you jump in the sack?"

"I didn't do that with you. We waited months. I knew you were different. I didn't want to mess it up."

"A fine job you've done."

"Jayne, please. Try to understand."

"Oh, I understand, all right. Sex is a way of saying hello. You think nothing of doing your thing and leaving the woman in the lurch. Or insisting that she 'take care of it.'"

"You're not being fair, Jayne."

"I'm not? Do you think it's fair to keep all this from me? To marry me knowing that you have all this stuff in the past?"

"That's just it. It's in the past. I know I did a lot of stupid stuff, but I don't want to be like that anymore. I'm *not* like that. I just want to forget about the past and have a future with you."

"It doesn't work that way, Mitchell." She slowly rose to her feet. "I need to know. How many women have had abortions because of you?"

"I'm not sure."

"That woman we met in the mall before our wedding? She looked like she felt awkward. Was she one?"

Mitchell nodded.

"How many in all?"

"Four, I think."

"Maybe more?"

He nodded shamefully. "It's possible."

"Have you ever even been tested for AIDS?"

His silence answered her question.

"How can you say you love me and put me at risk like that?"

"I'm not sick, Jayne. I don't have anything."

"I have to throw up."

Jayne hurled herself toward the bathroom, where she spent the next two hours emptying her stomach and ignoring Mitchell's pleas to let him in, to talk more, to try to understand.

Jayne fell into Noelle's embrace. She had nothing left to say, nothing left to feel.

"Oh, honey, honey, honey," Noelle murmured as she rocked with her arms tight around Jayne. "It's awful, it's terrible, it's horrendous."

The tears flowed, but the lump in Jayne's throat prevented any sound from escaping. After nearly half an hour, Jayne pulled away from Noelle and began to wipe her eyes with the back of her hand. Noelle handed her the tissue box she kept at the end of the sofa in her modest apartment.

"I'm so glad you came here," Noelle said softly.

"I had nowhere else to go," Jayne croaked. "We haven't known each other very long, but I feel like you're the only person in my life who could begin to understand what this feels like."

"I do know what feeling alone and abandoned is like. But I'm not anymore. And you don't have to be either."

Jayne nodded. "I know. I think that's why I came to you. I can't do this by myself. I need the kind of help that you got. But I'm not sure …"

Noelle grasped both of Jayne's hands.

"There's something else I have to tell you," Jayne said, her shoulders shaking. "I see things. Things that aren't there, that can't be there. Things that no one else sees. Sometimes I think I'm losing my mind. How can this be? Marble shelves that are way too heavy for the wall, and these creatures, these beings, they laugh at me, even if they don't make a sound. And I used to just ignore them, but now I can't, and they come all the time. I'm almost afraid to go to bed. Now when I tell them to go away, they don't."

Now that she had started, Jayne couldn't stop herself. The river of fear welled up into a torrent, pouring out of her beyond her control. "Mitchell doesn't see them. He says there's nothing there, that I'm having a bad dream, but it keeps happening. Do you think I'm crazy?"

Noelle shook her head and squeezed Jayne's hands. "There's nothing wrong with your brain, dearie. The Evil One wants to get in it, that's all."

"The Evil One?"

"You're getting closer and closer to walking in the light, and he's using whatever he can to make you turn around and go the other way."

"Walking in the light. That was in that part of the Bible you told me to read."

"You read it? Good. Do you remember the part about the love of the Father?"

"It's a great love. It makes us children of God."

"You got it! That love is more powerful than any creature or force in this world, and don't you ever forget that."

"But, what about whatever it is that makes Mitchell ... so ... well, the way he is?"

"Bigger than that. If we confess how messed up we are, how much we've messed things up, there's nothing that God won't forgive. Believe me, I know that better than anyone."

"So Mitchell—"

"And you, too, sweetie."

"When I told my therapist about the ... the beings ... he just said I had a lot of work to do to discover what's at the bottom of my dreams."

Noelle nodded. "You do have a lot of work to do. Just not the kind he's thinking of. Oh, I'm sure he can help you. God created the human mind, and he's the one who helps us understand it. But there's more to it than that."

"So you really believe these things are real? That I'm really seeing them?"

"I don't have a doubting bone in my body."

"You don't know how relieved that makes me feel." Jayne hesitated. "I've been afraid to tell anyone else, because I knew they would think I was crazy. I guess there's something to ... the way you talk about God."

"It's called faith, kiddo. And you're ready for it."

Jayne nodded.

~ 27 ~

Mitchell paced. It was three o'clock in the morning. He felt an unfamiliar panic. Jayne was different. She wasn't like all the others. He was going to do whatever it took to make her come back. There was more "truth" he could tell her, but if she knew it, she would never come back, Mitchell was certain of that. And there was no reason to tell her. They could move forward from here. He would make no more mistakes, no more slipups in the laundry, no more phone calls to overhear. How could he have let himself get caught like that?

At eight o'clock, he thought about the work day ahead of him. He had some legitimate appointments. An hour later, he called in sick and rescheduled two clients. He sat down. He paced some more. He sat somewhere else. He called Jayne's cell phone every twenty minutes. No answer. No answer.

At ten minutes to eleven, he heard the car in the driveway.

He stood up when he heard the back door open. "Baby, I'm so glad you came home."

Jayne sighed and hung her coat on the back of a kitchen chair. "Mitchell, I—"

"No, don't say anything. It's my fault, I know it is. No more secrets. We'll go forward from here. Together."

"Mitchell, something happened last night. Actually early this morning."

"You didn't have an accident, did you? You're all right?"

Jayne nodded. "I'm fine. Physically. I think. It's hard to tell right now."

"Have you had breakfast? I'll scramble you some eggs."

She shook her head briskly. "No, thanks. Let's sit down, Mitchell."

"Absolutely. I wanted to sit and talk last night, but I understand that you had good reason to be upset. I don't blame you for leaving."

Jayne carefully chose a seat across from Mitchell, out of his reach.

"I'm so sorry, Jayne. You've got to forgive me. I know that seems impossible, but, please, give me another chance." His eyes brimmed with tears that could only be real.

"Yes, Mitchell, I will." She spoke softly but sincerely.

He looked up at her, clearly shocked. "Oh, man, I'm so relieved."

"But I need to tell you why."

"Okay, anything, anything you want."

"Like I said, something happened early this morning. When I left here last night, I didn't know where I was going. For a long time I just drove around. Then I called Noelle, and she told me come to her place. I went there and I cried for a long time."

"You told Noelle? Jayne, honey, some things are private—"

"I had to talk to somebody, Mitchell. I couldn't hold all that in."

"But, Jayne, we'll work this out—"

"Mitchell, please." Was it really beyond his ability to at least imagine that she might feel like she had to talk to someone? If he objected again, Jayne was not sure she could maintain her composure.

He nodded reluctantly and pressed his lips together.

"So, yes, I told Noelle everything that happened last night. She knows about … everything. She didn't try to tell me what to do or how to think. She just held me while I cried. And then, when I had everything out on the table, she … I don't know how to explain it, she helped me to see things in a different light. We talked about walking in the light of Jesus, and I decided that's what I want to do. I know it sounds weird. You and I don't know much about the Bible. But last night I became a child of God. And there's a power in me now, it's not my power, but it's a power that will help me … through … all this crud that I can't even imagine how I'll handle. But I know God loves me, and I know he loves you. Noelle helped me to understand that God gives second chances, so who am I to say I won't give you a second chance?" She paused. "Does any of this make sense to you, Mitchell?"

"Well, I'm not sure I understand everything. But I have been reading a little in that Bible that guy gave me in the park. If this stuff is true, it would be really great."

Jayne nodded. "It's true. I don't know exactly what it all means, but it's true."

"We'll go to church on Sunday. Every Sunday. Both services. Anything you want, Jayne, I'll do it."

Jayne sank bank into the sofa with a sigh, or was it a groan? "I won't pretend that I don't feel horrible about everything I found out last night."

"I understand."

"But ... let's see where we can go from here."

"Oh, baby, you don't know how glad I am to hear you say that."

Jayne sighed deeply. "I think I'm going to try to sleep."

"That's an incredible story, Jayne," Dr. Lorimer said. "I can imagine you've been feeling like a train wreck the last few days."

Jayne had almost canceled her appointment. Still emotionally spent three days later, she wasn't sure she could talk coherently about Mitchell's revelations. But she hadn't canceled, and she had told Dr. Lorimer about Lizzie and the string of children.

"Would you mind talking about what drew you to Mitchell in the first place?" Dr. Lorimer asked.

Jayne blew out her breath to gain thinking time. "Well, he was so attentive. Right from the start. He still is, most of the time. There have been some times when I felt like I didn't see him enough, but when he's with me, he's with me. He's bringing me muffins, he's cooking breakfast, he's listening to my silly stories about my cousin. Do I need a sweater, an extra pillow? When we were dating, he always left me little cards in the back door so I knew he was thinking of me even when we couldn't be together."

"I can see how you would find that attractive. Anything else?"

Jayne shrugged. "I don't know. In many ways he's what I'm not."

"What do you mean?"

"He's so confident, so smooth. He knows what he wants. I feel like I have to work so hard to feel that way. Somehow it's comforting to be around someone who does it so naturally."

Dr. Lorimer nodded. "I think a lot of people feel the way you do. Is that how other people see Mitchell?"

"I'm sure they do. When he walks in a room, everyone wants to be around him. It's like he's a magnet. He knows the perfect thing to say to everybody, turns on the charm in a way that makes people feel good. He could have his pick of anyone he wants to be with. I don't know why he picked me."

"And his family?"

Jayne hesitated. "I'm not sure what they think. I mean, they're his family, so they care about him. But there's some strange stuff going on in that family."

"Like what?"

"His dad. He seems like a nice enough guy, but he and Mitchell have this thing. Everybody in the family knows it's there but no one wants to talk about it. When I try, they change the subject. Suddenly chopping up carrots or mixing Kool-Aid becomes really urgent, or whatever."

"And his mother?"

"She wants everybody to be happy. Or at least she wants to think they're happy."

"There's a difference."

"I know. But I don't think she does."

"Is Mitchell happy in his work?"

Jayne leaned back in her chair. "He seems to be. He's had a lot of different kinds of jobs in the past. He got the one he has now a few months before we got married, and he seems to like it okay."

"Is his income steady?"

"Well, I don't know exactly what he makes." In a moment of panic, Jayne realized the absurd truth of that statement. Would any explanation be believable? "We haven't been married that long. We haven't got the whole joint-finances thing worked out. We've just carried on the way we were before."

"So you don't know what he makes?"

"I have enough for what I need. He contributes plenty, like when we go out. It didn't seem important to know what his paycheck is."

"Have your recent discoveries changed your perspective?"

Jayne paused to think. "They make me feel sad. Not just because of the shock of it all. Also because, well, I guess he didn't have everything as under control as I thought."

"How does that make you feel?"

"It scares me a little, I guess."

"Just a little?"

"Maybe a lot," Jayne admitted.

"Do you think other people know how you feel?"

Jayne thought of Noelle and could feel her arms around her again. "Not really. Just my friend Noelle."

"And your other friends?"

"They think I have it all together. I guess that's what I want them to think. But underneath, that's not really true. I can't imagine telling them Mitchell has five children by five different women."

"What's different about your friend Noelle?"

"She makes me feel safe, like I have a place where I belong. She's not shocked by anything I say."

"Then I'm glad you have her. You've been through a significant shock, Jayne. We have to be careful not to minimize its impact on how you feel about Mitchell and how you feel about yourself. I hope you'll keep coming to see me."

The pounding woke Jayne abruptly, her heart instantly racing. She bolted upright in the bed, with Mitchell doing the same beside her.

"What is that? Who is at the door at this hour?" Through blurry eyes, she glanced at the clock—two thirty.

"I'll go. You stay here."

"Be careful, Mitchell."

She knew she shouldn't follow—who knew what Mitchell would encounter? But she did. She stood back, out of sight but within earshot.

Mitchell held the picture-window curtain back an inch and peered at the front door from an awkward angle. Then he moved to the door and opened it, flipping the porch light on as he did so. A young man in his early twenties stood in its glow.

"Can I help you?" Mitchell asked. He stood solidly in the narrow opening he had allowed.

"It's a little late to be asking that," the young man shouted.

"Excuse me? Who are you?"

Jayne inched closer to hear the answer, though the young man could probably be heard halfway down the block.

"I'm Jake." One fist pounded the door next to Mitchell's face.

"I'm sorry, I don't know you, Jake." Mitchell was amazingly calm, Jayne thought. But fear stirred in her—not fear for the moment, but fear of the truth. "Do you realize it's the middle of the night?" Mitchell made his irritation clear.

"Tricia is my mom."

"Tricia?"

"Yeah, Tricia. And don't say you don't know a Tricia."

Mitchell turned his palms up in question.

"High school? Junior year?"

Jayne saw the moment of recognition in Mitchell's posture, even from behind.

"Tricia Remmington?"

"That's right."

"Well, is your mother okay? I still don't understand why you are at my house in the middle of the night."

"Didn't you ever wonder where Tricia was your senior year?"

Mitchell shook his head. "I heard she moved away. It happens."

"Yeah, right. She moved away, all right. To a place where no one would know she was having a baby."

Jayne's heart lurched.

"What are you saying, Jake?"

"My mom stayed away all these years. She lied about her age and made up this story about being a widow before I was even born. But we came back to town a few weeks ago because my grandmother is sick."

"I'm sorry to hear that."

"You don't get it, do you? You're my old man! Mom saw you in a sandwich shop downtown and told me the truth. She figured I was old enough to know. I followed you for two days."

"Just how old are you?"

"Do the math. Junior year to now."

"Jake, I never knew why your mother went away. I didn't know her all that well, actually."

"Well enough to get what you wanted, apparently. I'm living proof of that! You're a scumbag, you know that?" Jake turned on his heel and marched down the front walk and slammed into his car.

Mitchell turned to find Jayne standing behind him, her faced blanched.

"Jayne, you have to believe me, I never knew. Tricia and I, we went out a few times when we were both sixteen. Then summer came and we lost touch. When school started again I heard she had moved. I never knew."

"But it could be true."

Reluctantly, Mitchell nodded. "I went to a lot of keg parties in those days. Stuff happens. But baby, I never knew. She never told me."

"You know what, Mitchell? I believe you. I believe you never knew Tricia was having your baby. What scares me is thinking about what you would have done if you had known. And what are you going to do now?"

That's six, she thought to herself as she returned to the bedroom, doubting that she would return to sleep. Was it really the end?

~ 28 ~

The black truck pulled away from the curb and eased into traffic.

Behind it, a nondescript beige compact followed, the sort of car that went unnoticed.

Inside the rented car, Jayne's hair was pulled back under a dark scarf. The bright late-winter day gave her a legitimate reason to wear new sunglasses. Her jacket was one she had borrowed a few weeks ago from Leslie and not yet returned. Still, Mitchell might recognize her, so she followed a steady and generous distance behind him.

He had called in the middle of the afternoon to say he was meeting a client after work. He would grab something to eat before going to check on the house he was still watching for his out-of-town friend. Despite her intuition that he was not entirely forthcoming, Jayne had cheerfully said she would see him at home later. After a few minutes she told Larry she had an appointment, backed up her day's work, and left the design shop. She walked the half mile down the street to the used-car dealership that also rented slightly used vehicles and picked out the most unassuming one in the lot. She hadn't really known where Mitchell called from. He said he was still at the office, which might or might not have been true. Jayne decided to start there. After a forty-five-minute wait parked down the street, she saw him emerge from the building and get into his truck.

Mitchell's first stop was a sandwich shop whose window advertised a specialty in Italian beef sandwiches, Chicago style. In Jayne's opinion it was more a dive than a shop. And she had never known Mitchell to show partiality to Italian beef. But of course she had discovered a lot of things about Mitchell that she had never known. He was inside for about ten minutes, then returned to his truck with two plain brown sacks. Surely he wasn't going to eat that all himself, and surely if he were trying to woo a client he would do better with a more sophisticated cuisine. When he pulled out into traffic, so did Jayne.

It wasn't long before the truck angled off onto a road that Jayne knew would bypass much of the afternoon traffic and disgorge travelers on the other side of town. His parents didn't live there, and neither did his sisters. In her mind Jayne conceded that it was still possible he was meeting a client, just not likely.

A few miles out of town, the truck lumbered off the main road and down a side street so full of potholes that it barely qualified as paved. Unbelievably it did have a stoplight. As the light turned yellow, Mitchell gunned the engine and sped through the intersection, not even close to beating the red but through nevertheless. A car coming from the cross street honked in protest as its brakes squealed.

Three cars back Jayne had no hope of keeping up. Craning her neck, she tried to keep track of his progress. She thought she saw him turn off to the right. Every other second she glanced at the traffic light. When it finally turned green, Jayne proceeded in the direction she had seen Mitchell go. A street angled to the right, but the main road also veered to the right. He could have gone down either route. By now several minutes had passed and he could be miles ahead of her in any direction.

Jayne pulled into a driveway and turned around, defeated. She would never know where he was going. But she was convinced that he had taken a route that was quite familiar to him. A few minutes later Jayne pulled into the lighted parking lot of a family restaurant. She would have to stop shaking before she could drive farther. Taking rapid, shallow breaths, she tried to think what to do next.

What would Noelle do? There was no question. Noelle would pray.

Jayne squeezed her eyes shut. She had never really prayed before and wasn't sure she knew what she was doing. She tried to think about the words that Noelle used when she prayed. But they weren't special words, just words that said how she felt.

"I can do that," Jayne said aloud. And she did. "God, I don't understand what's happening. But I believe you do. You have to help me know what to do, because I sure can't figure it out on my own. Please, God, help me know what to do, what to feel, what to think. I want to do the right thing, but I don't know what that is."

With a deep sigh Jayne let go of the constriction around her heart. She was ready to drive.

Bennett hoped Mitchell would keep his appointment this week. He had missed the last three.

The psychiatrist added things up in his head once again. The tally always came out the same: Mitchell Furst displayed a long list of classic symptoms of antisocial personality disorder. His life was a train wreck, even if he didn't recognize it. But two questions lingered unanswered in Bennett's mind: Why did Mitchell come to see him? And what was the truth about his relationship with his new wife? The fourth stair creaked, and Bennett hoped tonight would bring some answers.

"How are you doing, Dr. B?" Mitchell asked brightly.

Bennett smiled slightly. "I'm doing well, thank you. I wonder how you're doing. You haven't been here for quite a while."

"I should probably call when I can't make it."

Bennett said nothing. An interesting remark from a man who was supposed to be indifferent toward the feelings of others.

"Well," Mitchell began, "I'm doing pretty well, I think. Married life seems to agree with me."

Bennett raised an eyebrow. "How so?"

"It's really nice to have someone to come home to, someone who I know cares about me. I was getting kind of lonely living by myself, and now I know Jayne will always be there."

Bennett nodded. "Is Jayne as happy as you are?"

"Of course. We both know we made the right decision when we decided to get married."

"Some people have trouble adjusting to being married."

"I guess so. But it's going great for us."

Somehow Bennett doubted that. He'd seen this face of Mitchell many times, generally just before a belligerent rampage of accusations that placed the blame for everything that was wrong in the world on someone else.

"How's your job going?" Bennett asked.

"It's all right, I guess."

"Just all right? I thought you really liked this job?"

"I did at first. But I've got a new manager who is a nutcase. Believe me, he's the one who needs to come see you a lot more than I do."

Bennett forced a chuckle. "Feel free to give him my card."

"I might just do that. He's obsessive-compulsive, or maybe a full-blown lunatic. Just nitpicks at everything, wants everything just so. A guy who's that anal about details should be in the army."

"What sorts of details?"

"He wants to know where I am every minute of the day."

Bennett shrugged. "He's your manager. He must have some account-ability for how his staff spends their time."

"The bottom line is the business we bring in, and I bring in plenty. As long as I keep that up, why should he care about the rest?"

"Have you told him how you feel?"

"I should tell him that he's a nutcase?"

"No, of course not. Have you told him that you feel, oh, maybe 'scru-tinized' is the word."

"There's no point. He doesn't hear anything other people say."

Bennett coughed. "Well, I hope things work out. I know you've enjoyed the job up until now. Let me know if there's a way I can help you sort any issues out."

He paused to see if Mitchell would respond to the invitation to focus on himself rather than his manager.

"I can handle it," Mitchell said. "It's just aggravating, that's all."

"Well, we've talked about your wife and your job. Is there anything else? How is your father doing?"

Mitchell threw his head back and laughed heartily. "That's your favorite subject. You always want to talk about my old man."

Bennett allowed himself a smile.

"I haven't really seen him much lately. He's not usually around when I pick up my mail."

Bennett had no doubt that Mitchell chose the time to visit his par-ents' house very carefully. "Oh, let's just say it's this psychiatric fetish I have," Bennett said smoothly. "I happen to believe a father-child relation-ship is significant. If it goes bad, a lot of things go bad."

"We've been through this a hundred times." Mitchell remained calm outwardly, but Bennett knew him well enough to know what was going on underneath. "Dr. B., if you can't remember what we talked about last time, maybe I need to get myself a new shrink!"

"Then you'd just have to start all over," Bennett retorted, "and the new guy would ask about your father. So you might as well stick with me."

"Or maybe I don't need a shrink at all."

An opening. "Why *do* you come here, Mitchell? Most people come to see me because they're distraught about something or fundamentally unhappy. But you hardly ever talk about anything that's bothering you—except questions about your father. I wonder what keeps you coming."

Mitchell shrugged. "Maybe I just like you, you old buzzard."

Or maybe you're looking for a father to care about you, Bennett thought. "I'm here to help you, Mitchell. That's what I do. I care about you."

"Look, I don't claim to have a perfect relationship with my father. But it is what it is. And it's not as if I'm a nine-year-old kid. I make my own decisions, and he doesn't have much to do with anything anymore."

Bennett nodded. Just what he had expected Mitchell would say. The pain was good and deep.

Jayne closed the mailbox. It had been a long day, and she was ready for a hot soak and a good book. Mitchell had volunteered to stop and pick up Chinese takeout, and Jayne was smart enough not to protest. A bath, dinner out of a white carton, maybe a fire. It sounded good.

Inside the house she flipped through the stack of envelopes. Ever since finding the pink envelope from E. Furst, her whole body tensed as she went through the mundane process of sorting bills from advertisements. Her cell-phone bill, a grocery-store ad, her bank statement, a preapproved credit-card offer, a real-estate flier on a house for sale three blocks over. She stacked up the grocery ad, credit-card offer, and real-estate flier and prepared to push them into the trash under the kitchen sink.

Something made her stop. She transferred the credit-card offer to the other pile, did away with the rest, and turned back to open the envelope. She didn't use a credit card all that much; she didn't really need another one. But as she unfolded the canned letter full of promises and entreaties, she decided to actually read this one.

The credit limit was generous.

She was preapproved.

All she had to do was sign and return the form. The business reply was even postage-paid. A card would come in seven to ten days.

Jayne pulled a pen from the drawer and signed her name.

She hoped Mitchell would not reach for her tonight.

~ 29 ~

BJL062: Long time no hear from.

UNCLEB: Busy practice.

BJL062: Good problem to have. How's your ASPD?

UNCLEB: Still not talking. Says he is happily married.

BJL062: Wife may think differently.

UNCLEB: No way to ask her.

BJL062: Work?

UNCLEB: Mad at new manager.

BJL062: Reason?

UNCLEB: Accountability.

BJL062: Bingo!

UNCLEB: His pattern. Will probably quit soon.

BJL062: And it won't be his fault.

UNCLEB: No.

BJL062: Father?

UNCLEB: Off limits.

BJL062: Bingo again!

UNCLEB: Called me an old buzzard. But likes me.

BJL062: Father figure?

UNCLEB: My best guess.

BJL062: I have female client. Husband reminds me of your guy.

UNCLEB: Help her.

BJL062: Plan to.

UNCLEB: Wish I could help wife.

BJL062: Only person you can help.

UNCLEB: Not giving up.

BJL062: LOL.

UNCLEB: He has cracks. I will get into them.

BJL062: Cannot cure him.

UNCLEB: But he can get better.

BJL062: Mellow with age, perhaps. Maybe too late for her.

UNCLEB: Have not met her. Don't know.

BJL062: Ask to meet her.

UNCLEB: He will say no. Happy marriage. No reason.

BJL062: You can try.

UNCLEB: Will think about it. Don't think she knows he comes.

The stores were full of spring merchandise, even bathing suits promising a slender, golden summer. White sales dared buyers to redecorate for the new season, to start afresh. Out with the old, in with the new.

Leslie and Jayne, however, were scouting out the clearance racks of winter garb.

"This is perfect." Leslie shoved a black skirt toward Jayne. "Dressy, yet comfortable. You could wear it with just about anything. And it's your size."

Jayne took the hanger from her cousin's hand and held the skirt out in front of her. She did like the trim cut of it. Fingering the tag with three orange stickers stacked on top of each other, she found the price appealing as well. But she shook her head. "I don't know. I'll think about it and we can look at it again on the way out."

"At that price it won't be there when we come back through."

"Whatever. I don't really need a black skirt anyway."

"Of course you do. It's a wardrobe basic. Hey, why don't we go across the mall to that little shop you like so much? The one with the pantsuits you like to get for work."

"Okay."

Jayne kept pace with Leslie as they made their way across the mall. They managed to stop in only three stores along the way. Leslie bought earrings and a pair of shoes before they reached Jayne's store.

The huge red-lettered signs in the window said both "Clearance" and "Spring Sale." Jayne perked up momentarily and began shuffling through racks.

"What color are you looking for?" Leslie asked as she attacked the round rack next to Jayne's.

"I'm just looking. I don't know. I don't really have anything in mind." Jayne moved hangers around the metal rod automatically.

"Look at the markdown on that one you just passed."

Jayne picked up the tag. "Seventy percent."

"That's right, seventy percent, and you went right past it. It's even a color you like, burgundy."

Jayne looked at the suit. "I'm not so hot on burgundy these days."

"Trouble in paradise?" Leslie held a red blouse to her chest and checked the sleeve length.

"What do you mean?" Jayne fought to resist the internal alarm bells.

"I remember when everything you picked up was burgundy. Mitchell liked the 'rich' color."

"Still does, I guess. But how much burgundy can one person own?"

"It's about time you came to your senses on that one."

"Guess I'm just not in a shopping mood. No big deal."

"You can still look."

"There's not much point in looking if I'm not going to buy."

Leslie put the red blouse back on the rack. "You're being very weird today, Jayne."

"No, I'm not."

"Yes, you are."

"No, I'm not."

"What are we, five?" Leslie expressed her exasperation by shoving hangers around more roughly. "Okay, so maybe you're not weird, but you're not yourself."

Jayne silently pretended to look at a yellowish green shirt she would not be caught dead in.

"Aren't you going to tell me what's going on, Jayne?" Leslie's voice had softened a bit. "Please?"

"I'm sorry, Les. I'm just thinking about a lot of stuff."

"Duh. Mitchell, I presume."

"Not completely. Part of it is that I want to tell you something, but I'm not sure how."

Leslie turned to look her cousin in the face. "I know I sometimes over-react to things you tell me. I promise not to do that this time."

Jayne took a deep breath as she held her cousin's eyes. "Do you remember Noelle?"

"The wedding coordinator with the wild red hair?"

"Right. We've become friends."

"Well, she certainly seemed like an interesting type."

Jayne smiled. "She is. I enjoy her a lot. But it's more than that. We've had some really good talks."

"About?"

"Well, you're not going to believe this. About God."

"You gotta be kidding."

"No, I'm not." Jayne plunged ahead, feeling more comfortable now that she had blurted out that much. "She showed me some verses to read in the Bible, and I read them. I want God to be part of my life now. I want to be close to Jesus, the way Noelle is. She's helping me know how to do that."

"Wow. Jayne, I don't know what to say. All that joking we've done about Sunday school ..."

"I know. But you have to admit, there were some nice people there. We liked it when we were little."

"Then why did we stop going?"

"Why should we go if our parents didn't? I remember having that argument with my dad when I was about ten."

"Mine went once in a while."

"Yeah, but not much. I think some people who go to church don't really get it. It's just something to do. But Noelle gets it. And for the first time in my life, I'm starting to."

"I see." Leslie twisted her lip in a way that told Jayne she didn't see at all.

"Well, that's all I wanted to say." Jayne smiled brightly. "I think I'm ready to do some serious shopping now. Let's go back for my black skirt before someone else walks off with the buy of the century."

Mitchell cruised the parking lot, looking for a space as close to the store as possible. He had a theory that you could always find a spot close to the door if you took the trouble to look. Most people assumed a space that close wouldn't be available and settled for parking in the boonies.

Consequently, he reasoned, there was nearly always a convenient spot available for him.

As he slowed to pull into a space, he didn't see the older-model brown sedan backing out two spaces down. Mitchell swore at the impact and glanced at the rear of the brown car. An elderly man, clearly agitated, was wrestling with the seat belt so he could inspect the damage.

Mitchell didn't think it would amount to anything. No one was hurt. It was an old car, anyway. If you looked at it wrong, the bumper would probably fall off. It wasn't a hard hit, just a parking-lot fender bender. No one could prove anything.

He backed up, then revved the engine and pulled around the old man just as he finally managed to extricate himself. Mitchell heard the man yelling as he squealed out of the parking lot.

"Hey, babe. How was your morning?" A few minutes later, Mitchell bent to kiss Jayne, who was already seated at the table. "Did you buy anything?"

"A black skirt. It was on clearance."

"Sexy, I hope."

"Maybe with the right blouse." She wasn't planning to wear the right blouse anytime soon.

"I'm starved. Let's see if we can get the waiter over here." Mitchell put his hand in the air to signal for attention. A few minutes later they had cheese bread and peppered olive oil on the table to sustain them until their meals arrived.

"How's your cousin?" Mitchell asked.

"She's all right. She bought a lot more than I did."

"She always does."

"She's a shopaholic," Jayne agreed. "A lot of Saturdays, I just go along for the company."

"I'm glad I married the levelheaded cousin."

"Are you? Are you really?"

"Of course I am. How could you doubt that?"

"We've got some pretty serious problems to wade through. If you hadn't married me, you could just handle things however you like."

"Aw, babe, let's not bring that stuff up now. Can't we just have a nice lunch?"

"Of course." Jayne studied the tri-part dessert display on the table. "What did you do this morning?"

"Connor wiped the floor with me at the cages. Kinda hard on the ego."

Jayne laughed. "Baseball season will start soon. Then he'll have another outlet for his superiority."

"I dropped him back home and did a little shopping."

"You? Shopping? On a gorgeous Saturday?" Jayne feigned shock.

"Man stuff. We have our needs, you know. Then I worked out. Came straight here."

Before long their meals arrived. Jayne studied her husband as he plunged into his meal. He was ravenous despite the enormous breakfast she had witnessed him consume. He seemed a little too interested in his food, a little too eager to make light conversation. What was going on now?

~ 30 ~

"Jayne, I need to speak to Mitchell."

"Brenda?" Mitchell's sister had never phoned the house before.

"Yes, I'm sorry. This is Brenda. I need to speak with Mitchell."

"I'm sorry, he's not here. Why don't you try his cell?"

"I've tried it a thousand times. He's not picking up."

"He must be working out. Or he's gone out to check on the house. That's about the only time he turns it off."

"Well, he'd better turn it back on pretty soon."

Jayne didn't like the way this conversation was sounding. "Brenda, what's wrong? Are your parents okay?"

"No, as a matter of fact, they're not. My mother is a wreck."

"What happened?"

"The police showed up at their house with a warrant for Mitchell's arrest."

"Arrest! For what?"

"Hit-and-run. He hit an old man's car in a parking lot a few days ago and didn't even stay to see if the guy was all right."

"They're sure it was Mitchell?"

"Witnesses. Somebody got part of his plate number."

Jayne lowered herself onto a kitchen chair.

"My mother is falling apart," Brenda continued. "Mitchell has to stop doing this to them. If he's going to live like this, he has to stop using their address."

184

"Live like what?" Jayne asked, starting to tremble.

"He takes them for granted and treats them like trash. Then when he gets on the wrong side of the law, he leaves them to take the heat. It would be better if he didn't go there at all."

"I take it this is not the first time he's had a run-in with the police?" Jayne asked flatly.

"Honestly, I've lost count. But Mitchell is cunning. He always manages to get off. Nothing ever sticks on the record."

Brenda was fuming. The guardedness Jayne had become accustomed to at Furst gatherings had evaporated. Maybe Brenda would talk about things she usually avoided. Jayne plunged in.

"Brenda, I've found out some other things."

Brenda sighed. "It was only a matter of time, I suppose. What did you find?"

"I know that all those pictures of kids your mom has are not children of family friends. A lot of them are Mitchell's kids."

Silence. Awkward silence. "I didn't know you knew about the kids."

"Apparently none of you wanted me to know." Jayne fought to stay in control of her tone.

"It was Mitchell's place to tell you," Brenda said weakly.

"We both know that Mitchell isn't very good with the truth." Jayne wasn't going to let Brenda off easy. "And then there was Lizzie. He denies it, but I believe he was married to her, and he hurt her deeply."

"I'm sorry ... about the way you found out ... that we didn't ..." Brenda's voice faded into wordlessness.

The burning sensation flamed more intense by the second. "Marriages, children, arrests! If everybody in your family knew about Mitchell's past, why didn't you say something to me before Mitchell and I got married?" She heard a wild woman screaming. Was that really her?

"We could see he really cares about you. We thought he had changed." Despite the certainty of her words, Brenda's effort to speak was frail.

"But the past doesn't change! How could you let me walk into this blind?"

"We were never sure it was blind, Jayne. Mitchell didn't even bring you around until you were engaged."

"Well, then, what about then? Especially after we broke up for a while? Wasn't that a clue that something was wrong?"

"Debra and I, we wondered about that. But you did get back together, and you both seemed so happy."

"Ignorance is bliss." Jayne spat out the words.

"We all really liked you as soon as we met you. We could see the difference in Mitchell. It was incredible. You were so good for him. I guess we hoped that Mitchell had been honest and you loved him anyway."

"I might have. But he never gave me the chance. I tried doing it that way when I found out about Connor, and even after Shelbi. But all the others—you all let me walk right into it."

"I'm sorry, Jayne. We're all sorry."

Jayne paused, pondering the question that filled her head. "Are you afraid of him?"

"Well, not exactly afraid."

"Then what?"

"Just … not always sure how he's going to react. It's not pretty if you're in the way at the wrong time."

"So you didn't want to get in the way by telling me the truth." Jayne knew her tone was biting, but she had no regrets.

"I don't know what to say," Brenda said hoarsely.

Jayne reminded herself that Brenda was not responsible for Mitchell's choices. But Brenda had made some choices of her own—the whole family had.

"So what is Mitchell supposed to do now?" Jayne asked, resigned to the moment. "What does he have to do to clean up this mess?"

"The police are looking for him. He's going to have to go down to the station and face the music."

"What are the charges?"

"I'm not sure. But I'm sure it will only help if he goes down there on his own. Do you know when he'll be home?"

"He said he would be here for dinner."

"I'll come over about six. You shouldn't have to do this."

"Thank you, Brenda."

Jayne put down the phone and closed her eyes. She was new at praying. But it seemed like a good time to try it.

She would be sure to be gone by six.

Leslie looked across her living room at Jayne, her mouth hanging open, her breath held in disbelief.

"I can't believe you didn't tell me any of this when you found out. No wonder you haven't been yourself. Finding out about Connor and Shelbi was bad enough. But six kids! Arrested! What will that man do next?"

"I wanted to believe he was really trying to be different," Jayne moaned. "He cried in my lap, begging me to give him another chance. He promised he would be different. All those kids and abortions have already happened. He can't undo them. But this hit-and-run—he could have chosen to do the right thing. Why didn't he?"

"You gotta get rid of that jerk, Jayne. You've only been married a few months. You can probably still get an annulment. Surely you can't be legally bound to a marriage based on lies."

"I'm not sure what I want to do, Leslie," Jayne said, knowing it was not what her cousin wanted to hear.

True to form, Leslie erupted and was on her feet instantly. "What do you mean, you don't know what you want to do? You've got to get away from this loser. He's only going to hurt you. Why on earth would you stay around for that?"

Jayne was silent, waiting for the wave of Leslie's belligerence to pass. She had outwaited her cousin's impetuous fury before. Finally Leslie sat down again.

"Leslie, I need your support. Please let me have your support."

"Of course I support you. I just want what's best for you."

"I have to decide that myself. Maybe you're right, maybe I should get an annulment or a divorce. But I'm not ready to say that yet."

"I don't know what more you're waiting for that man to do. Sounds to me like he's done it all."

"It's not that simple. Maybe I shouldn't have married him, but I did. I married him because I loved him. And I still do." She held up a hand. "Don't say it. Don't tell me how idiotic that is. I love Mitchell Furst. I just do. He's my husband. And I'm trying to figure out what God wants me to do with all that."

"Where was God when you got into all this?"

"He was there. I just didn't know I needed him. Now I do."

"I don't see how God is going to get you out of this mess."

"Maybe he doesn't want me to get out of it."

"That's nonsense, Jayne. If God cares about you, he can't mean for you to live like this. Are you supposed to live through hell on earth before you can go to heaven? Do you get more spiritual points for that?"

"I can't explain it, Leslie. I don't understand it all myself. But deep in my gut, I don't think calling off the marriage is the right thing. At least not now."

Leslie blew out a long sigh and looked over Jayne's head at a seascape painting on the wall. "Will you at least let me help you get information?"

"What do you mean?"

"If you're going to muck around in the mud, at least you should know how deep it is. I think I know someone who might be able to help you find out about Mitchell's police record."

"We don't even know that he has a record, other than this one thing."

"I'd bet his sister would tell you different."

"She'd say he's been in plenty of trouble. But I don't think even she knows if he actually has a record."

"What can it hurt to find out?" Leslie pressed. "You deserve to know the truth, even if Mitchell won't tell it to you."

"It feels so sneaky, kind of dirty."

"You won't be doing anything illegal. How can you make a good decision if you don't have all the information?"

Jayne nodded. "All right. We'll do a little research."

Jayne was back at Leslie's apartment three evenings later.

"Here's the printout," Leslie said, handing her cousin a stack of papers.

It was thicker than Jayne had imagined. Words failed her as she began flipping pages.

"Jack's hunch is that it's mostly a bunch of small stuff, the sort of charges that get dropped if the guy pleads guilty to even smaller stuff. Like when you get a speeding ticket and plead down to a broken blinker so it doesn't go on your record."

"I wouldn't know. I've never had a speeding ticket."

"That's the way the system works. And it looks like Mitchell has been working the system for years."

"Has he been in jail?" Jayne asked, her voice hardly more than a whisper.

Leslie shook her head. "Not even overnight. Looks like he always talks his way out."

Jayne studied the papers silently for a few minutes. "Well, there's a lot here, but it looks pretty trivial to me. Nothing like hit-and-run or grand theft."

"There's one assault toward the back. But it was a bar fight and a bunch of guys got picked up. Jack says the charges didn't stick for anyone in that case."

Jayne flipped to the page. "Twelve years ago."

"Jack says you just have to know how to get this information. Even if it doesn't constitute an official 'record,' the information is accessible. Juvenile records, on the other hand, are sealed. There's no way to know what kind of stuff happened when Mitchell was a teenager."

"I'm not sure I'd want to know." She dropped the stack of papers on the table. "Besides, I did some research of my own."

Leslie's eyes widened.

"He never went to the university," Jayne said flatly. "Not anywhere in the state system. Not one single semester. The registrar's office has no file on him at all. Never even applied. And he never worked for Central Hospital Supply, either, much less for four years. And I'm pretty sure he didn't quit his last construction job—he was fired."

"Jayne, this just gets more and more unbelievable."

Jayne stared at the floor and whispered, "Who is this stranger I've been sleeping with?"

Halfway home, Jayne parked the car on the side of the road. Her hands barely felt the shape of the wheel, and she might have been staring across the Grand Canyon instead of watching traffic lights. Driving was a bad decision.

But she couldn't just sit there. If she didn't get out and move—well, she just had to. Jayne yanked on the door handle and swung herself out of the car.

The spring drizzle did not deter her. She was underdressed for the temperature of the cool evening, but she didn't care.

Leslie's friend and her own research had turned up information she wished were not true, but it was.

On the other hand, Mitchell had given her a wealth of information that he said was true, but it wasn't. Her thoughts tumbled quickly as she walked.

He talks about his best friends. Why have I never met them, or even talked to them on the phone?

No one outside his family came to the wedding. What did he do with those invitations I gave him?

He talks about the countries he has visited in Europe and Asia, but I've never seen a single picture. Who takes that kind of trip and doesn't take a single picture?

I have never seen any of the several houses he supposedly looks after. They can't all be gated communities. Where does he meet people who live in those kinds of houses, anyway?

Jayne's pace picked up as the rain slowed. She couldn't keep herself from breaking into a trot, then a full jog. Puddles, splashes from passing cars, backed-up drainage ditches—she ran through it all. Everything she'd said to Leslie about wanting God to help her sort things out was sincere. But the pain deepened every day, every hour, and now with every step. If she could have kept running until she reached the edge of the earth, she would have.

Mile after mile she ran till the hideous sounds surging from her depths were so frightening she could hardly stand to hear them. The rain started up again, chilling her, soaking her, spurring her on to keep pace with its rising rhythm. She ran until the catch in her side made her stumble, made it hard to breathe, made her want to throw up.

If she could regurgitate her life, she could choose a different menu the next time around.

She came to the town's central square. Perhaps this is where she had meant to come all along. Her father's old office building stood on the north side. The red brick glistened in the rain reflecting the late-afternoon light, luring her toward its consolation, toward the strength that her father would have offered. Gasping at the pain in her side, she stumbled around to the back, to the spot where he always parked his car. The parking curb had a strange name on it now, in half-faded yellow paint blurred by repeated spring rains.

Jayne collapsed on curb, the same parking curb where she used to wait for her father when she was a little girl, where she found the contentment and security every little girl needs because she knew he would come.

"Oh, Daddy, why aren't you here now? I need you now." Her sobbing wrenched her more terribly than it had since Claire died. She wrapped her arms around her head and hung it between her knees.

"Are you all right, ma'am?"

Jayne forced her eyes open and looked up at a middle-aged woman with a red umbrella.

"Well, of course you're not all right," the woman said, extending the umbrella to shield Jayne from the continuing rain. "That was a stupid question if ever I heard one. I meant to say, 'Can I help you?'"

Jayne nodded. "I got caught running in the rain. Could you give me a ride back to my car?"

~ 31 ~

I"I've never heard of antisocial personality disorder," Jayne told Brant Lorimer at her next session. After thirty minutes of telling Dr. Lorimer about Lizzie and Jake and the hit-and-run, the bulwark around her rage crumbled. Defenses constructed to hide the fury she felt compelled to control every minute of her day tumbled with her tears. He had quietly handed her a box of tissues and waited until her sobs abated. Then he simply said, "Jayne, I believe you are a victim of a man with antisocial personality disorder."

"Mitchell is not antisocial," Jayne continued. "He likes to be around people, the more the merrier. He's the biggest party animal you could ever meet."

"A lot of people use the word to mean someone who doesn't like to be around other people," Brant said. "In psychological circles it means something else. We use it to describe a person who chronically lives outside the boundaries of accepted societal norms. A person like this somehow doesn't think that the rules apply to him."

"What kind of rules?"

"Unspoken rules. The sort of behaviors and values that you learn as you grow up in a particular culture that someone from outside that culture might not know."

"I still don't understand."

"How old were you when you learned what a stop sign means? Could you read yet?"

"No, of course not. The shape and color—kids learn what that means very early."

"Right. That's a simplistic example, of course. But it illustrates my point that children internalize certain rules of behavior as they grow up. By a certain age, adults expect that they don't have to keep explaining the unspoken rules."

"I'm sorry, Dr. Lorimer, I'm not following."

"Think about your husband for a moment. What kind of unspoken rules of society do you think he has broken? What values has he compromised in his relationship with you?"

She wiped her nose one more time. "Well, he has lied to me about some pretty serious things."

Brant nodded. "We would probably agree that no one tells the truth one hundred percent of the time, but we do have an expectation in our society that people will be honest in intimate relationships. What else?"

Jayne swallowed a knot that didn't want to go down. "He's been irresponsible about … with all those women … and the children."

Brant nodded again. "We have an expectation of fidelity in a sexual relationship and responsibility for the children that result."

Jayne was beginning to understand. "His sister said he didn't see why it was such a big deal to leave the parking lot that day because the damage was minor, at least in his opinion. I still don't know what really happened. Sometimes it seems like he just does whatever he wants without thinking about how it affects other people. I guess there's a social rule that says we should care about how we affect others."

Brant was still nodding.

"But he's always sorry."

"Always?"

Jayne hedged. "Well, not always. He tells me he's sorry when he hurts me, but I don't think he ever apologizes to anyone else."

"Where does he think the fault lies when something goes wrong?"

"Like what?"

"Oh, a dispute at work, or a misunderstanding about some plans you make together."

"Nothing is ever his fault." She sank deeper into the couch.

"Does he care about your feelings after you tell him what they are?"

Jayne wanted to say, "Of course." But that wasn't true. A silent stillness wrapped itself around her as she reconciled herself to the truth. "First he tries to tell me why I shouldn't feel what I feel. He doesn't understand why the things he does make me feel the way they do. But later, he wants to make up. That's when he says he's sorry, that he doesn't want to hurt me, that he'll do anything I want him to do to make up for it."

"And you forgive him."

"Well, yes. That's part of love, isn't it? Besides, nobody's perfect. Lots of people have affairs and tell lies and cheat on their taxes and all that. I can't believe they all have this disorder." Jayne sighed and looked away.

"Of course not. Let me clarify that diagnosing this disorder is not based on one event or even a few occasions. We look for a long pattern of nonconforming behaviors, starting in childhood or adolescence."

Jayne remembered Leslie's report that juvenile records are sealed. She had no way to know what Mitchell was like in high school. But she could guess.

Brant continued, "A pattern is the key concept here, a consistent modus operandi that says, 'You can't make me.'"

"You've never even met Mitchell," Jayne said. "How can you be sure?"

"You make a very good point. Normally I wouldn't speculate a diagnosis for someone I haven't met. But I have a lot of experience with this particular disorder. And you've come to me for help. Part of helping you right now is making sure you understand the environment you're living in."

He paused, but Jayne was unable to speak.

"I'm going to give you some information to read about the disorder, and you can make up your own mind about what you see. We can talk more about the implications for you the next time you come. What I want you to remember, Jayne, is that you are a victim. You are not the one with a skewed view of the world or of what is right or wrong.

"People with this disorder can be unbelievably charming. They have you in the palm of their hands before you know it. They manipulate people in such a cunning way that makes you feel sure that they care about you. Then when they get what they want the game rules change. You haven't done anything wrong. You are the victim here, and you have every right to feel as violated as you do."

Jayne was crying again. "But ... is there anything ... can he get better?"

"Often there is some mellowing with middle age. The unacceptable behaviors become less frequent."

Jayne blew her nose, not knowing what to say.

"Take these articles," Brant said, handing her a small stack of papers. "If you want more information, I'll help you find it. I've included a card about a support group."

"A support group?"

"For you. To be with other people who know what it's like to be in this kind of relationship. To help you decide what your next steps will be."

Mitchell turned and pretended to look fully occupied with the display in the store window. But he had seen her too late to hide. She swaggered toward him, jaywalking oblivious to traffic with an undeniable expression of delighted recognition on her face. *Why couldn't there be more traffic on this street?* he grumbled inwardly.

She was underdressed for the weather, but a proper coat would have hidden her slinky skirt and long legs, and she would never abide disguising her greatest asset. Mitchell turned and started to walk down the sidewalk in the opposite direction.

"Hey, Mitchell!"

He pretended not to hear.

"Mitchell! Wait up."

He could tell from her enthusiastic tone that she would persist. Reluctantly he stopped.

"Well, hello there. I haven't seen you around the club lately." Her broad smile, so familiar, caused a strange tightness in his stomach.

Mitchell didn't say anything as she sidled in close to him, looking distinctly like she expected a kiss. He stepped back, away from the hand she had put on his chest to play with the top button of his shirt.

"What's the matter? I'm not good enough for you out in public?"

Mitchell remained silent.

"What's the matter with you? You're not acting like yourself at all." She swatted his arm.

"Maybe I don't want to be myself anymore."

"What in the world does that mean?"

"You don't know everything about me."

She laughed. "I know plenty. We've been running into each other at the club for years. I know more about you than most of your other women. I know not to expect anything long-term from you. And that's fine with you, and you know it."

"It's not that simple now."

She rolled her eyes. "Okay, if you want to play this game where we pretend we don't know each other outside the club, I can do that. I'll see you there soon enough."

"I'm not going to be coming around the Excelsior anymore."

"You really have gone off your rocker."

"No, I haven't."

"Then what's your explanation?"

"I got married."

"Married? *Married?* I thought you were never going to do that again."

"Yeah, well, I met someone who changed my mind."

"When did this happen?"

"A few months ago."

"But you've been coming to the club. I saw you there a couple of weeks ago."

"I know. But I'm done with that."

One side of her mouth twisted up in a doubtful smile. "We'll see about that."

"I mean it. I'm not going to screw up what I have."

"Where's the little woman now?"

"I have to be going. I have an appointment."

"Don't I even get a good-bye kiss?" Again, she leaned into him.

Again, he stepped back. "Good-bye."

"See you later, then."

He shook his head, pivoted, and walked down the street without looking back.

❧

Larry had gone out for lunch, and Mare had the day off. The office was all Jayne's for one secluded hour. She picked at the leftover ziti she had reheated for lunch without eating an actual bite.

At home she never knew when Mitchell might walk in. She would have to do this here at the office. Putting her fork down, Jayne opened a search engine and waited impatiently for the welcome screen to load. The search field came up and she typed in "antisocial personality disorder." She gasped at the number of results that spilled onto the screen almost instantly. Scanning the title lines, she began clicking on the ones that looked the most straightforward.

Is Your Loved One a Sociopath?

Signs and Tests of Antisocial Personality Disorder
- Lack of concern for society's expectations
- Unlawful behavior
- Violates rights of others
- Consistently deceitful
- Physical aggression
- Lack of stability in job and home life
- Lack of remorse
- Superficial charm and wit
- Failure to plan ahead
- Irritability
- Consistent irresponsibility
- At least eighteen years of age
- History of conduct disorder as adolescent

Are Antisocial Personalities Bad Guys?

We've all heard about the Hannibal Lecters and other extreme criminals. However, antisocial personality types are not always bad guys. Sometimes they are famous people and leaders of corporations. They accomplish a lot of good with their cunning, controlling personalities. The really smart ones never get caught. The pretty good ones have a reasonable degree of success in holding their lives together before they start to slip up. But they will slip up.

Are You a Victim?

If the person with antisocial personality disorder is getting what he wants, why should he change? He won't. It's up to the people in his life to look out for themselves. Insisting that he change is not usually productive. The people close to him have to learn new self-care skills. Victims spend far too much time questioning themselves or blaming themselves for the things that go wrong in the relationship.

Jayne leaned back in her chair and fought to breathe normally. This was all hitting a little too close to home. It all sounded like hopeless doom and gloom, with no way out. What had she gotten herself into? Was it really better to know these strange words and lose hope that her marriage could be salvaged? What did other people do?

She unlocked her bottom desk drawer and removed the packet of information Brant Lorimer had given her. Where was the card about the support group? Her fingers settled on it at last, and she stared at the phone number until it was burned into her memory.

Timidly Jayne entered the room in the lower level of the public library, unsure what to expect. Jayne had been in this room many times. Her father used to bring her for story hour when she was little, and after a renovation a few years ago, it had become a favorite room for local art exhibits. In her wildest imagination she never would have guessed that she would be here for the reason that brought her today.

Would there be a hundred people or four? In one corner an ordinary brown folding table was covered with a white plastic tablecloth, the sort that comes on a roll at the discount store. Someone had arranged an assortment of store-bought cookies on clear plastic serving trays and set them next to pitchers of ice water and a pot of coffee. A small display of fresh-cut flowers represented an effort toward cheer in the austere setting.

In the center of the room, two women chatted as they arranged chairs in a circle. They were using the new chairs that had come to the library with the renovation—folding metal chairs, but padded. From their effort Jayne judged that they expected a couple of dozen people. She turned away from them and studied her watch. How had she managed to arrive so early? Had she gotten the time wrong? The last thing she wanted to do was stick out.

To her relief the room soon filled. Everyone else seemed at least to recognize each other. More than once Jayne considered bolting before any organized discussion began. The muscle spasms deep in her calves screamed at her to run as far and fast as she could. No one would ever know she had been there. But she had run away from too many realities already.

Jayne picked up an oversized chocolate-chip cookie more to have something in her hand than because she wanted to eat it. A middle-aged woman who seemed to be in charge smiled at her and gestured for her to take a seat in the circle.

I'm sorry, I just remembered another engagement. Jayne tentatively smiled back.

Do you know where I can find the oversized art collection?

Don't let me interrupt your meeting. I'm researching my genealogy, and the reference librarian said there were some old records down here.

Would you mind if I took a rain check? I'm not feeling very well.

Nothing sounded credible. The woman once again gestured, this time more emphatically. Jayne obliged, forcing her feet to move toward the center of the room.

Jayne listened to several updates about members of the group who were not present and sat rigid as the leader asked several to share what had happened to them lately. The intimacy startled her: the details, the names—she was not prepared for it. Her frozen throat made it nearly impossible to say even her first name, but she listened intently.

Some group members, she learned, had left relationships they considered emotionally abusive because of deceit and manipulation and still bore the scars. Others had been physically abused. About half had been abandoned by spouses with the disorder and were still trying to pick up the pieces and build a life for their children. A couple had spouses serving prison time, which afforded them a period of safety during which they would decide what to do. Only two women currently lived with the men they were concerned about, and both were on the brink of leaving. They had to have a plan ready and find the right time.

The leader's eyes settled on Jayne, as she knew they would eventually. A hundred people or four, it didn't matter. She was the only newcomer tonight.

Am I like them? she wondered. *Does Mitchell really have this disorder? This can't be true. Wake up, Jayne.*

Jayne cleared her throat and began. She told her story, oddly keeping the tears in check. A bizarre detachment flowed through her tone. It was as if she were talking clinically about someone else, telling an unbelievable story that no one could possibly live through. Something from a supermarket tabloid or a scandalous movie. Yet she was in a room full of people who had done just that—lived through it.

Group members passed her their phone numbers. Call anytime day or night, they said. If you feel in danger, call. If you need help leaving, call.

No one said, "Call if you just need to talk."

Does no one stay? Jayne thought. *Is there no hope at all?*

She remembered the words of 1 Corinthians 13. She remembered the word pictures Noelle had painted as she talked about marriage, and Christ redeeming his bride.

I made promises, she thought. *And I meant them when I made them.*

But would you have made those promises if you had known the truth? A voice in her head challenged her. *Is your relationship really a marriage if it is based on lies?*

I love him. I love him. I love him! her heart screamed. She dared not say that aloud.

The meeting moved on and after another hour was dismissed. Jayne begged off further conversation over cookies and coffee with a previous commitment—a promise to herself to go home to bed.

Mitchell's truck was not in front of the house when she got home, and she couldn't remember if he had told her where he would be. Did it matter? It probably wasn't the truth anyway. She shut off the engine and pulled the key out of the ignition, but made no further movement. Jayne didn't want to go inside. It was *her* home. She had lived there for years before she met Mitchell, painting every room in soft, calming colors; carefully collecting the knickknacks and accent pieces; finding the perfect bedspread. It was *her* home, and she relished the cozy refuge it had always offered her. But now it was a peculiar, violated place. A place of insecurity, a place of surreal events. And she did not want to be there.

Jayne forced herself to go inside long enough to pack a bag. Remembering Larry, she left a voice mail for him explaining that she needed some time off again. She was very sorry, but it was unavoidable, she hoped he would understand. All her work was up-to-date. She would be in touch.

Checking to be sure she had her new credit card, the one Mitchell did not know she had, she left.

~ 32 ~

In the darkened room Jayne sat rock still. The heater kicked on and, after a first raucous burst, hummed contentedly. Her bag lay on the floor where she had dropped it just inside the door as she slumped into the straight-back chair at the cramped desk.

She had chosen a different motel this time, a place farther from home that had a kitchenette. Though small, the room was tidy and smelled fresh. Her bag was fuller than the last time, and she had plenty of money. If she wanted to, Jayne could stay away more than a couple of days.

The room was already dark when she arrived, and she made no effort to probe for light. Seeping darkness oozed under her skin and into her bones. She had gone so far as to unzip her jacket when the heater came on, but otherwise was clad as she had been three hours earlier when she checked in. The torrent of tears had ceased long ago, leaving her rung out and with a lump in her throat the size of a grapefruit.

By now Mitchell would be wondering where she was. She had left no note or phone message. How long would it take him to realize she was gone? On one level she hoped he hadn't missed her yet. The thought of a generous head start brought peculiar comfort. She had driven far enough, and in an unpredictable direction, that he wouldn't think to look for her here. On another level, though, she hoped he was panicked with worry, that he cared enough to be frantic. *He had been the last time*, she reminded herself. *The last time.* How ridiculous that there was a "last time" and a "this time." How many times would there be? Was this the last, either because she would never go back, or because they would work things out? Would Mitchell discover Jesus too, and together they would find out what 1 Corinthians 13 meant? Or maybe she would stay away and he would forget about her sooner than she wanted to think possible.

All those other women … had he felt anything for any of them? Was Dr. Lorimer right that Mitchell was a master of manipulation? Maybe he didn't really feel anything at all. Maybe he liked the semblance of normalcy that being married to Jayne gave him, without actually having to be normal himself.

"No!" she blurted. "What we feel for each other is real. Or at least it was."

She stumbled over to the bed before exhaustion cast her into a bottom-less sleep.

A stirring woke her; a rustling, a murmuring.

Jayne turned in bed and opened her eyes—then clutched the bedspread around her neck. The room was full. They were everywhere. Hundreds of them, perhaps thousands. They lined the walls and stood forty or fifty deep. It was on the shelf, of course, smugly presiding. They were people this time, not amorphous beings. All sorts of people: bent with weariness, tall with con-fidence, lost in despair, joyful in hope. Why did they despair? Why did they hope? Jayne's heart thundered. Never before had there been so many, never before had their faces been so human, so clear, or the color of their clothing so rich.

When the door opened, Jayne sat bolt upright. Despite her emotional wretchedness a few hours ago, she was certain she had turned the deadbolt and pushed the button in on the knob.

The murmuring rose to a new level, and she heard a wordless anxious-ness that had not been there before. The hundreds of people were slowly parting to make a pathway from the door to her bed.

Wake up! Jayne told herself. *Now is the time to wake up!*

She gaped up at the being on the shelf and tried to scream at it to go away. No words came through her swollen throat. The pathway continued to open. The room was small—tiny, really. How could the path from the door be so long? How could any of this be happening?

Wake up!

She saw it then. She saw why the crowd was parting, why they murmured anxiously. The brilliancy of the glow only flashed whiter and hotter as it came closer to her. But Jayne's fear had fled. Everything in the room faded into a pale gray against the light, mere shadows. Jayne blinked as she sought the source of the moving glow. Then they came into focus. Three of them.

Three ... men? Angels? Her breathing slowed and evened. She had no idea who they were, but they had come to help her. A certainty swelled through her as Jayne swung her legs over the side of the bed and sat up to greet them.

The being on the shelf did not look so smug any longer. Its fury boiled within as a hiss oozed visibly from its mouth. One of the Three looked at it and put up a hand. Instantaneously the hissing stopped.

The Three were wrapped in white brilliance. Not clothes, exactly, but an undulating covering that moved fluidly as they did. Two of them stopped, the hushed multitude behind them. The First stepped forward and knelt beside the bed. His eyes blazed into Jayne's but did not frighten her. How could she feel this balm, this placidity, in the midst of such an experience? But calm she was. In white brilliance at her feet he reached into swirling depths and pulled out a gift. This he placed on the bed next to Jayne. His hand traced Jayne's jawline as he stood and stepped back. Jayne looked at the gift but she could not make her eyes focus. Still the tranquility enveloped her.

She was about to reach for the gift, to touch it for herself, when the Second stepped forward and took both her hands in his. Gently he lifted her arms and stretched them out straight to her sides. When he let go, they remained in the air, buoyed effortlessly by something not visible, but palpable. Jayne wanted to stay in that position forever, never feeling the strain on her muscles. The Second, too, reached into his brilliance and pulled out a gift, laying it on the bed beside the first.

Jayne gazed at the Third as he glided toward her. He did not stop at her feet, but swirled around her, wrapping her in his sheath of light. The corners of her mouth turned up and the sound of her own laughter spilled out as he laid his gift on the bed beside the others. The wretchedness of the night was gone, and she felt a strange urge to sing.

The Three turned to leave. On the marble shelf, the being faded. A moment later, it was gone, shriveled into nothingness. They were all gone.

Jayne woke up.

The room was empty, dark and still, just as it had been when she went to bed.

The room was full, light and joyous as it had never been before.

Jayne sat up and felt on the bed for the gifts.

But they were not there, at least not anything that she could look at or touch.

As morning light seeped around the edges of the window shade, Jayne knew the gifts were real. Though she did not know what they were, gratitude swelled inside her as tears of relief slid down her cheeks.

~ 33 ~

Jayne was surprised when Brant Lorimer answered the phone. She had steeled herself to sound casual as she canceled an appointment with his receptionist. Something had come up, she would say, and she had to go out of town. All true.

But he picked up the phone himself.

"Oh, Dr. Lorimer. Hi, it's Jayne Paige-Hamilton."

"Hello, Jayne."

"I'm just calling to say I'm going to have to cancel my session tomorrow. I had to go out of town and I won't be back in time for the appointment."

"Jayne, is something wrong?"

She had tried so hard to sound normal. But what was "normal" anymore? Jayne swallowed hard while her mind flailed for coherent thought. Explaining to Dr. Lorimer what had happened last night was an impossibility. He would order the straight jacket immediately and fasten it on her himself.

Jayne fumbled for words. "I went to that support group, the one on the card you gave me."

"I'm glad. Was it helpful?" His voice carried a clear invitation to talk more.

"I'm not sure. But it made me decide I had to get away for a while to think things through."

"Where are you now, Jayne?"

She hesitated. She was one hundred fifty miles from home. A thousand miles from the pain she had driven away from. It didn't really matter where she was.

"I'm all right, Dr. Lorimer. I'm not going to hurt myself or anything. I just need to think."

"I have a few minutes before my next appointment. Why don't you tell me about the group."

Jayne really wanted to hang up. Now. Hard. "Well, I guess it was good to see that I'm not the only person going through this. Some of them have been through worse than I have."

"Why do I sense a 'but'?"

Now she really wanted to hang up the phone. She had not reckoned on having to talk about this with anyone just yet. And the support group was just a decoy for the real subject burning inside her. But she knew Dr. Lorimer was trying to help. "I guess because all they talked about was how to get out. No one talked about how to live in it."

"Is that what you want to do?"

"I don't know. But I want to believe I have a choice, that I can decide what's right in my situation."

"Of course you have a choice, Jayne. But sometimes people make choices for unhealthy reasons. There can be great wisdom in listening to the voice of experience in these people. Some stay too long because they think that if they can just get it right, the problems will go away."

"I don't think that. Not anymore."

"Good. I'm glad that you got away by yourself, actually. This may be just what you needed to do to be ready for the final break."

Jayne cringed at his choice of words. "What if there is not going to be a final break?"

"Jayne, I haven't met your husband. But from what you've told me about him, I believe he has a serious personality disorder. He can't help it. He didn't choose it. And it's dangerous. But *you* do have a choice. You can choose for yourself whether you are going to live under its rule. He has already shattered your faith in him several times. He's not really capable of the marriage you want. I think the healthy choice is to get out before he hurts you any more."

It was unlike Dr. Lorimer to tell Jayne what to do so clearly, so specifically. Her experience was that he preferred to lead her to her own discoveries. With images of the night before flowing through her, this was no time to debate that decision.

"Do you believe in God, Dr. Lorimer?"

Her question obviously caught him off guard. "I'm not sure my personal belief system is relevant here."

"I believe in God. I didn't used to, but I do now."

"Religion brings comfort to many people, and there is certainly a place for it in self-care. But—"

"I'm not talking about religion or self-care. I'm talking about really believing in God. There's a difference."

Dr. Lorimer was silent for a moment, perhaps waiting for her to say more. But Jayne had said what she wanted to say.

"Perhaps you should drive back into town for that session tomorrow," Dr. Lorimer urged. "We can talk about this further."

"No. I'm sorry, Dr. Lorimer. I can't make it. I'll call and reschedule after I sort things out a little more."

Jayne snapped her cell phone shut before he could protest further. The icon on the front screen told her she had several voice-mail messages. Mitchell. She ignored it and dialed another number.

"I can't believe you drove all the way out here to see me," Jayne said incredulously as she stared across the table at Noelle. On the phone she had tried to stop Noelle from such rash action, but her friend had already made up her mind. The best Jayne could do was look for a place to talk outside the confines of her motel room. They sat in a chain diner a couple of miles down the highway, a pot of coffee between them and any-time-of-day breakfasts before them.

"Dearie, when you called, I could tell from the sound of your voice that we needed a face-to-face, heart-to-heart, soul-to-soul."

"But I hardly said anything when I called you. I just felt like I had to talk to someone who might understand."

"I'm tickled pink that you picked me."

"Who else was I going to call? My cousin would drag me by the hair to a judge and tell me I could either get a divorce or commit myself to a mental-health facility."

"You do have some colorful characters in your life."

Jayne smiled. Noelle, of course, was the most colorful. "Still, you drove almost three hours to come out here. I wasn't expecting that."

"Gifts are not about what you expect, child."

"Thank you for the gift of your friendship, Noelle." She glanced around the diner. "I'm sorry that I didn't know a nicer place to have lunch."

"It matters not. Jesus ate in the homes of the dregs of society. But I would like to know why you are way out here in the first place."

Jayne twirled her fork in her salad without stabbing anything. "My therapist thinks there's something really wrong with Mitchell. Something called antisocial personality disorder. I did a little reading on it, and it's pretty scary."

"So you ran away in fear?"

"Not exactly. He suggested that I go to a support group and meet some others who've had spouses like Mitchell. You know, a lot of lying, promiscuity, being in control of everything. Nothing is ever their fault, all that stuff."

"So you went?"

Jayne nodded. "But most of them are already out of those relationships, either because they wanted to be or because the men left and they were glad to see them go. The rest are just waiting to get out."

"And?"

"And no one talks about keeping the promises they made when they got married, or finding a way to make the relationship work. I don't mean that women who are abused should stay, but doesn't anyone feel even a little bit of love, enough to make them keep at it?"

"And that's what you want?"

Jayne nodded. "I think so. Am I crazy?"

Noelle was silent, her eyes closed. When she opened them, she said, "I feel in my spirit that there is something else you want to talk about, something far more important than a depressing support group."

Jayne's heart leaped. How could she possibly put into human words what she had experienced last night? She wanted to try.

"Do you remember that I told you sometimes I get visitors during the night?"

"Yes, ma'am, I surely do." Noelle's tone sounded light, but she set her fork down and fixed her attention on Jayne.

"I had some last night," Jayne continued quietly. "But this time it was very different than it ever has been before."

Neither of them touched their food as Jayne recounted to Noelle the details of last night's visit.

"When I woke up this morning, I actually reached for the gifts, as if they were real, like they should have been there on the bed."

"What makes you think they weren't real?" Noelle challenged.

"They weren't. I wanted to look at them and see what they really were, but they weren't there."

"That doesn't mean they weren't real."

"I was hoping you would say that! I can't remember what they were, but I know they were important, and I was hoping you could help."

"You didn't see or touch the gifts, but you felt them all the same. You told me very clearly what you felt with each one even though you didn't see what it was."

Jayne pursed her lips. "I felt really, really calm with the first one. A hundred times more calm than I have felt since this all began."

"God's peace surrounding you."

"Then I felt like my arms would never get tired."

"Christ's strength. He's holding you up."

"Then I wanted to laugh and sing."

"The Holy Spirit's joy bubbling out of you."

"Wow, it really sounds simple when you put it like that."

"Sometimes people make walking with Jesus a lot more complicated than it really is."

"So these gifts are from God, and they're going to help me, no matter what happens from here on out."

"Now you're catching on."

"Do you think this means I should go back, talk to Mitchell, try to figure things out?"

"I'm going to stop short of telling you what to do. It's not time for that just now. But I am going to tell you something to read."

"What's that?"

"Did you pack a Bible?"

Jayne blushed. "Sorry. I'm still new at this. I didn't think of it. Besides, the one at home really belongs to Mitchell."

"Check the desk drawer in your room. I'll bet the Gideons have been there."

"Okay, so what should I read?"

"Genesis twenty-nine has an outrageous story about a most remarkable marriage arrangement."

"But things were different back then, weren't they? Polygamy, arranged marriages, and all that. Are you sure it's going to apply to my situation?"

"You can decide that for yourself. If you want to talk more about it, call me after you read it. Now let's have some dessert!"

Jayne laughed and relaxed. How was it possible that she could feel so good? She devoured an enormous piece of double-chocolate fudge cake with raspberry filling.

By the time Noelle got in her car for the trip home, Jayne felt drenched in gratitude and hope. A part of her brain told her it was impossible to feel hopeful in her situation. It made no sense, but that is what she felt.

Alone in her room later that afternoon, Jayne slid the desk drawer open and lifted out the red Bible. Just as Noelle predicted, it read, "Placed by the Gideons." She found the story quickly and began to read, with a notepad and pencil nearby, also courtesy of the establishment. She jotted down the basics of the story:

> Jacob loved Rachel.
>> Worked seven years to marry Rachel.
>> Was tricked into marrying Leah.
>> Still wanted Rachel, worked seven more years.

Jayne stuck the end of the pencil in her mouth as she thought about the story, wondering what Noelle thought she would see in it. She jotted down more phrases.

> Jacob's love strong.
>> Laban lied. Marriage based on lie.
>> Jacob did right by Leah anyway.
>> Loved Rachel enough to work seven more years.

Love and lies. Lies and love. Those two words bounced back and forth in Jayne's head. How could she have missed such an obvious point? Jacob's marriage to Leah was based on lies, not love. But he still considered himself married and did the right thing by staying with Leah. And his love for Rachel was strong enough to make him stay in a situation where he had been lied to and cheated.

Well, the point is certainly clear, she thought. Jayne tore the sheet off the notepad, creased it in half, and tucked it in a discreet pocket in her purse. Anyone who thought this was a cut-and-dried, black-and-white decision was wrong. How could anyone be positive which side was black and which was white?

A sun-catcher hung in the window. The late-afternoon sun beat right in the window, sending hues of gold, blue, green, and violet streaking across the room. Jayne smiled at the playful power of light in unexpected places.

~ 34 ~

Bennett Grey waited for his patient to speak. The session had gotten off to a slow start. Mitchell had come in with a can of pop and a bag of chips that seemed to interest him more than anything Bennett had said in the last fifteen minutes. But Bennett would wait. He felt sure the window would open soon.

Mitchell tipped back his can of Coke and emptied it down his throat. He wasn't looking at Bennett, and his left foot was tapping, details Bennett did not fail to note. Mitchell's usual self-assured, everything's-under-control countenance had faded into a gray internal muddle he didn't want to talk about.

"Why are you here, Mitchell?"

Mitchell stared out the window at the streetlight that had just come on.

"I just thought it would be good to talk, that's all," he finally said, tossing his pop can into the wastebasket next to Bennett's desk.

"You haven't said very much."

Mitchell shrugged.

"We talk about a lot of different things when you come. Is there something specific you want to talk about this time?"

"Not really." Mitchell forced a laugh. "Aren't you going to ask me about my father? That's what you usually do."

"I'm very interested to know more about your relationship with your father. I think it is far more significant than you think."

"You know what, Dr. B.? You're right. My relationship with my father is totally screwed up. We have never really gotten along. He doesn't care a flying fig about me, never has, and I don't even like being around him."

"That's quite a step for you to verbalize those feelings."

"It's what you wanted to hear, isn't it?"

Bennett raised an eyebrow at the unusual edge in Mitchell's voice. "Is that why you said it?"

"Maybe it wasn't such a good idea to come here today." Mitchell crunched up his chips bag and tossed it at the wastebasket. He missed.

"We can talk about something else. How is your wife?" Bennett asked casually.

"What makes you ask about her?"

"No reason. You've said a number of times how happy you are with her."

"I love Jayne. I guess that's why I'm a little upset today."

Ah, now we're getting somewhere, Bennett thought. "Why is that?"

"Something's happened to her. I came home from work a couple of nights ago, after a late appointment, and she wasn't home. She's always home at that hour."

"What do you think happened?"

"I don't know. I've called all the hospitals and she hasn't been in an accident. That's a relief, of course, but what if she was snatched or something?"

"Is there any reason someone would want to hurt Jayne?"

"Who would want to hurt Jayne? She's ... no one would want to hurt Jayne."

"Does she carry a cell phone?"

"Not answering. That's what makes me think something's wrong."

"Have you contacted the police?"

"I'm thinking I'd better. She's been gone long enough to be a missing person. They could at least look for her car."

Bennett decided to take a risk. "Was everything all right between the two of you the last time you saw her?"

Mitchell's head snapped up. "What do you mean? I tell you my wife is missing and you start accusing me!"

Bingo. Bennett cocked his head to one side. "I'm not accusing you of anything, Mitchell. I was just wondering if she was upset about anything before she disappeared."

Mitchell's foot started tapping again. "Not really."

"Has she ever done anything like this before?"

"Not really. Well, once, before we got married, she thought she wanted to call off the wedding. But it was just jitters like everyone gets. She got over it."

"So you believe she's happy?"

"Of course. I do everything I can to make her happy."

"Can you think of anything that might have upset her recently?"

"Maybe something at work. Or maybe her mom's having a problem. Or her cousin. I don't know."

"Wouldn't she tell you about something like that?"

"We try not to talk about work when we're together."

"What about the other things? Her mother?"

"It's probably personal stuff that she can't talk about without breaking a confidence."

Bennett nodded. Plausible, but not likely. "So maybe she's upset about something, but it doesn't have to do with your relationship."

"I don't think so. I mean, we've had a couple little glitches lately, but nothing big enough that she should leave."

"Anything big enough to make her at least think about leaving?"

"She didn't leave." Mitchell sighed. "Well, something happened a few days ago, but if it made her leave, then she's taking it all out of proportion."

"Why don't you tell me about it."

"It's nothing really. This kid, well, a young man, showed up at our door in the middle of the night. He claimed that his mother was a girl I knew in high school. She told him that I was his father."

"Are you?"

"I don't know. I could be, I guess. We only went out a few times. She moved away. I never knew she was pregnant."

"How did Jayne react?"

"She wasn't real happy. But she believed me when I told her that I never knew anything about this one."

"This one? Are there others?"

"I misspoke."

"Are you sure?"

"I have a son from my first marriage. You know that."

"Right. Anyone else?"

"What is this, the Inquisition?"

"I'm just trying to help you think through why Jayne might have left you."

"Jayne didn't leave me! We love each other. She knows I would do anything for her."

"Can you think of anything in particular that she would like you to do? Something she has asked you to do?"

Bennett watched Mitchell carefully. The leg had stopped twitching. Bennett could see a look of closed composure ooze across Mitchell's face. The window was closing.

Mitchell looked at his watch. "I think I have to be going."

"We still have twenty minutes."

"That's all right. I'll catch you next time."

"What about Jayne?"

Mitchell shrugged. "She probably left a message on my cell phone that I didn't get, or something like that."

"So you're not worried."

"Not really. Jayne can take care of herself. She'll be back."

The window slammed shut.

Jayne had stocked the little refrigerator in her motel room so she could eat simply, on her own schedule. Yogurt, juice, deli meats, cheese, fruit. She walked down the road to the diner when she wanted something more substantial.

Four days had passed, and Jayne had never felt better. On the second day she had made a delightful discovery of a walking path that ran alongside a small stream. Traffic on the path was light, and Jayne enjoyed long walks during which she could talk aloud to God. Speaking to him this way was a little easier than praying silently, and she wondered if she was really praying. Noelle assured her she was.

She slept heavily at night, and easily, without the worry that the being would come to taunt her. As she descended into her dreams, she hoped that the white visitors would come again, or that she could picture more clearly their gifts. Even though she did not see the gifts again, they were with her, bound up in her in a way that kept her safe and inviolable. Nothing Mitchell might do could destroy the gifts.

At a small bookstore Jayne purchased a Bible. She wanted to be able to mark the passages that Noelle suggested she read. The story of Jacob, Leah, and Rachel burned in her heart. Despite the rough beginning, it ended with a lasting love between Jacob and Rachel.

Four days of resting, walking, praying, and reading had brought good results. The reality of Mitchell's past still made her stomach lurch several times a day, but it did not overwhelm her. The gift of hope buoyed her to look to the future, rather than abandon it because of the past.

Jayne called Noelle twice daily as she agreed to do. Noelle was a lifeline. Without her, Jayne was sure she would have felt so confused that she would have gone home without sorting things out. With Noelle's support she took her time and felt more sure of herself than she had in a long time. Noelle's gentle interpretation of the white visitors had calmed Jayne. Befuddlement was gone, and in its place had come contentment.

Contentment. Jayne laughed aloud as she thought of it. How could she possibly feel content in her circumstances? It made no sense. But she was.

It was time to call Mitchell.

Jayne sat on the little stool in the phone booth across the street from the motel, her new credit card in hand. The instructions for using it to make a call were printed in the tiniest type she had ever seen. As she dialed the numbers, she hoped he would answer. The thought of leaving a message and then waiting for him to phone back was unattractive. This conversation needed to happen in a moment of preparedness and resolution.

"Hello."

"Hello, Mitchell."

"Jayne! Oh, baby, I've been so worried about you. Are you okay?"

"I'm more than okay." And she was.

"Where are you? I'll come and get you."

"No, Mitchell, let's not do that. I just wanted to talk for a little bit."

"Can't we talk when I pick you up?"

"I don't want you to pick me up, Mitchell."

"Aren't you coming home?"

"That depends."

"On what?"

"On how you respond to what I'm going to say."

Mitchell was silent, but Jayne could hear him breathing.

"I have a feeling I'm not going to like what you say," he finally said. "But go ahead."

"First of all, I want to say that I love you. I really do."

"I love you, too," he said apprehensively.

"I know. We wouldn't be together if we didn't care so much for each other. But things are pretty complicated between us. We need some time to sort them out."

"What are you saying, Jayne?"

"I want to come home, but I don't think we should be together right now."

"You want a divorce!"

"No, no! Nothing like that. A lot has happened to me in the last few days, things that change the way I look at things and how I feel about everything. It's been really good, actually, and I want to share it with you."

"And I want to hear it."

"But I think we need to step back and take a look at our relationship and decide what we both want out of this marriage."

"I want this marriage more than anything I've ever wanted, Jayne. I'll do anything to make it work. You name the terms."

Jayne drew in a deep breath. "Well, the first term is that I think we should live apart while we sort things out. If we live together, it will be too easy to slip into the old patterns that got us where we are now. I want to make some new patterns."

"I do too. This is a fresh start."

"So you're willing to live apart?"

"We'd still see each other, right?"

"Of course. But we won't be physically intimate."

"No sex?"

"No sex."

"But Jayne, that's a natural way for us to express our love."

"I know. But just for now, I want us to keep our heads clear even of that." *Especially of that.* "I would like to stay in the house and have you go somewhere else."

"Well, I suppose I could stay with my parents, or at one of the houses I'm watching. It's only temporary, right?"

"I hope so."

"Okay, then, I can do that."

"Thanks." Jayne swallowed and prepared to continue. "I also want to be able to see where you're living."

"If I'm at my parents' you can come there anytime."

"And I want to see all your mail."

"My mail?"

"Yes."

"Don't you trust me, Jayne?"

She was aghast at his question and didn't answer.

"That was dumb. I'm sorry," he said. "Of course you can see my mail. I won't even open it until you see it. Not even the junk. My life is an open book from now on, as long as we get back together."

"That's what I want too, Mitchell. Please believe me."

"I do, babe. Can I come and get you now?"

"I have my car," she reminded him. "I'll give you a day or so to get moved, then I'll come home. I'll call you as soon as I get there."

"Love you."

"Love you."

And she did love him. She was not afraid.

~ 35 ~

UNCLEB: News on your private practice?

BJL062: Going well. Busy. Would like to get out of prison work.

UNCLEB: Thought you liked it.

BJL062: Too much ASPD. Would like to help people who actually want to get better.

UNCLEB: Like the young woman.

BJL062: Concerned about her. Won't come to see me.

UNCLEB: Maybe things are okay.

BJL062: No. She left him.

UNCLEB: When?

BJL062: Few days ago. Called to cancel appt. Out of town.

UNCLEB: Will she go back?

BJL062: Afraid she will.

UNCLEB: Loves him?

BJL062: Of course. Will miss him and give in and go back.

UNCLEB: Maybe has better reason.

BJL062: Can't think what it would be.

UNCLEB: Hope? Commitment?

BJL062: Wonderful woman. Deserves better. Can't see that for herself. Your patient?

UNCLEB: Still showing conflicting signs. Starting to break down. I'm hopeful.

Bennett leaned back in his chair and stared at the fragments of dialogue still hanging on the screen. Such a coincidence was not possible, was it? BJL062's patient had left her husband. Mitchell had admitted that his wife was "missing." At about the same time.

In every chat BJL062 persisted in his message that there was no hope for individuals with antisocial personality disorder to get better. So of course he would think the woman should get out as fast as she could. But if he could meet Mitchell, maybe the iron strapping around his theory would give way a bit. If Mitchell's wife saw the glints of hope that Bennett saw, no wonder she was hanging in.

But was she hanging in? Would she come back? And for the right reasons? Bennett sighed. Maybe there were no good reasons for her to come back.

No, of course it couldn't be the same couple. The city was not large, but there were plenty of outlying towns. Plenty of room for dysfunctional relationships.

Still, the thought nagged at Bennett. If only he and BJL062 could talk freely about their patients, they might both get a clearer picture. But of course he would never violate patient confidentiality and certainly would never suggest that a colleague should do so. It was frustrating not to have all the pieces of the puzzle on the table. Perhaps he should suggest to Mitchell that his wife join them for a few sessions.

He had no idea if she would come. And he wouldn't blame her if she didn't.

Unless she still believed in hope.

No, it couldn't be the same couple.

Although Jayne and Mitchell had only lived together for a few months, the tiny bungalow felt odd without him. Jayne expected to glance across the room and see him snoozing on the sofa, or find him whipping up Saturday-morning pancakes, or hear his even breathing beside her in bed. She missed his presence, but she was relieved to have her refuge to herself.

Mitchell was staying with his parents. Whenever Jayne called him, she purposefully used their home number rather than his cell-phone number. So far—it had only been a few days—he always seemed to be where he said he would be. He called her freely, just like the old days.

"This is Jayne."

"And I'm so glad it is."

"Hi, Mitchell," she replied with genuine if subdued enthusiasm.

"How about some coffee downstairs. Meet you in twenty minutes."

"Sounds good."

"Love you."

"Love you."

She did love him. Still, it felt awkward saying that under the circumstances. They started slowly: coffee, a casual lunch, talking about doing something together with Connor on the weekend. On Sunday she wanted to go to church. He wanted to be wherever she was, so he went as well. In the afternoon, in the warm calm of the newspaper spread around her living room and Chinese food on the coffee table, Jayne was ready to tell Mitchell about the white visitors.

"Mitchell, do you remember that night on our honeymoon, the time I woke up in the middle of the night?"

Mitchell repositioned the throw pillow behind his head on the sofa. "Yeah, you were having a bad dream or something. You kept talking about, I don't know, something that wasn't there. That's what you do every time."

"Most of the time I just ignore them and they go away."

"Is it still happening?"

Jayne shook her head.

"Well, that's good, isn't it?"

"I think so. Yes, I know so. But there's more."

"Oh?" Mitchell pushed himself upright on the sofa.

"I had a different kind of visitor while I was away. I think they were angels."

"Angels? Like with wings and halos?" He raised an eyebrow skeptically.

"They brought me gifts, things that I need at this point in my life."

"What were the gifts?"

"I can't describe what they looked like, but I know how they made me feel. Peace. Strength. Joy. Things that don't make a lot of sense considering the circumstances of my life, but that's what I felt. I could never have those things on my own."

"Do you really think they were angels? From God?"

"I do."

Mitchell silently considered what she said. "And that's why you're willing to give me another chance?" he finally asked.

Jayne nodded. "This is all really hard for me, Mitchell. I won't pretend it isn't. Some days I just want to walk away from it all or wake up from a bad dream. And if I thought I had to go through it alone, I would bail yesterday. But that's not how I feel. I'm not alone. So I can do this."

Mitchell let out a long, slow breath. "Wow. When you were gone I told God I would do anything if he would just bring you back to me. I've messed things up, but he can help me get it right."

"Do you really believe that?"

"On my honor." Mitchell held up three fingers.

"You were never a Boy Scout."

The days turned into weeks. They met for breakfast before work, went out to dinner, played racquetball on the weekends, watched Connor play baseball as spring training turned into real games, ate dinner with Mitchell's family. He sent Jayne flowers at work with sweet notes tucked into the blossoms. After a few weeks of not knowing what to say, Mare was beginning to rave about Mitchell again. But even as Jayne breathed in the fragrance of the flowers, she held fast to her resolution that they work things out before getting carried away. She still talked to Noelle frequently, who gently urged her to think of someone she and Mitchell could talk to together. She had some names to suggest when Jayne was ready.

Leslie, of course, was a stalwart supporter of taking it slow—moving backward slowly would have suited her fine. But after an initial outburst *(Are you insane!)*, she held her tongue out of respect for Jayne's right to make her own decisions. Jayne enjoyed her time with Leslie—an island of relief, away from thinking about Mitchell, time when she could gently try to explain to Leslie what had happened inside her.

Mitchell and Jayne strolled through the mall one evening, hand in hand, their mouths still savoring the taste of the hot fudge sundae they had shared. Jayne had been working up to asking a question all day.

"Mitchell, whatever happened about that accident you had in the parking lot?"

"Nothing really."

"Didn't you have to go to court?"

"The court date has been moved twice. I guess the old guy's health is not so great."

"I hope not because of the accident."

"No, he's been sick a long time, they tell me."

"Who tells you?"

"My lawyer, who talks to his lawyer."

"I didn't know you had a lawyer."

"He thinks he can get the charge reduced, so delaying the court date is a good thing. I might not have to go at all."

An old man was sick, so the court date changed. Mitchell had consulted a lawyer. It sounded credible. Jayne wanted so much to believe him. But she had believed credible explanations before that had turned out to be outrageous fiction. Caution curbed further conversation.

When he took her home that night, he stood at the door and kissed her in a way that made his desires known. Pulling back, she pushed her hands against his chest. "Not yet, Mitchell."

"I can't stand to leave you here. I just want to be with you." He bent to kiss her again, but she turned her head.

"I know. But it's not time yet."

He sighed. "Okay. I can be as patient as you need me to be. As long as you know I want to come home."

"That's very clear," she said, breathing in his scent. "And I want you to come home."

"I've changed, Jayne, really I have. I'm not keeping anything from you, and I never will again. I don't even want to imagine my future without you."

"I know, I know. I just want to be sure we do this right so we never have to go through anything like this again."

Jayne leaned against the door after she closed it behind him. She wanted to trust him again. She wanted the love that bears no record of wrongs. Was it possible?

"I don't know if I'll ever trust him again," Jayne said to Noelle over the enchiladas that had become their favorite. "I want to. I love him and I want to be with him. How can I love someone so much if I don't trust him?"

"Love and trust are not the same thing." Noelle plopped a generous helping of salsa on her plate. "Love is something you give freely. On a human level trust is something you have to earn, no matter what relationship you're in. Mitchell hasn't earned your trust."

"But can he ever? If he asked me what would it take for me to trust him again, I wouldn't have a clue what to say."

"Maybe he's not the one you need to trust."

"Well, of course, I'm trusting God. I mean, I'm trying to."

"What are you trusting him for?"

Jayne looked at Noelle in confusion. "I trust him to help Mitchell be different. I would love it if Mitchell would really understand about Jesus."

"What if it doesn't happen?"

The waitress hovered at their booth to refill their water glasses. Jayne broke off a tortilla chip and dipped it in salsa. When the waitress had gone, Jayne looked at her friend, wide-eyed. "But you always say God can do anything. He can change anybody. You're the one who told me to read about Paul in the Bible. If God can change Saul into Paul, can't he change Mitchell?"

"Certainly God can do all that."

"Well, Mitchell keeps saying he wants to be different."

Noelle shoved enough salsa in her mouth to make Jayne think her taste buds must be dead. "Do you think he's capable of making that choice?"

"He wants to, and if he lets God help him …"

"You told me once that your father's sister was clinically depressed."

Jayne's expression showed the bewilderment she felt.

"Did she have a depressing life?" Noelle persisted.

Jayne shook her head. "Not really. Her husband loved her, and my cousin was always a good kid. They had a comfortable life."

"So why was she depressed?"

"Brain chemistry. That's what the doctors said. When she was on the right medications, she was happy. But if she went off, it would start all over again."

Noelle stabbed a bite of enchilada and lifted it toward her mouth. "Do you think she could choose not to be depressed?"

"No, I don't. She did try to choose, but she just couldn't. She needed the medications." Jayne stopped. "I see where you're going. If it's a disease or a disorder, Mitchell can't just choose to be different."

Noelle nodded.

"But if he can't choose and there's no medicine to help him either—what hope is there? His only chance is for God to do something."

"Why doesn't God just heal all the people with depression or diabetes, instead of making them take medicine every day?"

"I don't know. Why?"

Noelle laughed. "If I knew the answer to that one! God can heal. You must always believe that. You've experienced your own sort of healing in the last few weeks. But lots of people are sick, and God doesn't choose to heal them all."

"What are you saying, Noelle?"

"What are you trusting God for, Jayne?"

~ 36 ~

The pastor raised his arm as he spoke the benediction. "To him who is able to keep you from falling and to present you before his glorious presence without fault and with great joy—to the only God our Savior, be glory, majesty, power, and authority, through Jesus Christ our Lord, before all ages, now and forevermore!"

Jayne joined the congregation's responsive "Amen." As the organ swelled with the postlude, she squeezed Mitchell's hand and glanced around. She had spotted Noelle in her usual pew early in the service. Now her fiery friend was deftly dodging and ducking her way through the crowd toward Jayne and Mitchell. As small as she was, and as big as he was, Noelle nearly tackled Mitchell when she reached him.

Jayne smiled as she caught Mitchell's eye over Noelle's shoulder. Obviously he had not expected such an enthusiastic welcome. Jayne had not demanded that he come to church; he had come willingly. Still, she knew that he was uncomfortable with the intimate knowledge that Noelle held. Jayne was thrilled with the generous, nonjudging welcome Noelle offered. Accepting it might be an important step for Mitchell.

Noelle patted Mitchell's cheek and stepped back. "How utterly scrumptious to see you here again," she said with a grin that would have looked ludicrous on anyone else.

"I want to be here," Mitchell responded, glancing at Jayne again. "I need to be here."

"If only more folks had that attitude!" Noelle held Mitchell's eyes with the sparkle in her own. "How are the two of you getting on these days?"

Mitchell felt awkward, Jayne knew. Still, she wondered what he would say.

"We're doing pretty well," he said. Noelle continued to look him in the eye until he continued. "I know we've got some work to do. Well, me, anyway. And I'm going to do whatever it takes, anything Jayne asks me to do, to work this out."

Noelle turned her eyes to Jayne, still speaking to Mitchell. "Well, your lovely bride certainly looks happy today."

Jayne blushed. "I am happy." She squeezed Mitchell's hand again.

Noelle patted Jayne's cheek. "And what are you two happy people going to be doing on this glorious day that the Lord has made?"

"Connor has a baseball game at four," Jayne said cheerfully. "We are going to cheer him on."

"He's pitching," Mitchell added. "There's nothing he loves more."

"Have a delightful day." And Noelle was gone. She knew just how far to press and no further.

The metal bleachers rattled under each step as Jayne made her way to where Mitchell had parked himself. She brought a soda for each of them from the concession stand. "Here you go." She handed her husband the taller of the two.

Mitchell took a long sip. "If you get hungry, let me know. I'll go next time."

"My stomach is still trying to figure out what to do with lunch," Jayne answered. She scanned the field. "I don't see Connor."

Mitchell pointed. "There. Behind third base, talking to the coach."

"Ah, yes. He told me this team was tough. Do you think he's ready?"

"He's always up for a challenge, I've got to give him credit for that."

"Did he say whether Rachelle is coming to watch?"

"She's at a baby shower or something. Might make it in the later innings."

Jayne set her drink down, leaned back, and hung her feet over the bench in front of her. Noelle was right: It was a glorious day. It felt so good to just do something normal, to sit beside her husband and watch a baseball game. Mitchell was regularly spouting praise for Connor's baseball prowess, and

Jayne had to admit the boy looked good. When he pitched, his focus was intent. When he fielded, his responses were precise. When he batted, his swing was solid and well placed. She could easily believe that in a couple of years minor league scouts would be checking out Connor Furst, perhaps even surreptitiously from these very bleachers. And wouldn't that make Mitchell proud.

Mitchell *was* proud of his son. Even though the game had not yet started, his eyes were fixed on Connor, following his every movement, hoping the boy would glance at the stands and see his father rooting for him. The pleasure in his face was undeniable. As Jayne watched Mitchell, she shared his pleasure. And she found her own in seeing his affection for Connor, especially because she knew it had not always been that way. Mitchell had told Jayne on more than one occasion that he regretted the years that he was not very involved in Connor's life. He couldn't make up for them, he said, but he could do better in the future. And he was doing better in so many ways.

But Jayne wondered about his other children, the ones who didn't have an interested father. The ones who perhaps did not even know who or where their father was. The ones who would grow up angry, like Jake. What could Mitchell do for them?

Sometimes when she pondered that question, Jayne could do nothing more than stare and sigh. It was not difficult to understand that Mitchell would be overwhelmed at the prospect of scaling the brick wall of his past. Wouldn't it be easier just to find a gate or go around and start over on the other side? Yes, for Jayne and Mitchell, of course that would be easier. A fresh start, focused on just the two of them. But Jayne did not forget. Sometimes as she tweaked a book cover or placed an image in a document, she saw the faces of children staring back at her. And she thought of the pictures Mitchell's mother kept.

Jayne had not been to the Furst home in the eight weeks that she and Mitchell had been living apart. She was not ready to see the pictures held to the refrigerator by assorted appliance-company magnets or hanging on the wall in their tidy frames. At first she had not wanted even to see the faces of anyone in Mitchell's family—anyone who had known the truth and withheld it from her, leaving her to plunge into the pit they knew was there. When she had first returned home and Mitchell had moved out, Jayne had contemplated confronting Mitchell's parents as she had his sister. Why had no one told her the truth about Mitchell's past? How could they have let her innocently walk into this nightmare? But wrapped in the contentment of remembering the three gifts, the urge soon passed. Roger and Leona were Mitchell's parents. Didn't they deserve the same second chance she was giving their son?

Jayne had invited Roger and Leona to her home on several occasions—for a simple supper or a backyard lunch. Once Roger had started to tell Jayne that he had tried to warn her about Mitchell a year ago, but Leona cut him off, for which Jayne was grateful. When they visited, Leona prattled on about trivialities that held not the least bit of interest for anyone else. Jayne supposed that Leona did not know what else to do with her nervousness. Jayne had no idea what Mitchell had told his parents about why he needed to move back into their home, while it was obvious that he saw Jayne nearly every day.

The fans scattered around the bleachers began to clap as the teams took the field. Connor strode confidently toward the pitcher's mound. Connor pitched well, holding the opposing team to only one run in five innings while his own team scored four. He contributed a solid double in the bottom of the second that had Mitchell up on his feet, stomping and shaking the bleachers. Jayne laughed and playfully tugged him back down beside her.

In the later innings Mitchell wrapped an arm around Jayne's shoulder, and she let herself relax into the niche his form created for her. Connor was tiring, she could see that, and there were still two innings left. Mitchell groaned when a pitch went wide and runners on two bases advanced. The coach lumbered out to the mound and bent his head in to talk to Connor.

"Leave him in, leave him in," Mitchell muttered. "He'll pull it together."

And he did. The runners got no farther, and after a spell sitting on the bench while his team batted, Connor roared through the top of the ninth with three snappy outs. The final score was four to one. Connor Furst had outpitched the toughest team in the league.

Connor chattered all through dinner at his favorite hamburger place, where Rachelle caught up with them and had to settle for the verbal replays. Connor asked for ice cream and his father immediately consented as Rachelle and Jayne sat with their mouths gaping at the amount of food the boy was consuming. The evening flew by. Rachelle took Connor home, and Mitchell and Jayne headed to her bungalow, where they passed several more hours talking and watching a movie. Mitchell nuzzled up to Jayne on the couch and kissed her deeply. She responded with sincerity. His hand stroked her thigh enticingly, then moved across her stomach.

But it was getting late. She gently pushed him away and pointed at the clock. He grumbled, but he put his shoes on and left a few minutes later.

Standing in an oversized T-shirt, Jayne brushed her teeth and eyed the phone beside her bed. Waiting for it to ring. Waiting for Mitchell to call. Finally it rang. She plopped into bed and grabbed the phone.

"This is Jayne."

"And I'm so glad it is."

When he first started calling almost as soon as he had left her, no matter how late, Jayne found it amusing. Now she looked forward to it. She could enjoy his nearness and attention without having to push him away.

"Hello, Mitchell." Jayne settled back against a pile of pillows for a long talk.

~ 37 ~

Her computer calendar beeped to remind her she had fifteen minutes before her appointment. She paid such little attention to time when she worked that she depended on the audible reminder.

Mare glanced up from her desk. "Meeting Mitchell for coffee again?"

Jayne smiled. It had become a daily ritual, either midmorning or midafternoon. Mitchell would manage to break away from his work and arrive promptly at the coffee shop below Jayne's office. When she went downstairs, he would be waiting as she came through the door. Often her steaming latte would also be waiting for her.

"Why don't you surprise him and be first?" Mare suggested.

Jayne liked that idea. She was at a good stopping point anyway. Hitting the button to save her work with one hand, she grabbed her purse with the other. "Maybe I'll even treat today."

"I have to admit, you seem happy these days, considering what you've been through."

"I am happy," Jayne said simply. Mare had only a skeletal idea of what had gone on between Jayne and Mitchell, and Jayne planned to leave it that way. She thought, *Mitchell's been patient for three months, and he's done everything I've asked him to do and then some.*

Pushing open the door to the coffee shop, Jayne glanced at her watch. Ten minutes early. She was already planning what she would order to surprise Mitchell when she caught sight of him at a corner table. He didn't seem to notice her entrance. Puzzled, Jayne looked closer and saw he was engrossed in a book laid flat on the table. Quietly she walked toward him until she was standing beside him, looking over his shoulder.

"You're reading your Bible!"

Mitchell glanced up. "Oh, hi, babe. You're early."

Jayne bent to kiss him. "And you're earlier." She sat down across from him. "And you're reading your Bible."

"You said that already."

"It's not a sight I'm used to."

Mitchell smiled. "I keep it in my briefcase. I pull it out whenever I have a few minutes."

"Every day?"

He nodded. "Pretty much."

"Why haven't you told me this?"

He shrugged. "I don't know. I just started doing it one day and found out it was more interesting than I thought."

"Wow, Mitchell. I don't know what to say."

"I told you I was going to be different, Jayne."

"You have been."

"I know I've said that before, but this time is different. This time I'm not on my own."

"What do you mean?"

"I'm asking God to help me this time. I'm not trying to do something so huge on my own."

"I can't tell you how great that is to hear."

"It's pretty great to say it. What would you like to order? The usual?"

Jayne swallowed hard and nodded. She was not going to cry. She was going to have coffee with her husband.

Back at the office Jayne's mind was only half on her work the rest of the day. Twelve *weeks,* she reminded herself. They had lived apart for twelve weeks, and Mitchell had been perfect. No mysterious absences. Dinner together most evenings. Sports and movies on the weekend. Real conversation, a predictable schedule. Yes, he was trying as hard as he could. She had no doubt that he wanted their marriage to work as much as she did. Recently she had suggested that they see a counselor, and he had not objected even to that. He had a lot of baggage, a lot of dirty laundry. It couldn't be easy for him to lay all that out before a stranger and have it picked apart. All Mitchell ever said was that he would do anything she asked if it meant they could stay together.

Jayne was not naive enough to think every difficult moment was behind them. Those six children still existed, and their mothers were still out there. Mitchell had responsibilities that would always be with them. And there were other women Mitchell had hurt. As much as Mitchell simply wanted to move forward and leave the past behind, Jayne knew it was not that simple. Mitchell's past would always be with them. And she, for one, needed help knowing how to stay afloat.

She did not think she wanted to take Mitchell to see Brant Lorimer, however. The good doctor was already persuaded that the relationship was doomed, so what would be the point of seeing him? Sometimes the crushing weight of what she and Mitchell faced overwhelmed her, made her think Dr. Lorimer was right, that living through the days ahead would be too much for her. She shook those thoughts aside, as she always did. The doubts dissipated more and more easily as her and Mitchell's relationship strengthened. They were both committed; they would need help, just not from Brant Lorimer. They would have to find someone else. She would ask Noelle, she decided, the next time she saw her.

The computer screen flickered and morphed as Jayne touched various keys and clicked here and there. The text of the book she was working on was a little too long for the template, and she was toying with ways to make it fit. The publisher was adamant about not adding pages. Jayne squeezed in almost another full chapter, but progress was slow. Mare left at lunchtime as usual, and Larry shuffled papers on his desk most of the afternoon before leaving for a late-afternoon doctor's appointment. Jayne stayed another hour to answer the phone. It rang only twice with questions she easily answered. Alone, Jayne wandered to the window and gazed at the street below. Her mind's eye saw Mitchell standing down there, his cell phone to his ear, his face cracked by a wide grin as he lifted his face toward her window. And then she saw him at the coffee-shop table with his Bible open in front of him.

Perhaps it's time, she thought. She had wondered for weeks how she would know it was time. Being ready to have Mitchell home again had more to do with her than it did with him. He had never really wanted to leave. But perhaps it was time.

Mitchell tapped his desk with the end of a pencil. Somehow he would have to get these figures to work or he was going to lose his client. He'd been over them four times already, digging for any wiggling room even on one small item. He'd found a few dollars, but not enough. He pushed out his breath, thinking that maybe he needed to clear his head and come back to it. Just a few minutes away from the office would help. He had to have something to present in the morning.

As he punched buttons on his calculator yet again, Mitchell hoped Jayne would not mind if he showed up for dinner with his briefcase in tow. Actually, he was sure she wouldn't. She would just be glad to know where he was, that he was right across the room from her. Or maybe he should just have dinner with her and excuse himself to go work at home. No, his parents' house would not be quiet enough for the kind of thinking he had to do. Jayne's would be better. He would work, and she could sketch or read.

But he would need a break first. He'd been glued to his office chair all afternoon, something he generally avoided. He much preferred to be out on appointments, with freedom to make small detours if he liked. He needed a detour now. Maybe a walk. Maybe a quick beer. Maybe some music.

Jayne did not understand how hard this new lifestyle was for him, what she had asked him to give up. She really had no clue, no clue at all. But she was convinced he was doing his best, and she claimed that was all she asked. There were things she just never needed to know.

The phone rang. He muttered into it, "Mitchell Furst."

"Hi there."

"Jayne! Hello. I was just thinking of you," he said truthfully.

"Good thoughts, I hope."

"Is there any other kind?"

"Mmm. Are you coming for dinner?"

"A man's got to eat." He glanced at the papers strewn across his desk. "But then I've got to work some more. I just can't get these numbers to work."

"I was hoping I could make you a better offer. One that you couldn't resist."

"You can try. After all, I'm putty in your hands."

"Well, after dinner maybe you'd like to stay."

"Stay for what?"

Jayne was silent.

"Stay the night?" he speculated.

"That would be a good place to start, yes."

"Well, now that is a tantalizing option. Are you sure?" The desire for a beer and some music pounded against Jayne's offer in a familiar tension. But he would handle it. The pounding would stop.

"Yes, Mitchell, I'm sure. It's been three months. It's time."

"I would love nothing more, babe. Let me make a quick stop for a client errand, and I can be there in about an hour."

She laughed. "Do you want to eat first or later?"

Jayne woke the next morning to the smell of bacon. She lay in bed, her eyes closed, savoring the memory of last night. Their reunion had been both tender and passionate. Still deeply satisfied, she sighed and listened to the sounds of Mitchell in the kitchen. He would scramble the eggs just the way she liked them, soft but not runny with a sprinkle of cheddar cheese.

It wasn't long before he arrived with the tray. Jayne sat up in the bed and smoothed the sheet around her, and Mitchell set the tray down on the bed. "You're going to make me wonder how I ever got along without you."

"I'm going to make sure you never think you can again."

Her eyes widened at the feast the tray held. In addition to the eggs and bacon—prepared perfectly—she saw a bowl of fruit, a glass of orange juice, and two warm blueberry scones.

"Where did you get these?"

"Where do you think?"

"How long have you been up? Are they even open this early?"

"Let's just say I was the first customer."

Mitchell sat beside her on the bed. He was wearing the shirt and trousers he'd had on yesterday, of course. All his things were still at his parents'. "I guess you've got a little packing to do today," she said, tearing off a piece of scone and stuffing it in her mouth. "You can't keep wearing those same clothes forever."

"But if I wear them today, the client will think I've been working all night, and that can only be good."

"Ah. Did you figure out what you're going to do?"

"Not yet. But I still have forty minutes."

"Then you'd better hit the shower."

Jayne listened to the water running while she sampled every part of her breakfast. Mitchell was home where he belonged.

Mitchell stuck his head out of the bathroom, rubbing the stubble on his face. "I'm going to have to use your razor, babe."

"Fine by me."

He emerged a few minutes later, properly groomed. Jayne swallowed the last of her eggs and lifted her face for a kiss. Mitchell obliged, holding her chin in his hands and kissing her deeply.

"So I'll see you tonight," she finally said, catching her breath. "With your stuff."

"Count on it."

Outside in his truck Mitchell scrunched up the receipt from the stop he'd made last night and tossed it out the window.

~ 38 ~

The summer was getting away from her.

Jayne sat at the kitchen table on a Saturday morning staring at the calendar, wondering if the middle of July was too late to put in some ground cover beside the walking path in the backyard. The major jobs were under control. Mitchell had seen to that, starting the very week that they met. He had laid a flagstone path from the driveway to the back door, in a stretch of ground where grass refused to grow. A bed of perennials had bloomed beautifully this year, and Jayne had meant to add more color with annuals. But the weeks had flown by, and the spring gardening magazines purchased with earnest intent lay stacked on the baker's rack.

But there would be next summer. Or maybe she and Mitchell would buy a home of their own where she could plan the backyard from scratch. And Connor would have his own room for when he stayed over, instead of sleeping on a futon in her home office.

Mitchell and Connor had headed out bright and early for a baseball tournament that would last all day. Jayne was free to dream leisurely of the months and years ahead. The weeks since Mitchell had come home had been the best they had ever had in Jayne's opinion, and she was pretty sure Mitchell felt the same way. A time of separation had been wise. What were a few months apart when they had their whole lives ahead of them?

Jayne got up from the table and went looking for her gardening tools. She refused to believe it was too late.

Mitchell thought about not going. Monday had come too quickly after a satisfying weekend with Jayne and Connor. He was not in the mood for Bennett Grey's questions. But, of course, if he did not want to play Bennett's games, it would be simple enough to avoid them. Mitchell revved the engine and turned toward the downtown district.

Inside the old building he climbed the steps, stepping especially hard on the fourth one to make sure it creaked, and pushed open the door to the outer office. As usual, Dr. Bennett was waiting for him and waved him in to the familiar couch.

"What's up, Doctor B.?"

Bennett raised an eyebrow. "You sound like you're doing well."

"Why wouldn't I be?" Mitchell answered a little too cheerfully.

"I'm glad to see that things seem to be going well. Why don't you tell me about it?"

"Oh, it's not anything in particular," Mitchell said lightly. "I'm just in a good place all around. I landed a big client last week. I'm thinking of surprising Jayne with a weekend away."

"I'm sure she'd like that. What do you have in mind?"

"Oh, she'd probably like one of those bed-and-breakfast places, you know, the old Victorian houses."

"And what about you? What would you like?"

"I just want to make Jayne happy."

Mitchell did not like the way Bennett was looking at him—as if he did not quite believe him, or expected him to say more.

"Jayne and I are doing really great these days."

"In what way?"

Those stupid questions. Why had he come? Why did he ever come?

"We're not fighting, she trusts me more."

"More than when?"

Mitchell laughed. "You know, Doc, whatever I say, you're going to be suspicious about what I mean. Why can't you just take things at face value?"

"Call it an occupational hazard. I've been trained to look behind the face."

"Does it ever occur to you that you give people more problems by doing that?"

"What do you mean?"

"There you go again."

Bennett smiled slightly.

"See?" Mitchell said. "You know you drive people crazy with all your questions. You're just trying to keep them coming to see you."

"An interesting business strategy. I'll have to give that some thought."

"If you have a sudden boom in patients, I should get a cut, don't you think?"

Bennett pressed his fingertips together in front of his chest. Mitchell did not like it when that happened.

"Would you mind if we followed up on something we talked about a few weeks ago?"

"And what would that be?" Mitchell was prepared to humor Bennett without actually disclosing anything significant. He was smugly confident about his ability to do so.

"Do you remember when you thought Jayne was missing, that something had happened to her?"

Mitchell rolled his eyes. "That was ages ago."

"Yes, four months or so. You seemed upset that night, but you were better the next time. We didn't talk further about it. I never quite understood what happened."

"Jayne's fine."

"Yes, I understand that. But she must have had a reason for leaving, and I just want to be sure we examine your feelings about such a significant event."

"She didn't leave. I mean, of course, she went away for a few days. It's not like she actually left me. She called me and explained. She just needed some time to think."

"This was after the young man came to your door and claimed to be your son."

"Yeah, I guess it was about that time. I don't remember exactly." Mitchell shifted in his seat and crossed his legs. "Why does it matter?"

"You seem so anxious to make Jayne happy. I find myself wondering if there's anything else you should tell her so she won't have any lingering doubts."

"Lingering doubts about what?"

"Any other pieces of your past."

"Am I supposed to give her a moment-by-moment narrative of every-thing that happened before I met her?"

Bennett let silence have its effect.

"I've made some bad decisions in the past. Who hasn't?"

Bennett continued his silence.

"But that's all in the past. I'm not making those kinds of decisions anymore."

"Choices always have consequences."

"What are you getting at?"

"Choices we've made in the past have consequences that we carry into the future."

"You're talking in riddles, Doc."

"Then let me ask a plain question. Does Jayne know everything she needs to know about your past so that she can make her choices for the future?"

"That's not such a plain question." Mitchell looked uncomfortable. "Look, Jayne and I are in a good place. There may be a few small things I haven't told her about, but I don't want to focus on that stuff. I just want to focus on us, on the future."

"Are you sure you're being fair to Jayne?"

"Why all these questions about Jayne? I thought you had this thing about my father."

"As I recall, you didn't like to talk about that either."

Mitchell sat silently for several minutes. "Look, Doctor B., if I tell her this other stuff, it'll just wreck what we have. She'll make a bigger deal out of it than it really is. What's the point of that? I love Jayne. I don't want to lose her."

"I believe that you care for her deeply, Mitchell. I'm trying to give you the best chance you can have for a long future with her."

"Well, there's where you and I disagree. I think our best shot is a fresh start, not dredging up the past and dragging it with us everywhere we go."

Mitchell left the session with twenty minutes still on the clock. He'd had enough of Bennett Grey for one day. Maybe for good.

"I can't fix the past," he said aloud as he returned to his truck. "I can only worry about the future."

He had not seen Corrine in months and did not answer Sadie's calls. But if Jayne found out about Corrine—he couldn't think about that.

His cell phone rang. It was Jayne.

"Hi, babe."

"Hello there."

"What can I do for the light of my life?"

Jayne laughed. "When do you think you'll be home?"

"Oh, maybe an hour or so. Why?"

"I want to make that cheesy chicken chowder you like, but we don't have enough milk. Will you be anywhere near a grocery store?"

"Just tell me how many gallons you want."

"Just one."

"Not a problem."

"Thanks. See you in an hour."

"Love you."

"Love you."

Mitchell set the phone on the seat beside him. Milk. To make soup. The truth was she liked that soup a lot more than he did. Such simple things made Jayne happy. Didn't she ever feel the need for some excitement? Soup, of all things.

He would get her milk. He started the truck and scanned the nearest intersection to get his bearings. Where was the closest grocery store?

Jayne chopped potato, carrots, onions, and green pepper for the chowder. She decided to make a double batch so they would have plenty of leftovers. Lifting the lid on the soup pot, she checked the chicken, then snapped off the burner to let the chicken finish cooking in the hot broth. She liked preparing a meal that she knew Mitchell was especially enthusiastic about. The cheese was ready for grating.

Mitchell spotted the small market up ahead, just beyond the Excelsior and around the corner. As he drove past the club, he slowed ever so slightly, glancing at the entrance, wondering who might be inside. It was still early. The usual crowd would not be there yet, not for hours. The after-work crowd was probably in there, stopping for a drink on the way home. No one he knew should be there yet. The band was not even playing yet.

I don't care about that crowd, he thought. *Jayne is waiting for me.* Still, he cruised past the grocery store and circled the block. He knew a good place to park behind the Excelsior. He could go in the back door and check things out.

He went around the block one more time before finally pulling into the secluded parking lot. She wouldn't be there this early anyway. What was the harm? Just a handful of people having a drink after work. He wouldn't have to talk to anyone. It would help him calm down. He had plenty of time; he had told Jayne he wouldn't be home for an hour.

~ 39 ~

"Can you believe it's the end of August already?" Leslie slammed the driver's door and clicked the button on her key chain to lock her car.

"Clearance sales!" Jayne responded gleefully as she led the way toward the mall entrance.

"You got that right. And we even have a purpose. We *must* have something new and summery to wear to the birthday party."

"Absolutely. Though I do wonder why our mothers decided to have a joint birthday party this year. They usually are more than happy to forget they have birthdays, much less throw themselves a party. Not that I'm complaining about a chance to see my mom. I'm thrilled that she is flying in."

"Hey, it's an excuse to shop."

"Like you need an excuse."

"You're no slouch either."

"I'm just a thrifty spender. Mitchell often tells me he's glad he married the sensible cousin."

Leslie feigned offense. "He just doesn't know me well enough to recognize my true inner value."

Jayne laughed. "That's because you don't want to be in the same room long enough for him to try to understand you."

Leslie shrugged. "That's true. Although I have to admit he's been better lately. When I stopped by your place to pick up that skirt you borrowed, he

240

was downright friendly. Acted like he was interested in how I spend my days cleaning teeth. No one in their right mind is interested in that."

"You are."

"Like I said ..."

Jayne chuckled again. "He's really making an effort."

"Well, as much as I hate to admit it, I have to give him credit for that." Leslie held the mall door open for Jayne. "Whatever happened to finding a counselor?"

"We're still talking about it. But everything's going so well, it just hasn't seemed urgent to find someone."

Leslie's tone turned somber. "I know you love the guy, and you do seem happy, but you've got to look out for yourself, Jayne. He comes with a lot of crud that he tends to ignore."

"I know, I know. I'll find someone. I will."

"Oh, look, sixty percent off!" Leslie made a beeline into a shop.

That afternoon Jayne hung the pale pink linen shift she'd found on sale in her closet. It would be perfect for an outdoor birthday party in a couple of weeks. She could always wear a light sweater if the afternoon turned cool.

The doorbell rang. Mitchell had gone to the gym, so Jayne padded out to the front door and pulled it open.

"Leona! Hi, what are you doing here?" Jayne pulled the door open wide for her mother-in-law.

"I can't stay long. Roger is out in the car. We had to come to this neck of the woods for some errands and thought we might as well drop off Mitchell's mail. He's hasn't been by for a while."

"He's getting mail here now," Jayne explained.

"He must have missed a few people with his change-of-address cards, then, because I've got quite a bundle. Two weeks' worth."

"Oh." Jayne took the plastic grocery sack from Leona. "I'll make sure he gets it."

When Leona and Roger had pulled away, Jayne dropped the sack on the kitchen table. Mitchell had told her weeks ago that he had put in a forwarding address at the post office. If the choice came down to trusting the post office or trusting Mitchell, she would pick the post office. It was true that he had started receiving some mail at the bungalow, but obviously he had not let the post office know where to send his mail.

She reached for the bag and dumped the contents on the table. Quickly she sorted out the obvious junk mail. Among the letters that remained were some business envelopes.

Jayne's heart lurched. Two envelopes looked official, like government correspondence. She recognized the state logo. Cautiously she pried the flap open on a subtle gray envelope and extracted the document.

Rusty's mother claimed that Mitchell had not sent her any money for three years. Rusty was nearly seven. The state child-support enforcement agency planned to garnishee Mitchell's wages.

Trembling, Jayne opened the other envelope. Mitchell owed back child support for a little girl named Corrine. Sadie somebody was her mother. According to her, Mitchell had not sent her any money in a year and a half. Jayne stared at the age of this child she had never heard of. She had been born about the time Jayne met Mitchell.

Tens of thousands of dollars, between the two.

Another lie. He had sworn that he had told her about all his children. She was not foolish enough to believe he had not known about this one.

How many? How much more back child support was accumulating?

Jayne collapsed into a chair and put her head down on the table. How could she stand by and knowingly let Mitchell neglect his responsibility to his children? But it was a financial impossibility. Without knowing his exact income, Jayne still knew that even Mitchell never would be able to make those numbers work. Offering part of her income would barely make a dent—and she was not sure at the moment that she wanted to do that.

And legal fees. If he hired legal representation, the debt would only increase. He would probably have to cover the legal expenses of the two mothers as well.

Paralysis swept through her. Jayne had no idea what her next step should be. How could she stand by and knowingly let Mitchell deceive her again? Had she made an enormous mistake when she invited him home? She should have asked for his paychecks. She should have scrutinized every penny. She should have insisted on knowing the specifics of all his legal obligations.

But the thought of confronting him yet again was more than she could comprehend.

But she wanted to trust.

But the three visitors.

But Jacob and Leah and Rachel.

But 1 Corinthians 13.

When she lifted her face, her cheeks were streaked with tears. "Oh God, what have I done?" she said aloud, her face turned upward. "I tried to do the right thing, I really did. But now I don't know. I don't know what you have in mind for Mitchell. I've prayed and prayed for you to heal him, I've prayed for him to really understand that you care about him, and I wanted to believe …"

With a deep sigh, Jayne folded the documents and returned them to their envelopes. "God, you have to help me. I'm the one who needs healing here. I'm the one who needs to know that you care about *me*."

Jayne glanced at the baker's rack behind her. The main surface was clear of clutter. If she put the envelopes there, Mitchell could not help but see them. She tucked the flaps neatly back into place and set the envelopes on the rack in front of the rest of Mitchell's mail—a credit-card bill, a reminder from his dentist that he was due for a cleaning, an auto-insurance bill, a bank statement. Jayne was tempted to open the bank statement, but she resisted. Leaving his mail—including the junk mail—in plain view would be an experiment in trust. She wouldn't say anything. It was obvious the legal envelopes had been opened, so he would know she had seen the contents. Would he do the right thing?

Mitchell would be home from the gym soon. They were planning to go out to dinner. Jayne went in the bathroom and splashed cold water on her face. She would get through this somehow.

As she toweled her face dry, she heard the back door open.

"I'm home, babe."

Jayne forced a smile as she turned to greet the man she had promised her life to.

~ 40 ~

They ate steak for dinner, accompanied by enormous baked potatoes and a house salad. Jayne marveled as she always did at the quantity of food Mitchell could consume without discomfort.

Jayne smiled as Mitchell recounted Connor's latest baseball triumphs, while wondering silently about Rusty, about Corrine, about the others who would not know their father's pride. As glad as she was that Connor received generous portions of his father's attention, she grieved for the others. Did Mitchell think he could make it all right by lavishing affection on one son? Or was it just that he had been married to Connor's mother and somehow felt more obligation?

The steak and potato on Jayne's plate were formidable opponents, and she opted not to put up much of a fight. Her appetite was fleeting, so she poked at the vegetables in her salad and had the server pack up most of the rest of her meal to take home. Sustaining a facade of peace during dinner had depleted her severely. But she had gotten through it, chuckling at Mitchell's humor and steadily looking him in the eye, giving him no reason to ask what was bothering her. Not that he ever would. She didn't know why she ever worried about that.

When she declined dessert, Mitchell asked if she wanted to go dancing. It was Saturday night after all. His lively eyes told her how badly he wanted to go, but Jayne pled fatigue and they went home. She went to bed early, relieved that rather than join her Mitchell ensconced himself in the living room with the cable sports channel and a piece of apple pie he'd brought home from the restaurant.

In the morning Jayne got up before Mitchell. It was still early, barely light outside. She was not a morning person, but her fitful sleep had reached a stage where it seemed impractical to remain in bed with Mitchell breathing evenly beside her. All night long she had alternated between wanting to shake him awake and demand an explanation—although she knew none would satisfy her—and wanting to sink into a cavern of sleep far away from reality. Deep sleep never really came, so she got up.

With her robe wrapped around her, she shuffled into the kitchen to get the coffee pot started. Her eyes fell on the baker's rack. Mitchell's pile of mail was untouched.

Or was it?

She wasn't sure.

She picked up one envelope. The flap was not tucked in the way she had left it.

So he knows, she thought.

Jayne made the coffee and carried a mug into the living room. Waiting for Mitchell to wake up. Waiting for what he would say. Waiting for what he would do. Waiting to know if love could bear all things.

He kissed the top of her head, startling Jayne out of her doze.

"Did you leave any of that stuff for me?" he asked, eyeing her oversized mug.

She smiled. "There's plenty. It should still be hot."

Mitchell went into the kitchen, continuing to converse. "How about we go to the early service today? Then maybe we can grab an open tennis court at City Park."

She heard him set a mug on the counter and close the cabinet. Coffee splashed into the mug. He always poured too fast. She would have to wipe the counter up later.

"Jayne? Babe, you okay?" Mitchell was back, mug in hand.

Jayne roused. "Yes, of course, I'm fine. Just still a little drowsy, I guess."

"So, church? Early service?"

"Yes, that's fine." Noelle would not be there. She always went to the later service.

"Tennis later?"

"Yes. Sure." She looked up at him and smiled.

"Why don't you hit the shower first? I'll make some breakfast."

"I'm not really very hungry today, Mitchell." A faint wave of nausea rolled through her at the thought of one of his breakfast feasts.

"Just some toast, then."

"Maybe. I don't know. I'll fix myself something later. Thanks anyway."

"Okay, then. I'll go get the paper."

Jayne stayed in the shower longer than usual. He had seen the envelopes. He had to know she had opened them. But, watching Mitchell, an outsider would never have guessed anything was amiss. *How in the world does he do that?* she wondered. Keeping up the front was exhausting her, and it had been only a little more than twelve hours since Leona stopped by with the mail.

Mitchell held her hand during the opening praise songs, and when the sermon began he settled in with his arm around her shoulders.

Jayne couldn't concentrate on the lesson. Maybe she had not tucked that flap in after all. Maybe Mitchell had watched the sports channel and come to bed without ever looking at his mail. Maybe she was jumping to conclusions that were unfair to Mitchell.

She didn't know what to think and played tennis badly that afternoon.

On Monday morning Mitchell was up and out before Jayne even opened her eyes. With a start she looked at the clock and realized she had overslept. At the same time she was relieved that she had slept deeply enough not to hear Mitchell get up and leave.

A note on the kitchen table said, "Breakfast meeting across town. Probably can't make coffee today. Will call. Love you. M."

Deliverance from having to see Mitchell for the next ten hours revived Jayne. Concentrating on getting to work on time, she hurtled through her morning routine. Once she was at the office, she would be able to absorb herself in the latest deadline, a welcome challenge.

Every time the office phone rang, Jayne jumped but answered it calmly. It was never Mitchell. Jayne checked her cell phone three times to make sure she had not turned off the ringer. No missed calls.

At noon she went downstairs for a sandwich with Mare. At five she said good night to Larry and drove home.

She knew right away. Even before she opened the door. The emptiness swarmed her as soon as she walked through the back door.

Mitchell was gone.

After a frozen moment Jayne opened a kitchen cupboard to look for the electric griddle that Mitchell had contributed to the household, the one he used for Saturday-morning pancakes. Gone.

In the bedroom the closet door was open. His clothes were gone. His sports equipment, usually piled at the bottom of the closet was gone. Even the hamper was empty.

Jayne looked in the spare room, the one she used as a home office. Mitchell had put a floor lamp in there. Gone. And a small bookcase. Gone.

At first she did not notice anything in the living room. But she finally saw it, the empty space where the DVD player should have been. He had given that to her last Christmas. Hers had stopped working, and she hadn't gotten around to shopping for a new one. The gap in the entertainment center revealed that the extension cord was gone as well. Mitchell had thought of everything.

Instinctively she knew she was lucky he had left her the television.

In the space of five minutes, Jayne had accounted for all the material goods Mitchell had contributed to the household. No trace of his presence remained.

He would not be back, she was sure of that.

UNCLEB: How's your patient?
BJL062: Stopped coming.
UNCLEB: Sorry.
BJL062: Yours?
UNCLEB: Agitated. Think he's gone.
BJL062: His wife?
UNCLEB: Think she may be your patient.
BJL062: Oh? How so.
UNCLEB: Many similarities.
BJL062: Have been careful to protect confidentiality.
UNCLEB: Agree. Still, many coincidences.
BJL062: Then for her sake, hope he's gone.
UNCLEB: For his sake, hope he's not. Beginning to feel serious emotion.
BJL062: Good reason to run.
UNCLEB: Only hope is to stay and work.
BJL062: Keep me posted.

~ 41 ~

"Come on in, the door's open."

"All right, we're prepared for anything now." Leslie set a grocery sack on the coffee table and began to pull out items.

"What do you have there?" Jayne asked, rescuing her sketch pad from underneath the sack of unknown contents.

"I brought dinner."

"Oh, I don't know, Leslie. I don't really feel all that much like eating." The truth was that she could barely keep food down one bite at a time, much less by the grocery sack.

"You have to eat."

"It smells like Mexican."

"It is."

"Too spicy."

"Don't try to pull that on me. You love Mexican. You order it every chance you get."

"Well, yes, normally, but lately it's hard to eat."

"That's why we're starting with your favorites. It'll give you a little motivation."

"Where did you get this, anyway?"

"Mom told me about an old Mexican restaurant out their way. She only recently discovered it herself, but apparently it's been there for decades."

"You drove all the way out there for takeout?"

"No, silly, I went to see my parents this afternoon, remember? I picked this up on the way back."

"It must be cold by now."

Leslie felt one of the cardboard dishes. "So-so. But you have an oven."

"What's this place called?"

"El Señor's. It's kind of a dive actually, but everyone says the food is really good."

"I've heard of it. Noelle mentioned it once." Jayne laughed inwardly at the irony of Leslie picking up food at Noelle's old haunt.

"You stay put," Leslie said. "I'll put this stuff in the oven to warm up a little more."

"Really, Leslie, I don't think I could eat Mexican tonight. My stomach ..."

"You've got to eat, Jayne. That creep took a lot away from you. You can't let him take your health as well." Leslie went around the corner into the kitchen.

"I wish you wouldn't refer to Mitchell that way."

"Do you have a more accurate description? Where are your cookie sheets?"

"Bottom cupboard to the left of the sink. He's my husband."

"I hope you're going to get that fixed real fast." Leslie slammed the oven door closed and reappeared in the living room.

"I really haven't thought that far ahead."

"It's been a month, Jayne. You haven't heard from him. His boss called you twice wanting to know where Mitchell was. Face it, he's gone."

"I know that."

"You should have dumped him a long time ago."

"You're not making this any easier, Les." Jayne swallowed the nausea that had become her companion since Mitchell left.

"All he ever brought you was hardship."

"That's not true. We had some good times."

"Mostly because you made them happen. He never picked up his end."

"That's not true either."

"I know it hurts now, but you'll be better off without him. Just like Chuck."

Jayne had heard the same diatribe for weeks. If Leslie's plan was to make her feel relieved he was gone, it wasn't working. Leslie expected her to pick up her life as if Mitchell had never been part of it, but it was not that simple. Jayne had given up trying to make Leslie understand.

"I never liked him," Leslie prattled on. "For your sake I tried to give him the benefit of the doubt. But I was always looking out for you."

"Thank you," Jayne said automatically. Maybe the nausea would abate if she ate something. She just wasn't sure Mexican was a good idea. Crackers, maybe. Why couldn't she just throw up and get it over with, the way she had the other times when she was upset about Mitchell?

"I wanted to believe I was wrong," Leslie continued. "You seemed so happy. I thought maybe he really had changed. I'm sorry to say that my first instinct was right."

"For something you're sorry to say, you say it an awful lot."

"Sorry." Leslie's tone softened.

"I'm not sure you are. You keep doing it. It's getting really old." Jayne heard the edge in her own voice, but at the moment quelling nausea and remaining polite at the same time was too much to ask.

"So now you're trying to pick a fight with me?" Leslie exclaimed. "Mitchell's the one you should be angry with."

"I know. I am."

"You don't act like it."

"It's not the only thing I'm feeling. If you'd stop bad-mouthing Mitchell for half a second, you'd realize that."

"Sorry. Really."

Neither of them spoke.

Finally Leslie said, "Would you like to eat in here or sit at the table?"

Jayne sighed. "The table, I guess."

"I'll check on the food."

Jayne heard Leslie take plates from the cabinet and open the silverware drawer. She remembered Mitchell offering to make her breakfast, hearing him move around the kitchen just the way Leslie was now. That was the first day she had not been able to eat. It seemed like forever ago.

"What do you want to drink?" Leslie called.

"Water."

"Come and get it."

Jayne moved reluctantly to the kitchen and sat across from Leslie. A tray of cheese enchiladas steamed between them, with a plate of tacos to the side.

"Just how hungry did you think I was?" Jayne asked.

"Leftovers. You won't have to cook tomorrow." Leslie lifted Jayne's plate and slid an enchilada onto it. "There. Dig in."

Jayne picked up her fork, not at all sure she could eat. But Leslie was staring at her, so she felt compelled to try. She took one bite and chewed slowly.

"It is good," Jayne admitted after she finally swallowed. "It's not as spicy as I expected, very cheesy."

Leslie nodded in agreement. For a while the only sounds were their forks scraping across their plates and the crunch of a taco shell when Leslie bit into it.

"I'm sorry things didn't work out for you and Mitchell," Leslie said softly.

"Thank you. I know how hard that was for you to say."

"And I give you credit for hanging in there a lot longer than I would have, than most women would have."

"Thank you."

"That doesn't mean I understand why you did it."

"I know that." Jayne put her fork down. "Obviously I wanted my marriage to work out. I didn't make my vows lightly. And the thing is, I really think Mitchell wanted it to work too. I never doubted that he loved me."

"He had an awful lot of baggage."

"I know. He couldn't carry it any longer. He had to just put it down and leave. I'm just sorry that he'll never find out ..."

"Find out what, Jayne?"

"That God is a God of second chances. If Mitchell had stayed and faced his past, God would have been there with him. But he ran away. Now he might never know what it could have been like. That makes me sad."

"How noble of you to be thinking of him."

Jayne ignored Leslie's sarcasm. "Not really. I'm plenty angry, too. And in a lot of pain. You know that. I'm still figuring out what to do with all these feelings."

"Punch a wall, cut up your wedding pictures, scream at his family."

"You're full of suggestions."

"There's plenty more where those came from."

Jayne stood up. "I'll get something to put these leftovers in."

"I can do that."

"It's fine, Leslie. You said so yourself, I have to get on with my life. I can manage to put a little food away."

"All right." Leslie set her empty plate in the sink.

"You know," Jayne said, "Noelle likes Mexican food too. Maybe the three of us could go out to El Señor's one Sunday after church."

"*After* church," Leslie stressed. "As in, I'll meet you *after* church."

"Okay, you don't have to go to church." *But you can meet Noelle. It's a first step,* Jayne thought. *Wait till you spend some time with Noelle.*

~ 42 ~

Jayne stood in the bathroom and stared at the white stick in her hand.

Blue meant positive. She double-checked the back of the box. Yes, blue meant positive. Positive meant pregnant. The ever-present queasy stomach was not from stress. It had nothing to do with Mitchell's sudden departure.

She had not really needed the stick to tell her what she already knew, had suspected for several weeks, but perhaps had not wanted to believe. She had been so careful. They had not even talked about having a child. Under the circumstances, it would have been ludicrous.

What should I feel? Jayne wondered. Mitchell was gone, but his baby was coming in the spring. Did that make Jayne another in his long line of victims?

Should I be frightened? I'm not.

Should I be angry? I'm not.

Should I be stunned? Well, yes, I am that.

She put her hand on her belly and remembered Claire, the early movement that had startled her and made her long for the warmth of her child in her arms. The tuft of hair on the top of her head that made Jayne never want to put her down. The swell of emotions Jayne had never before experienced. Would she feel that way about this child? She had not planned on Claire, either, and had loved her no less for the circumstances of her birth, had grieved her no less on her death.

Noelle was waiting. Jayne set the white stick on the back of the sink and went to meet her friend at Peace Chapel.

"You have such an artist's eye," Noelle said, standing back to take in the floral arrangements. "The florists come in and do their thing, and then you come in and make it better. And the candles and lighting—you're so good with the personal touches for each couple."

Jayne blushed. "Come on, Noelle. You were doing this for years without me. You're the one with the great touch."

Noelle paused to consider her friend. "You all right, dearie?"

Jayne nodded. "Very."

"It's not too hard to be here, in this place?"

"Where I got married?" Jayne shook her head. "I'm fine. Better than fine. I love this place. Something much more important than my wedding happened here."

"I remember." Noelle paused. "Sometimes we don't understand God's timing, why he called you to himself and let Mitchell's illness overtake him."

"I admit I do wonder about that. It's hard for me to think of it as illness, when it seems like choices that Mitchell made."

"Some of both, perhaps. For whatever reason, Mitchell ran away. But you ran toward something. That's the difference."

"I think about him all the time."

"God's timing may yet bring hope."

Jayne adjusted the position of a vase. "Noelle, do you remember when you asked me what I was trusting God for?"

"I do."

"I thought the answer was about Mitchell. But it wasn't. It was about me. I'm trusting God to take care of me. No matter what happens, I'm safe."

Noelle leaned over and kissed Jayne on the cheek, a gesture that always made Jayne giggle inside, as if she were being tickled.

"I knew you would figure that out," Noelle said.

"Something is not right about this vase," Jayne said. "Too many flowers for how slender it is, I think." She held the vase in one hand and began pulling out stems with the other.

She never felt it slip. Suddenly the vase was on the floor, a puddle seeping into the carpet.

"Oh, goodness." Noelle stooped to pick up the vase and turned it over. "It's cracked."

Jayne took it from her and held it up to the light. "I can see right through it." She pivoted until a rainbow of light from the window blazed through the crack.

"I'll look in the closet and see if there's another one," Noelle said. She reached to take the vase back from Jayne. "This one won't hold water; we won't be able to use it."

"I'd like to have it," Jayne blurted.

"A cracked vase?"

Jayne nodded. "It's still beautiful. I know it sounds silly, but it reminds me ... of me."

Noelle smiled and placed the vase back in Jayne's hand. "That's not silly at all. It won't hold water, but it will show the light."

Noelle went in search of another vase. Jayne cradled the cracked one, a sign of triumph.

She would not be a victim.

She would not be beaten down.

She would let the light blaze through her.

Additional copies of *THE LATEST MRS. FURST*
are available wherever good books are sold.

If you have enjoyed this book, or if it has had an impact on your life,
we would like to hear from you.

Please contact us at:

RiverOak Books
Cook Communications Ministries, Dept. 201
4050 Lee Vance View
Colorado Springs, CO 80918

Or visit our Web site:
www.cookministries.com

RiverOak®
Good News in Fiction